DIVINE GRACE

VIRGINIA CANTRELL

HOT TREE PUBLISHING

DIVINE GRACE

DIVINE

BOOK TWO

VIRGINIA CANTRELL

HOT TREE PUBLISHING

For information, contact the publisher, Hot Tree Publishing.

www.hottreepublishing.com

Editing: Hot Tree Editing

Ebook ISBN: 978-1-925655-77-3

Paperback ISBN: 978-1-925655-80-3

SECOND EDITION

Also by Virginia Cantrell

Divine Merit

Divine Grace

*To all of you who cannot see yourself clearly. I see you.
You're amazing!*

ONE

The quiet was deafening. The only respite was the soft creaking of the rope against the rafter. Inaya's eyes were locked on that spot. Why was the rope still moving?

Maybe she wasn't too late, but she'd have to allow her eyes to travel down the length of the rope to find out. Her heart raced frantically in her chest and tears began to blur her vision as she watched the rope sway once more in the stillness.

She had to do it. She had to check. If there was even the slightest chance that she had made it in time, she had to know. Taking a deep breath and releasing it slowly, her eyes began their descent, inch by never-ending inch.

Her mother's silky blonde tresses came into view first. Breathing became difficult, and she squeezed her eyes shut. Not wanting to see, but knowing she had to, she began to count. One. It'll be okay. Two. I can do this. Three. She forced her eyes to pop open, quickly taking in the entire scene.

"Momma." It came out as a whimper.

The lifeless body hung listlessly from the rope. Inaya's stomach churned, and she wrapped her arms tightly around her waist. It was clearly too late. Her momma's spirit was no longer there. Numbness came with acceptance. She examined her momma's once beautiful face. It was twisted in anguish. She remembered hearing that there was peace in death. Why wasn't Momma peaceful?

Suddenly, her mother's eyes flew open. Inaya yelped and stumbled backward; feet tangling together, she landed hard on her bottom as bloodshot eyes pinned her to the floor.

"There is no peace because it was all your fault." Momma's voice was harsh with anger. Then something in her expression twisted and a deep, masculine voice emerged from her pale pink lips. "It was never meant to be. There is no such thing as love or fate. You're pathetic. How could you ever believe that I would want you?"

Heart pounding, Inaya awoke to her own sobs. The nightmare had returned. She sat up in bed, bringing her back against the headboard, drawing her knees to her chest and wrapping her arms around her legs. As she rocked herself back and forth, she tried to breathe through the pain. Until recently, it had been years since she had dreamed of her mother, but the nightmare was just as powerful as ever. With the details still fresh in her mind, she was afraid to even look around her room for fear certain aspects of her dream would seep into her present reality.

As a child, she had been plagued with this same dream after she had come to live in the Palace of Velius. She could remember many nights when King Vidar himself had been woken by her cries and would rush to her room to comfort her. He would sit at her bedside and distract her with stories of the great angels they were descendants of and tell her of the legend of how their home, the island of Cashile, had been created by the angels as a sanctuary for all Nephilim.

She tried using that same coping technique now to calm her racing heart and her terrified mind. She thought about the angels who had fallen from grace and lost their dignity to be with the human women, thus creating her people. Was it worth it? Did they regret their decisions? Were they, too, plagued with nightmares for all they had lost?

Knowing the impossibility of ever having answers to her questions, and too afraid to return to sleep, she pushed herself out of bed. It was just as well; there was much to do to prepare for the festivities. Tonight was the celebration of the launch of the new scout, and the dignitaries from the other territories would all be in attendance. It was time to earn her keep and get to work—not that King Vidar or Princess Amira ever asked for any service from her, but still, she felt obligated. When she had first been brought to the palace to be Amira's companion sixteen years ago, she had tried to find her place amongst the palace servants, but when King Vidar caught her trying to polish the floor, he strictly forbade it.

"My dear Inaya," he had said, "you were not brought here for labor. You were brought here to be a companion for my daughter, but more importantly, you were brought here to become part of our family. You are a very special girl. You are Lady Inaya of Velius, so no more of this servant business." He paused and kissed her on the forehead. "Go play. Be a child."

Just thinking about King Vidar brought a smile to her face and eased the heaviness from her chest that the nightmare had caused. He chased away the fear, just as he had when she was a child. He became the father she never had.

That was why it was so important for her to be useful to him. He had saved her from her past. Somehow, she hoped to be able to repay his kindness. Until then, she would work to ease his burden by making sure his household ran smoothly.

~

Trevin left the soldiers' keep with a shake of his head, wondering why he even bothered to try to talk sense into Caeden's thick skull. If it had been anyone else, he would have just saved his breath, but Caeden was not just his commander and captain of the Royal Guard. He was Trevin's best friend and the closest thing he now had to a brother.

It frustrated him to watch Caeden continue to deny what was right in front of his face. Caeden and Princess Amira were destined to be together. It was clear to all, except Caeden. Watching the two dance around each other was getting painful.

Hearing heavy footsteps rushing in his direction from behind, his hand automatically fell to his weapon as he turned to see who approached. His stance relaxed as he recognized his fellow Guard member Murdock.

"Hey, I just wanted to ask a favor of you, no need to strike me down," Murdock joked, motioning to where Trevin still clutched his sword.

"Depends on the favor."

Murdock smiled briefly before his face turned serious. "You're on guard duty this afternoon and tonight, correct?"

Trevin raised his chin in a "yeah, what do you need?" motion.

"I need you to take care of my sister."

Well, that certainly got his attention. His body tensed again as the image of Inaya's long, golden blonde hair, incredible turquoise eyes, and curvy body flashed through his mind. He shook his head to dislodge the vision, trying to recall her as the skinny tomboy who had followed him around during her teenage years, but the image was lost to him.

Being a male of few words, he got right to the point. "Why?"

"Sorin of Ammon will be present," Murdock said in answer.

No one could stand that bastard, and his presence put them all on alert, but this was something different. Whatever it was brought a sick twisting to his gut.

"And?" Trevin prompted.

"And he can't be permitted to get close to Inaya."

"Agreed, but you seem to have a reason to make an issue of this fact. What is it?" Trevin felt his anger rising as the possible scenarios raced through his thoughts.

Murdock's gaze drifted to the side uncomfortably. "I don't have the time to get into it right now. I need to be at training." His dark, piercing eyes locked with Trevin's. "Will you look after her?"

"Absolutely, but you and I are going to find the time to talk." If Inaya was in danger, he needed to know.

Murdock hesitated, but there was no way to miss the steel-like determination in Trevin's eyes. He gave in with a slight nod. "Thanks, brother."

"No need to thank me for something I would have done anyway," Trevin answered. Throughout the years, it had taken both her brothers and Trevin's help to contain her impulsive nature and keep her out of trouble. As he turned away, he saw the look of displeasure cross Murdock's face, but he really couldn't care less.

Two

"Lady Inaya."

Inaya turned to see Endora, the palace's kitchen manager, rushing in her direction. She took in Endora's harried appearance and took a deep, calming breath and silently reminded herself that whatever the problem, she could handle it. She placed a welcoming smile on her face. "Endo—"

"You have to do something about that dreadful female," Endora interrupted.

Inaya's thoughts bounced around, trying to determine which "dreadful female" she could be referring to. All the palace servants were in a tizzy preparing for tonight, but so far, there had only been minor problems that had been easily rectified. So Inaya was coming up blank.

"What is the problem?" she asked as she watched

Endora wringing her hands and shifting from foot to foot.

"It's Lady Marcelle," Endora hissed.

Well, that was not an easily solved problem. "What has she done now?"

"It's less than two hours until supper and she has demanded the menu be changed! 'Roast duck,' she says. That witch has no idea how long it takes to roast a duck, let alone how many it would take to feed a party that size!"

"Endora. Endora, calm yourself. There is no need to worry. There will be no changes to the menu. The meal has been planned and approved by King Vidar himself. Just go about your duties as usual."

"But—"

"Did she come to the kitchen herself to tell you?" Inaya asked.

"Of course not. She sent a maid."

"Right. I highly doubt Lady Marcelle is even aware of the location of the kitchen. So, breathe easy. Any further requests or complaints can be directed to me."

"You're an angel!" Endora said with a bright smile as she grabbed Inaya's hand. "I know I've told you before, but it's true. We are blessed to have you with us."

"Thank you," Inaya mumbled with embarrassment, the praise making her uncomfortable. With a pat of her hand, Endora went back to work, her departure leaving an echo of unease.

Inaya did not look forward to dealing with Marcelle. Being King Vidar's deceased wife's sister and the Supreme Healer, Marcelle deserved a fair amount of respect. But Endora was right; Marcelle was a dreadful female, and that was a kind description. Marcelle didn't live in the palace, but when she came to visit, she made Inaya's life a misery by lording over and disrupting the entire palace staff.

This would not be the first or last time Inaya had a confrontation with her. But for now, she would deal with that problem when it came to a head. Right now, she knew Amira needed her. Earlier, she had seen the princess rush to her chambers through the hidden servants' pathway, obviously upset. Knowing Amira like she did, Inaya had given Amira some time to collect herself and think things through. But now was the time to go to her friend and help pick up the pieces. She finished grabbing the supplies she would need and headed toward the stairs.

At the foot of the stairs, she was once again halted by her name being called. She paused as tingles shot through her body at the sound of Trevin's deep voice.

She forced herself to wear a look of indifference as she turned to greet him. Hoping her eyes didn't give her away, she allowed herself a moment to quickly appreciate his defined chest and broad, muscular shoulders. As her eyes trailed upward, she took in his strong jaw, covered in a day's worth of scruffy facial hair, which only added to his rugged appeal, and his disheveled, dark brown hair. Not wanting to get caught admiring his spectacular physique, she forced herself to meet his molten chocolate brown eyes.

"Trevin," she greeted simply.

"What is your relationship with Sorin of Ammon?" he asked brusquely, getting straight to the point. His mind had been racing since he'd spoken with Murdock.

He was unused to this feeling of jealousy, which aggravated his usual calm demeanor to near fury. They would settle this issue now, and if Inaya had any sort of feelings toward Sorin, well, he'd see to it that they ceased immediately.

"Excuse me?" she questioned with a look of confusion.

"You will answer the question," he stated, not being one to repeat himself.

Inaya's spine stiffened and her look of confusion turned to one of pure stubbornness. "I don't believe that is any of your business."

"You know very well that it is," he forced out through clenched teeth.

"If I remember correctly, you refused that right."

Her voice had quivered at the end of her statement, causing a dull ache of regret to form in his chest. By her stiff posture and her refusal to meet his gaze,

Trevin knew any advance he made to comfort her would be refused or misconstrued. He'd made many mistakes in handling this female, he admitted to himself, but that didn't excuse any possible entanglement she might have with Sorin.

Knowing she would be unreceptive to any mending of their personal relationship, he continued with the pressing issue at hand.

"Any association you have with Sorin will cease immediately," he declared.

"I will associate with anyone I please," she snapped, her angry turquoise eyes finally meeting his.

He grabbed her arm firmly when she moved to turn away, careful not to hurt her, but he needed her to understand. He closed his eyes briefly to calm himself before saying, "Sorin is dangerous. He will think nothing of using you, and then disposing of you. Or worse."

"I'm very aware of what he is capable of. I don't need—"

Taking a step forward and placing a hand on her nape, Trevin growled, "How? Has he done something to you? Hurt you?"

Inaya's eyes grew soft, and he felt her tremble at his words. Without intention, his thumb caressed the soft skin of her throat, inciting yet another shiver. Instinctively, he drew forward until their breath became one. He'd never touched her like this before, but in the moment, it felt right.

He watched as her eyes suddenly cleared and then hardened. With her walls firmly in place, she stepped away from him and out of his reach. "I would never let a male close enough to harm me," she said with indifference as she turned and made her way up the stairs.

This time, he let her go. He was not one who second-guessed his decisions, but as he watched Inaya's curvy figure ascending the stairs, for the first time, he wondered if he had made the wrong one all those months ago.

With regards to being a Nephilim, a descendant of the angels and humans combined, Inaya was considered young, just having reached her full maturity in the previous months. But as she finished readying for the evening's festivities and made her way to Amira's chambers, she felt much older and far more cynical than she should for only being twenty-five.

She thought back to her maturity celebration. She had been so sure Trevin was finally going to claim her as his own. She could still remember the moment she had naively decided he was her fated mate. Despite her only being a teenager at the time, their eyes had met and her heart raced. She swore she had felt an arc of electricity pass between them. It was the same electricity she'd felt today as he touched her. It was as if her skin craved contact with his. She detested the weakness in herself.

Throughout the years, she had gone out of her way to gain his attention, earning herself the reputation among the soldiers as being reckless and impulsive. She knew he had felt their connection as well, but he had remained distant and aloof. Yet it had always been Trevin—along with her brothers Murdock and Alyx, of course—who had gone out of his way to ensure she stayed out of trouble and never came to any harm.

As she'd grown older, she'd convinced herself that it was only a matter of time until he made his move. The tension between them had grown unbearable, and as her maturity celebration had approached, she'd known it was time for something to give. And it did, but just not in the way she had expected.

She had dressed in her finest gown and glowed with excitement. She couldn't remember a time when she had ever been more excited or felt more alive. King Vidar and Princess Amira had thrown her a grand ball to celebrate. She had danced and laughed, but kept constant watch toward the door, waiting for Trevin to make his appearance. As the night wore on and her feet began to ache, she started to lose hope, and her patience. Finally, she cornered Alyx and demanded he tell her where Trevin would be. Alyx had been confused, but he had never denied his little sister a thing in her life, so he told her what she wanted to know.

Trevin had specifically requested guard duty on the southern perimeter wall that night, which was just about as far away from her celebration as he could get and still be in Velius. Validating her reputation, Inaya acted on impulse at this information. She snatched off her shoes and ran for the nearest exit, uncaring of the commotion her actions caused.

By the time she reached the southern wall, she was out of breath and had a terrible ache in her side, but her fury kept her moving. On bare feet, she silently climbed the stairs and spotted him about a hundred yards down. He was staring off into the night, but she knew by his stance he was aware of her presence. The closer she came, the stiffer his posture, but he never once looked her way.

"You didn't come," she accused, and was frustrated further by the quiver in her voice.

"There was no need," he stated calmly, still staring off into the darkness.

"N-n-no need?" she stammered in disbelief.

Finally, he turned to her with an enquiring expression, but said nothing. She'd always loved how he was the strong, silent type, but his silence now cut her deeply and she finally lost all restraint.

"Being with me wasn't reason enough to tear you away from this wall? Celebrating and dancing with me? I wore this stupid dress for you!" she yelled through her tears as she indicated the low-cut, silver dress that hugged and exposed her breasts to perfection. She wasn't sure if he'd had an answer, but she didn't give him the chance. "I know this isn't one-sided. I know you feel this, too. I foolishly thought tonight was the night. I've been dreaming of the day you'd finally claim me, but you had no intention, did you? You were just going to stand up here on this wall and do *nothing*!" Without thought, one of her shoes flew from her hand. Trevin swiftly caught it before it hit his chest. For some reason, that angered her even more, so she threw the other one at him as well. Unfortunately, he caught that one too.

"Inaya," he said in warning. She angrily wiped the tears from her face, but said nothing, hoping her silence would force him to communicate. She waited him out, and finally he said, "You're right, I had no intention of claiming you tonight, nor did I give you reason to believe I would." It was her turn to stare out into the darkness. There was no way she could look at him as he so casually ripped her heart out with his words.

"I understand," she said in a near whisper through her tears. And she did. She now understood that she had gotten the whole situation wrong. She had been wrong about Trevin's intentions toward her. The pain in her chest threatened to bring her to her knees, but she refused to show him any more emotion.

"Inaya, I'm just doing my duty." His voice was much gentler as he said this.

"I understand," she repeated as she turned and made her way back to the palace.

The morning after, she had found her shoes sitting neatly outside of her bedroom door, spotless. She had never shared the details about that night with anyone. Nor had she revealed how her nightmares had returned that night as well, reminding her of her mother's hard-learned lesson. There was no such thing as love, fate, or meant to be. And she was pathetic for ever dreaming there was.

Bringing herself back to the here and now, she paused outside of Princess Amira's door. Feeling unworthy and hurt from reliving that night, she straightened her silky, turquoise gown and took a moment to collect herself before knocking. She knew from experience that the best way to get out of self-pity was to be of service to someone else, and by Amira's behavior today, she knew her dearest friend needed her now.

"Amira, may I come in?" she said softly, tapping lightly on the door. "It's an hour until supper. Would you like me to help you prepare?"

Amira's blotchy, tearstained face and her puffy, red eyes peeked around the door as it barely opened. "Yes, I do believe I could use your help tonight."

"Oh, dear...," Inaya breathed softly as she pulled Amira close for a comforting hug, closing the door firmly behind her. She had anticipated Amira being upset, but was taken aback by the state her friend was in.

Amira was the future ruler of the Nephilim and the island of Cashile, and she took that responsibility seriously, working hard to always project herself as the perfectly poised and gracious princess. Through her bloodline, their island sanctuary would remain hidden and protected by the blood bond forged by the angels, which tied the royal family to the shield surrounding the island. Carrying this heavy burden, Amira was careful to never let her guard down with anyone but Inaya.

Unloading her supplies, Inaya quickly took charge. "I've brought a cold compress. Here, hold this on your eyes to help the swelling while I redo your hair."

Amira briefly looked surprised before saying, "You are such a blessing. How did you know?"

As she worked, Inaya explained how she had seen Amira retreat to her chambers through the hidden servants' entrance, and knowing her friend, when she didn't come back, she knew there was a problem. They fell into a comfortable silence as she finished Amira's hair. Figuring she had given her enough time, and impatient to know the problem, Inaya finally asked, "Are you ready to talk about it yet?"

With a chin quiver, Amira admitted, "I overheard a conversation between Caeden and Trevin." Inaya's heart skipped a beat at hearing Trevin's name, but she kept her face impassive and her feelings in check as she tried to focus on Amira's story. "I was returning a towel to the soldiers' keep after my self-defense lesson with Caeden, but before I got there, I heard voices. I... well, I guess I stopped to listen."

Inaya saw the embarrassment staining Amira's cheeks and struggled not to smile at her admission. Amira would feel guilty for eavesdropping, but Inaya lived for moments like that. Having two soldiers as older brothers, Inaya spent a lot of time around them and knew from experience the juicy gossip and wild tales the soldiers would share.

"They were discussing me, Inaya," she continued. "Caeden admitted he only sees me as a naive child who follows him around and chases away all other females. Other females! Can you believe it? I'm just so embarrassed! I have been in love with him for years, and he sees me as nothing but a nuisance."

Inaya shook her head, because, honestly, no, she couldn't believe it. Caeden, the captain of the Royal Guard, and Princess Amira had been circling each other for a while now. It was obvious to everyone that these two would be perfect together. Although Inaya no longer believed in a "meant to be," she had to admit, if there were such a thing, it would apply to Amira and Caeden.

"What?" Amira asked.

"That just doesn't make sense. I've seen you two together, and there are definitely sparks on both sides," Inaya tried to explain. "I think you rattle him. Males, especially soldiers, like to be in control. I think Caeden does want you, but deep down you scare him senseless. He knows he cannot control you; you're the princess, for crying out loud."

"He said he wanted other women!" Amira shouted in rare, unprincesslike behavior, causing Inaya to giggle.

"What's so funny?" Amira asked indignantly, making it even more difficult for Inaya to contain her laughter.

"I just remembered a conversation I heard between Murdock and a couple of the other Guard." There were six Royal Guard members in all, who were in charge of protecting the royal family and commanding the soldiers of Velius. Caeden was the captain, and Trevin was his second-in-command. Her oldest brother, Murdock, along with Levi, Osmond, and Dalek made up the remaining members. "I swear, the soldiers gossip worse than females," Inaya continued with another giggle.

"What did they say?" Amira asked with a grin, catching Inaya's amusement.

"I heard Dalek telling the other guards that he thought Caeden must be going daft because he saw that hussy, Sadie, all but strip naked and throw herself at Caeden's feet in the middle of the courtyard, yet Caeden barely spared her a glance." Inaya didn't feel any guilt for spreading this gossip. Neither of them held any love for Sadie, and although Amira would never speak badly of any of her people, Inaya knew she would enjoy hearing how Caeden turned her down.

She continued by telling the opinion of the others. "Murdock said Caeden was just showing good sense by staying clear of that viper, but Levi seemed to think Caeden was developing an aversion to females. Then the conversation digressed into crude jokes and caveman-like behavior, which would scald your innocent little ears." What Inaya didn't share was how Trevin had also been present at this conversation. As per his custom, he had not voiced his outlook on the situation, but, as per *her* custom, Inaya had been watching him closely and noticed how his lips had tipped up in a knowing grin at the mention of Sadie. She couldn't help but wonder just how "knowing" he was of Sadie.

"That doesn't mean anything; maybe I should just give up and accept that he doesn't want me," Amira said, interrupting Inaya's unwanted thoughts.

Inaya eyed her closely, and then decided to offer her the same plan she had been implementing with Trevin. Although she was no longer allowing herself to want him, she was going to make darn sure he still wanted her, hence her sexy turquoise gown. "Or maybe you should show him what he is missing," Inaya suggested.

THREE

Perched on the edge of the table, Lahash endeavored to contain his anticipation as he pulled the strings of his favorite puppet. Centuries of manipulation and persuasion, and finally, his retribution was at hand. Soon, the abominable Nephilim would cease to exist and so would the reason for his fall. The Creator Upon High would then be forced to remove his status of disgrace and restore him to his full glory of exalted angel.

Lahash watched in amusement as Sorin gracefully manipulated Marcelle into doing his bidding. The male was almost as skilled as Lahash himself, as he should be. Lahash had invested much time in molding Sorin into his blade of deliverance. In fact, Sorin was born for the simple purpose of being Lahash's puppet. From the beginning, he had watched his direct lineage from afar, but only in the last few generations did

Lahash realize their potential. Since, he had taken a firmer, more active role in fashioning them to fit his design.

Unlike others of his progeny, Sorin required a more subtle, indirect approach. He was Lahash's most vital and useful instrument, but his ego and selfishness necessitated that he be played carefully to cultivate the depravity and self-entitlement needed for the task at hand. During Sorin's childhood, Lahash had learned that delicate mental pushes and suggestive taunts were most effective in bringing about the desired outcome, unlike with Sorin's predecessor, with whom direct contact was vital.

Before his fall, obscurity and invisibility were instinctive and effortless, but that was taken, right along with the Creator's divine grace. His magnificent obsidian wings were defiled and tainted opalescent, exposing Lahash and his misdeeds to all. With time and effort, he was able to cultivate the ability to camouflage himself and perfect the ability to influence susceptible minds, which had been forbidden in his angelic status.

Cocking his head to the side, he brought his focus back to the scene before him.

"But what if she won't listen?" Marcelle's husky voice took on an unnaturally shrill pitch, as was her custom when addressing Sorin, which grated on Lahash's nerves. Although she was not one of his own, she had her usefulness for the time being. As soon as that was depleted, he would ensure she was properly disposed of.

Sorin was well-trained and needed no interference as he maneuvered Marcelle. "Are you unworthy of being my queen? Of ruling Cashile at my side?"

"Of course not, my lord, it's just—"

"Then you will do your duty and persuade Princess Amira to obey. She must choose me as her suitor for us to take our rightful places as King and Queen of Velius. Surely you are more intelligent than that sheltered, naïve girl, are you not?"

"Well, of course—"

Sorin's tone gentled and his thumb lovingly caressed her cheek as he interrupted, "Then there should be no problem."

"None," Marcelle quickly agreed.

Lahash watched as Marcelle winced as Sorin's fingers tangled in her unnaturally red hair and violently jerked her head back.

"There had better not be. You will not enjoy what comes next if you fail," Sorin promised, his lips brushing hers in a tender kiss that contradicted the painful hold he retained on her hair.

Lahash barely contained his glee at witnessing Sorin masterly manipulate the female physically, mentally, and emotionally all at the same time.

"It's time, my love," Sorin whispered. "You will make me proud."

Marcelle's dark, beady eyes looked dazed and her

sharp nose flared with arousal as she eagerly nodded in agreement.

Without another word, Sorin pushed her away and dismissed her from his thoughts as he turned to exit the chamber. Lahash focused his attention to the weak-willed female before him. She was nothing like the arbiter of his disgrace, the wicked human seductress who had rejected him after his fall. He longed to snuff out Marcelle's existence.

A commotion just outside the door captured his attention. Curiosity had him utilizing his mental capability to manifest himself at that location. Lahash found himself witness to a confrontation between a fierce, dark-haired warrior who served as a palace guard and Sorin, who appeared weak and pathetic in comparison.

"You are not permitted in this area of the palace," the guard called Trevin informed Sorin.

"I-I go where I please," Sorin stammered, fronting a brave façade, but failing.

His discomfort amused Lahash. It was productive for Sorin's ego to be trampled occasionally. It forced him to recognize his impotence, which fanned the flames of his fury.

Trevin didn't acknowledge Sorin's words. He merely arched his brow and calmly stated, "I'll escort you," before stretching out his arm to prompt Sorin to proceed.

When it looked as if Sorin's arrogant temper was

about to emerge, possibly compromising the future outcome of Lahash's plan, he quickly stepped in, giving Sorin a mental push.

This is a standoff you are incapable of winning. Adapt. Adjust. Be smart. When you are king, you will seek your revenge for this injustice.

Sorin, accustomed to Lahash's subtle influence, calmed immediately, arrogantly cocked his head, and strutted away. Lahash watched as Trevin shook his head in what could only be disgust before following behind Sorin.

Beings such as the warrior Trevin discomfited Lahash. They were unyielding in their righteousness and immune to his influence. There were many such as Trevin within the walls of this palace, thus the reason Lahash had selected residence in the other territories of Cashile to carry out his will. He reminded himself that soon it would all be rectified.

The creak of a door behind him gained his attention. It gained Trevin's as well. They both turned to witness Marcelle exiting the chamber Sorin had just left. Turning back to Trevin, Lahash watched as he struggled to fit the pieces together. It was obvious something was amiss, but it looked as if Trevin lacked the essential details needed to create a clear picture.

Since Marcelle was technically of royal blood, being the late Queen Maryam's only sibling, and Supreme Healer, it was within her rights to have access to this portion of the palace. Therefore, Trevin was not entitled to question her or remove her along with Sorin, although Lahash could perceive that was Trevin's desire. Wordlessly, Trevin turned to carry out his task.

Marcelle had paused, guilt and indecision apparent in her features, as she noticed Trevin. Relief flooded her face as Trevin simply turned and walked away. Her beady eyes roamed the hallway once more before she slunk away to do Sorin's bidding. She must assume all was well and her rendezvous with Sorin had gone unnoticed, but Lahash knew differently. This guard in particular was observant and intuitive. Given enough time, he would become a problem. The Royal Guard as a whole was a problem. They would need to be dealt with quickly.

FOUR

Inaya grinned from ear to ear as she watched Amira twirl in front of the mirror. The sleeveless, champagne-gold-colored silk gown had been the perfect choice for her, and by the look on her face, for once, Amira was actually viewing herself as the rest of the world saw her. She was practically glowing.

But then the excitement fell from her face when a husky voice called through the closed door, "Amira, darling, the guests are arriving."

Damn that woman for putting that insecure, cautious look back on Amira's face. Inaya clenched her jaw tightly to prevent the unkind reprimand from escaping. She would like nothing more than to send Marcelle away for good.

She concentrated on calming herself as Amira admitted her aunt into the chamber and began to make small talk, but couldn't hold back when she heard Marcelle mention the importance of impressing *Lord Sorin of Ammon*. The combination of Marcelle's pretentious attitude and the reminder of Sorin's presence made her want to gag.

"Yes, one must always try to impress Lord Sorin," condescendingly slipped from Inaya's lips.

She knew it was childish and regretted the moment it was said. Not only did it bring her presence to Marcelle's attention, but it also brought a look of panic to Amira's face. Amira had enough pressure and worry; she didn't need Inaya adding to it.

Ever the peacekeeper, Amira automatically jumped in to distract her aunt. "You look lovely as well, Aunt Marcelle," she said, returning Marcelle's previous compliment. Vain and narcissistic as she was, Marcelle easily fell for it.

With one last venomous look in Inaya's direction, Marcelle wrapped her arm around Amira's shoulders and pulled her further away from Inaya, surely so the "lower class" creature in the room wouldn't be privy to the conversation between her betters. Being used to that type of treatment from Marcelle, she didn't allow it to affect her. She knew it said less about her, and more about Marcelle's character, which could only be described as twisted and cruel. It was difficult to believe that such a being could hold such a vital role to their culture and well-being as the title of Supreme Healer. It was her responsibility to safeguard the ancient traditions and ceremonies passed down from their first ancestors. She was to care for the injured and the vulnerable young ones who hadn't yet reached full maturity. In Inaya's opinion, this was not a job the heartless female was qualified for, but unfortunately for all Nephilim, it was her birthright.

Inaya let her mind wander while she waited for Marcelle to take her leave. She found herself mentally rearranging Marcelle's appearance. She'd begin with removing the artificial red hair tint and give her back her natural dark brown locks, which would help her eyes look less beady and abnormal. With the red hair gone, Marcelle would have no use for the shocking red lip color she used to match. Inaya imagined herself gleefully wiping it off her face. Finally, she would adorn her in a gown befitting her station, something with class instead of the racy red dress she had chosen for this evening. Of course, those changes would only decorate the outside; the inside would remain rotten.

The next words to enter her awareness had her seeing red for a completely different reason.

"I'd like you to keep in mind your duty tonight, Amira. Soon it will be your turn to lead our people. You will need a strong, worthy male at your side as your consort and king. Keep an open mind about our guests tonight. For me?" Marcelle begged.

That request was wrong on too many levels. Inaya impulsively interrupted, "She is aware of her duty, Marcelle. Why must she dwell on it tonight? She hasn't even reached her full maturity and cannot join into a bond of marriage until she does."

"This does not concern you, girl," Marcelle snapped, cutting her dark eyes to Inaya.

She opened her mouth to finally tell this horrible female what she thought of her, but Amira was quick to interfere.

"Aunt Marcelle, this is a formal dinner to celebrate the launch of the new scout. This dinner has nothing to do with my future consort."

Inaya held her tongue for the rest of the conversation, mostly out of shock and disgust as she listened to Marcelle sing the virtues of *Lord Sorin* and the "advantages" of a match between him and Amira. By the time Marcelle finally departed, Inaya's head was pounding and she was dreading the evening to come.

As soon as they entered the dining area, Caeden's eyes were immediately drawn to Amira, just as Inaya had known they would be. He wasted no time approaching and requesting a private moment with Amira. Inaya gave her an encouraging smile before she left them to, hopefully, sort things out.

A hand snapped forward and firmly grabbed Inaya's arm as she entered the seating area, effectively stopping her at the entryway. She barely withheld a yelp, which would no doubt attract everyone's attention. Jerking her head to the right, she found eyes the color of molten chocolate staring down at her, threating to draw her into their spell.

"Trevin." It came out as a husky whisper.

"The seating arrangements could not be altered, but I trust you will take heed of our earlier conversation. You may be polite, but you will not pursue Sorin's attention," Trevin decreed.

Inaya ripped her arm from his grasp. "I don't need you to instruct me on how to behave. I've been adequately put in my place once already today and reminded not to interfere with my betters."

"How's that?" His body was tense and his eyes fierce.

She felt a flutter in her lower belly, the unwanted attraction flaring at his intensity and show of strength. She shifted away from him and tried for a look of indifference. "Nothing for you to worry about."

Trevin quickly scanned the room before his eyes came back to her. "We'll discuss it later." His warm hand settled on the small of her back as he escorted Inaya to her seat. "For now, safeguard yourself from unnecessary trouble, for both of us," he said the last on a whisper in her ear as he helped her settle in her seat before taking his position across the room to stand guard. Her eyes followed him the entire way.

"I didn't realize this was a charity event." Sorin's snide comment reached her from across the table, as he had intended.

Inaya was temporarily distracted by Marcelle choking on her water at Sorin's comment, but quickly turned back to address him. "Meaning?"

"Meaning the rest of us are forced to endure the company of a street urchin," he gave her a scathing once-over before continuing, "because King Vidar is weak-willed and gullible, which works out well for you, but is unfortunate for the rest of us."

Inaya could practically feel the hatred being thrown at her through Sorin's words. Her brief interactions with him in the past hadn't been pleasant, but never had he spoken to her in this manner before. Too stunned to speak, she glanced to the head of the table where King Vidar sat conversing with Lord Donovan, Lady Ferrara, and Kearney, the new scout.

Inaya was grateful the king hadn't heard the slight against him, but as the shock wore off, indignation and hurt began to surface, quickly followed by untamed fury. Just as she opened her mouth, ready to let this arrogant swine know exactly what she thought of him, Amira came sweeping in the room, gaining everyone's attention. Always the proper princess, Amira greeted each of her guests before taking her seat at the end of the table opposite of her father.

The stress of the day, added to the fact she was sitting across the table from Sorin, was beginning to wear on Inaya. She tried to keep her head down and her temper contained, but the emotions inside her were churning, threatening to erupt. This dinner couldn't end quickly enough; the urge to run, to escape, to yell, to hit something—anything to release this painful energy inside her—was overwhelming her.

Taking deep, slow breaths to calm herself, she tried to concentrate on her dinner, but Sorin's arrogant and annoying voice broke into her awareness. "...is difficult to find good help. They sometimes forget their place."

Inaya looked up to see him staring at her as he made that statement. She once again opened her mouth to let him have it, but a movement on the other side of the room behind Sorin caught her attention. Trevin had merely shifted his stance, but it was enough. When he caught her eye, he made a slight gesture with his head, not quite a shake, but Inaya understood what he was saying.

She met Sorin's gaze and narrowed her eyes, hoping he saw in them all the words she was unable to say. He met her look with a scornful expression of his own before slapping on a falsely charming smile and addressing Amira again. Inaya tried to tune him out once more, but the strange tone of Amira's voice caught her attention, slightly alarming her.

"Speaking of hands, please remove yours from my person before I have my guards do it for you."

Inaya gasped in shock. She had never heard Amira speak in such a harsh and commanding tone.

Then the princess continued. "For future reference, and so there will not be any more confusion, the Lady Inaya is not a servant but an honorary part of the royal family and will be addressed with the respect she deserves. Furthermore, since I must instruct you on what is proper, you will address me as 'Princess,' not 'doll.' Is that understood?"

Amira was not only standing up for herself; she was defending Inaya as well. She was so proud of her friend, she couldn't contain her excitement. And the look of disbelief and frustration on Sorin's face made the entire situation hilarious. Her pent-up emotions and energy had finally found an outlet in her laughter, and before long, she had attracted the attention of the entire table.

"Inaya, sweetheart, would you like to share your amusement with the rest of us?" the king asked, smiling down the table at her.

Trying to control her giggles, she said, "Oh no, I couldn't. Amira was just sharing with us her outlook. You know how charming and entertaining she is. I apologize for interrupting your conversation." She had finally gotten herself under control.

King Vidar looked fondly at Inaya, and then turned his attention to his daughter, his smile dimming a bit.

"My dear, are you feeling all right?" he asked with concern, drawing Inaya's attention to her friend as well. She was pale, and her anxiety could clearly be read on her face. Seeing that sobered Inaya completely.

"Father and dear guests, I'm going to have to excuse myself for the rest of the evening. I find that I am feeling a little unwell," Amira announced. Inaya tried catching her eye as she passed, but was unsuccessful.

Sorin immediately leapt to his feet to follow Amira out the door. Childish, yes, but as he passed Inaya's chair, she "accidentally" stuck her foot out, making him stumble. Unfortunately, he was able to catch himself before he tumbled to the ground. He sneered at her as he straightened and then made his way out into the hall, only to return minutes later.

As he glared at her from across the table, Inaya thought tripping him might have been going a step too far. Inaya prayed dinner would be over soon; only one last course to go. Maybe this night could end with no more conflict. As she had that last thought, Sorin sat up and leaned toward her across the table.

"You may wash up nicely, but I can see right through you. You're garbage, just like your mother." Inaya gasped at Sorin's words, causing a smirk to cross his cruel features. "Oh yes, I knew your mother. In fact, there aren't too many males in that area who didn't know your mother."

Her fists were clenched so hard that her fingernails were cutting into her palms, not that she cared.

"You're a liar," she hissed.

"Am I?" he asked with a wide grin and sat back.

She needed to leave. She needed to leave right now or else she was going to hurl herself over this table and beat him senseless. She may be an honorary member of the royal family, but she didn't think that would free her of punishment should she assault a royal dignitary.

As gracefully as she was able, she stood and folded her napkin beside her plate and addressed the table. "Please excuse me also. I find that I, too, am not feeling well." She waited for King Vidar's nod of consent before exiting.

Trevin took a deep breath and forced his jaw to unclench. He was ready to just end Sorin and save everyone the aggravation, but he wasn't about to let his inner rage be seen. He had learned early to keep a close hold on his emotions. To display them would leave him vulnerable, and that was a position he would not put himself in again.

Before the meal had even begun, Sorin had somehow upset Inaya, and the urge to drag her away and lock her up until their "guest" left was nearly overwhelming. Instead, he did his duty and stood silently, watching, guarding, waiting for the provocation needed to take Sorin down. It had come close when he had gotten into a verbal confrontation with Princess Amira. Sorin was lucky Caeden had so much self-control, or else, with the black mood the captain of the Royal Guard had been in lately, Sorin wouldn't have made it alive through the second course.

When Inaya had excused herself before the meal

was complete, every instinct screamed for him to follow her out, but duty demanded he stay. His duty to the Royal Guard was what gave him purpose; it was what he lived for. It kept him grounded and in control. Inaya was his one exception, his only vulnerability. She was young and impulsive. And she needed him. He both loved her and despised himself for that.

Trouble was coming. He could sense it, and until it presented itself and he was able to rectify whatever it may be, he didn't have time to consider his feelings for Inaya. It was best for everyone involved if he kept her at a distance. He would protect her and keep her safe, that was part of his duty after all, but that's all there was to it.

Angry voices met Trevin's ears as he entered the guards' keep.

"What do you mean 'She's taken Knight'?" Murdock's voice thundered as Trevin entered the commons area.

A red-faced Murdock was standing in the middle of the room toe-to-toe with his younger brother, Alyx, who had the good sense to look worried. Normally, Trevin would go about his business and let others sort out their own affairs, but he'd been around these siblings enough to have seen this situation before. Inaya was up to something. Murdock was the overly protective brother, whereas Alyx was the unknowing accomplice or condoner, often precipitating this very scenario.

Trevin leaned against the wall, crossing one leg over the other, waiting to see if this required his attention. He had last seen Inaya only a short time ago when she had excused herself from the dining hall, so surely she couldn't have created too much trouble.

"Well...," Alyx hedged, "she wanted to go for a ride."

"Therefore you allowed our little sister to take your fastest and most unpredictable stallion out on a joyride through the countryside *in the dark*! Do you have any sense at all? If she'd have asked for a dagger to slit her throat with, would you have provided that too?"

Trevin was only slightly alarmed by her actions. It was dangerous, but he knew she was an accomplished rider, and it wasn't the first time she'd pulled a stunt like this.

"It's not like you can tell Inaya no. Besides, she didn't actually ask permission," Alyx answered defensively.

"So, she stole your horse." Murdock threw up his arms in exasperation and began to pace but stopped midstep when he noticed Trevin. "You!" Murdock pointed and made his way to Trevin. "You were supposed to be watching her."

"And I did," Trevin answered calmly, Murdock's bluster not affecting him.

"Well, not well enough. She's upset and has run off to break her foolish neck!"

"I did my duty," Trevin growled as he pushed off

the wall to stand straight. "Sorin didn't get close enough to lay a single finger on her. In fact, someone needed to guard him from her. She nearly had him flat on his face by tripping him."

Murdock's lips twitched with a grin before turning serious once again. "I wasn't worried about him touching her. I was worried about what he might say to her, and obviously I had reason."

Trevin wasn't sure what Murdock meant, but he remembered the fire and unknown emotion that flashed in her eyes before she excused herself earlier. A knot formed in his stomach. "I'll go get her."

"No, I'll go get her," Murdock contradicted. Trevin started to protest, but Murdock cut him off. "Inaya is my responsibility."

As much as it angered him to admit it, Murdock was right. A growl of frustration left his lips as he watched Murdock leave.

"Did she really almost knock Sorin on his ass?" Alyx's amused question brought Trevin's attention to the younger male. He'd almost forgotten he was even present.

Instead of answering, Trevin gave the boy a word of advice. "You're going to have to learn to stand up to her sometime. One day your sister is going to get herself in more trouble than she can handle."

"You try telling her no," Alyx shot back.

"I have."

"Yeah, and how'd that go?"

"Not well," Trevin was forced to admit, causing Alyx to snicker.

"That's what I thought. Besides, I know you and Murdock would never allow her to get in any trouble you couldn't get her out of."

"No, we wouldn't," Trevin said as he left the room.

FIVE

Inaya slid from the heaving stallion and began to pace, her chest rising and falling in anger almost as quickly as the exhausted horse's. The break-neck-paced ride was supposed to be a release for the turmoil raging inside her, but it hadn't helped. Her chest ached, breathing was difficult, and her mind raced, never settling on one thought. She felt ready to burst into tiny, unsalvageable pieces.

Looking to the heavens, she screamed out in anguish as she fell to her knees, tears falling uncontrollably. She wanted to be mad at Sorin. She wanted to indulge her indignation, because how dare he say such things to her? But out here, alone, at the edge of their world, with nothing but ocean and sky before her, she could be honest with herself. She was angry, and she was hurt, but it was directed at the one person it truly belonged to—her mother.

There was much about her childhood that she couldn't remember, or refused to let herself think about, but from what she did know of her mother's character, Sorin's words very well could be true.

As her tears began to ease, she slowly became aware of her surroundings. First, she felt the cool, damp ground underneath her, saturating her gown. Next to enter her consciousness was the rhythmic whoosh of the waves meeting the shore and the moist, salt-laced air encircling her. And finally, the silent, steel-like form sitting just an arm's length away.

She wiped her face with her sleeve quickly before turning her full attention to her brother. His shoulders were tense, his jaw was clenched, and his eyes were locked on the untamable waves before them. Murdock could be quite intimidating, and she knew he would be displeased by her reckless behavior this evening. A shiver of apprehension ran up her spine.

Murdock, who missed nothing, wrapped his arm around her and pulled her into his embrace. Her automatic response was to stiffen at the physical contact, but she forced herself to relax. He was her brother; he'd never harm her. Besides, Murdock never allowed her to distance herself anyway, knowing she needed the affection even if it didn't come naturally. He pressed a kiss against her temple when he felt her settle in to his embrace and gruffly whispered, "I'm sorry."

"Wh-why are you sorry?" she questioned, shocked.

"I couldn't prevent this."

"Murdock, you can't safeguard me from every little thing."

"I'm—"

She raised her hand to stop him and quickly interrupted. "I got upset, but I'm a grown woman. I can handle it and get over it."

Murdock let out a heavy sigh and his body relaxed minutely. "You will always be my baby sister, grown or not, and it's my responsibility to look after you. I have failed you before." Inaya tried to interrupt again, but he wouldn't let her. "I will do everything in my power to never let it happen again."

"Murdock—"

"Inaya, I know you don't hold me responsible, and I cherish how forgiving you are, but that doesn't change the past."

She knew it was pointless to have this conversation once again. He would not let her ease his guilt. Instead, she did something she hadn't ever done before; she asked about the past.

"Tell me about Momma?"

Murdock's head snapped to the side to look at her in shock and, maybe, a little apprehension. For years, he had tried to get her to discuss the past with him and she had refused. She was still unable to tell him what he wanted to know, but she was hoping he could give her the information she needed to reconcile her fragmented memories and, hopefully, be able to objectively evaluate Sorin's accusation.

"Momma was not well—"

"No," she cut him off, "not that part. I know that part. Tell me about before. Tell me about what she was like when you were young."

Silently, his eyes searched hers. She was unsure what he searched for and if he'd even be able to find it with only the light of the moon to see by, but he must have because he began to speak.

"She was beautiful, almost as beautiful as you are." He turned to stare back out at the ocean before he continued. "She had a great voice," he said with a wistful smile. "She and Father would sing together as they worked in the garden. Alyx and I would willingly help, just to listen."

"They were happy together?"

"They were."

"What happened?"

"I don't know, Inaya," he answered with a heavy sigh. "Alyx and I joined the army. Life got in the way, and it was hard to find the time to visit. Many years passed as I fought my way up the ranks to the Royal Guard, and when I finally came home, Father was dead. Momma had sent no word to me or Alyx. Our father died, and she didn't even see fit to tell us."

Inaya heard the hurt and anger in his voice. She clutched his hand, wanting to comfort him.

Murdock audibly swallowed before continuing. "She claimed he had died peacefully in his sleep almost two years prior."

A memory flashed in Inaya's mind, pulling her from the present.

"You challenged my husband for me, and yet you refuse to claim me," a female voice screeched.

"But I already have you. What need is there to claim you?" a rough voice answered with a cruel laugh.

Inaya's heart pounded and her breath caught. Murdock gave her a questioning look. Guilt engulfed her. Keeping secrets from her brother felt wrong, but that particular memory would bring nothing but pain and more questions. She justified her silence by reminding herself that she didn't have the details needed to provide an answer; her memory was faulty. She shook her head and gave him a weak smile, letting him know it was okay to continue.

"My resentment toward her kept me away after that. I only returned home decades later because I had heard word of your birth. I came back for you." He briefly met her eyes with that statement.

"Were you angry?" Inaya asked fearfully.

"Why would I have been angry?"

"That Momma had had a baby with another male," she said quietly.

"Angry, no. Concerned, yes. I was worried for you. She was alone with you, no male present to provide for you and protect you, and she was getting up in age. I tried to persuade her to allow me to care for you, to let me take you with me, but she refused. I couldn't stay there; my life was in Velius, but I visited as often as I could. I know that wasn't enough. I hadn't realized just how unwell she was until it was too late." His voice trailed off.

This conversation was skating the edge of a path she just couldn't allow it to go down. So instead, Inaya steadied herself and finally asked the question she had always wanted to know the answer to, but had been too afraid to ask.

"Did she tell you who my father is?"

Murdock shifted uneasily before answering. "No. I'd asked her several times, but she never would say."

Inaya didn't think he was lying, but she had the feeling he wasn't telling her everything. They both sat quietly for a while, each lost in their own thoughts. Finally, Murdock broke the silence by asking, "Tell me about her death?"

Inaya's heart froze in her chest before picking up a frenzied tempo. "I-I can't...."

He let out a disappointed sigh, but didn't push, only asked, "Someday?"

"I'll try," she promised with a weak smile.

Murdock pushed to his feet and held his hand down to help her up. "So, young lady, let's discuss your new talent for horse thievery."

Inaya couldn't prevent her smile. Now this was a conversation she could handle.

~

Trevin watched as Inaya shuffled her way down the hallway, looking half-asleep. Her head hung low, and therefore she hadn't even noticed his presence outside of Princess Amira's chambers. Her vibrant energy was lacking this morning, and the possible reasoning behind it infuriated him, bringing back his feelings of impotence from the previous night.

"Does your word mean nothing?" he growled in her ear. Those were not the words he had planned. For someone who guarded his words carefully, he seemed to have lost the ability in her presence.

Her head snapped up, and he was taken aback by the dark circles beneath her weary eyes.

"And good morning to you as well, Trevin," she sassed to his amusement, but he didn't let her distract him from his purpose.

"I need to be able to trust you," he stated, putting himself out there.

A hurt look crossed her face before she slipped on her impassive mask, the one she was getting so good at wearing. "And you believe I'm untrustworthy?"

"I believe you are young and impulsive and do not think before you act. I asked something very small of you yesterday, and you failed to honor your word." He knew that statement was unfair and harsh, but he needed her to understand the seriousness of this issue. This wasn't just about this singular event, but about her future. Their future.

Her mask slipped, and her anger shone through.

"You asked nothing of me yesterday, and therefore, I agreed to nothing. You made declarations and commanded me about as if you have the right," she said through clenched teeth.

"I have every right."

"Who do you think you are?" Inaya yelled directly into his face, her vibrant energy returning with her passionate anger.

"Sweetheart, you know exactly who I am," he growled back at her.

A sharp intake of breath coming from his right snapped him out of his angry standoff with Inaya. He turned his attention to Princess Amira, who stood in her bedroom doorway with a shocked expression on her face, her mouth hanging open slightly. Confusion swarmed her eyes as she looked between them, taking in the tense atmosphere. His eyes traveled back to Inaya. Her eyes flashed with her fury as her chest rose and fell heavily from her anger. By the angels, she was beautiful.

The princess's arrival broke the spell Inaya's presence put him under. He was on duty, and duty came first, he reminded himself.

"Good morning, Princess," he greeted formally, once more containing his inner turmoil, at least on the outside, but as much as he wanted, he was still unable to pull his eyes away from Inaya. When startled by the princess's arrival, Inaya had jumped away from him and even now refused to meet his gaze.

"Trevin," the princess responded politely, her voice soft and unsure as she held her door open for Inaya to enter.

As Inaya brushed past him, the urge to pull her body back to his pushed at him, demanding contact, insisting on her attention. His eyes closed briefly as he fought to keep in control. Duty came first.

"The send-off is in an hour, Princess," he reminded her before heading back to his post, needing the distance.

He couldn't keep doing this; it wasn't fair to either of them. He wouldn't be claiming her, and acting as if she were his just played havoc with both of their emotions. Inaya had looked exhausted; whatever caused that haunted look in her eyes, his mixed signals were not helping. He had been right in the past to keep his distance; this just reaffirmed it. She was Murdock's little sister, the broken and scared girl brought to the palace years ago. He shouldn't be having these thoughts and feelings about her. As he waited for when it was time to escort the princess to send off the dignitaries—thankfully, Sorin would be part of the group leaving—he recommitted to his plan of action, or inaction, as it were.

Once the dignitaries were gone and the heightened security was no longer needed within the palace, he'd be free to focus on the danger he could feel stalking them, as well as create some much-needed distance between the two of them.

Dreamless sleep had been elusive for Inaya, so she fought sleep altogether. She had hoped it would pass with the relief of the stress that came with the departure of the dignitaries, but that had been two days ago, and the lack of sleep was wearing on her. Seemingly only minutes after her eyes had closed, screams echoed through the room. Panicked, Inaya scurried to the headboard, trying to make herself as small as possible. The bed shook, and the walls shuddered. She watched in shock as the chair next to the desk crashed to the floor, but the trembling ceased as quickly as it had started. If there weren't physical evidence, she would think she had imagined it. Fear clouded her sleep-filled mind as she desperately surveyed her bedroom, looking for danger, but finding nothing. It was an odd feeling to be awoken by screams other than her own. A commotion in the hallway drew her attention. It sounded as if a battalion of soldiers was trampling just outside her door. Could there be a fire and everyone was evacuating?

Cautiously, she climbed from her bed and made her way to the door. Opening it just enough to peek out, she realized there really was a battalion, or very near to, rushing through the hallway, made up of palace servants and soldiers. No one seemed to know what was happening. Quickly, she closed the door and rushed to get dressed before making her way back into the hallway.

Spying a familiar face, she darted across and latched onto Dalek's arm, stopping him in midmotion. With Dalek being a member of the Royal Guard, surely he would be able to tell her what was going on.

"Dalek, what is all of this?"

Dalek was the most carefree and fun-loving Guard member, so seeing the despair and reluctance on his face sent a chill up her spine.

"Dalek?"

His large hand wrapped around her bicep as he pulled her to the side and out of everyone's way.

"He's dead. The king is dead," he choked out quietly.

His words didn't make sense. All the commotion surrounding them faded away as her mind tried to make reason of his words. It seemed as if even her heart had stopped beating for a moment.

"Inaya?"

Her head snapped up; only then did she realize her mind had shut down and she had been staring blankly in front of her at Dalek's chest.

"I'm sorry, what?"

"The king was murdered sometime during the night," he said quietly. Her face must have shown her confusion because he continued. "We're not sure who is responsible, but we will find out," he promised fiercely.

"Oh..." was all she could say to acknowledge his words, but she felt her head shaking in denial. This wasn't making sense. How could this have happened? It couldn't be real.

"Hey," he said sharply, gaining her attention once again, "stay with me, girl. I know you were close to the king, but you gotta keep it together. We're going to need you." She took a deep, shaky breath and nodded. "Good." His eyes left hers as he quickly looked around, taking in the activity around them. Palace servants lingered about in various stages of fear and confusion as soldiers rushed around on high alert as they searched the palace. Dalek's rusty brown eyes met hers once more as he softly admitted, "We have no idea how this will affect the island and our protective shield. Earthquakes have already begun. We need to avoid panic as much as possible."

She nodded again, and his piercing eyes searched her face, probably trying to judge her stability. She squared her shoulders and asked, "How can I help?"

Apparently deeming her competent, he began, "The princess—"

"Oh God, Amira!"

Inaya turned to rush to her friend, but Dalek forcibly stopped her by once again grabbing her arm.

"I need to—"

"Shh," Dalek interrupted. In what was meant to be a calming gesture, he brought his hand up to brush a strand of her long, blonde hair from her face, but on instinct, she flinched and ripped herself away from him before she had a chance to control the impulse. With confusion in his eyes, he raised his hands in front of himself in a surrendering motion. "Hey, hey, I'm not going to hurt you."

Embarrassment stained her cheeks. "I need to check on Amira." Her mind was racing, but she latched on to that thought, that purpose, to help stifle the fear and grief that threatened to overwhelm her.

"I get that, but you need to know, the princess is unconscious. Lady Marcelle is with her now. She believes it's due to the blood bond shifting from King Vidar to Princess Amira. You're the closest thing we have to a member of the royal family right now." He paused to survey their surroundings again. "Listen, word of the king's death has already started to spread, but it would probably be easier to take if it came from someone they trusted, if it came from you."

She closed her eyes in resignation; this was not a task she wanted, but she would do what she must. "Okay, but... are you sure?" she asked, uselessly hoping there might be some doubt regarding Vidar's death.

Sympathy and grief filled his eyes. "Inaya, I witnessed the body," he admitted carefully.

Tears filled her eyes, and she felt her chin quiver, but she refused to allow herself to break down.

"Okay," she whispered, "but if Amira—"

"The Guard is meeting there now. If something changes, someone will notify you." He paused, as if something just occurred to him. "Try to get everyone rounded up and see if anyone else is missing; then you can join Amira."

"Else?"

"Levi can't be located," he admitted softly, "but that information isn't to be shared, understand?"

"Of course," she agreed quickly. Levi's disappearance was strange, but it was the least of her worries. The Guard member was probably snuggled up to some random female right now.

With a nod, Dalek continued, "Keep an eye out for anything suspicious." With her nod of agreement, he went about his business, leaving her to a task she desperately dreaded.

Six

Lahash watched the whimpering, sniveling huddled mass with disdain. How simple it would be to strike them down and end their miserable existence. But that would be considered unethical. They must destruct by their own doing. To directly cause their obliteration would not serve his purpose in the eyes of his maker.

A small, curvy, blonde female drew his attention. He'd seen her before in passing, but never paid her any mind. Now he could see he had been amiss in doing so. Familiar turquoise eyes flashed in his direction, and the oxygen caught in his throat. If he were capable of such a feeling, he would describe the tightening sensation in his chest and the prickle of goose bumps that ruffled the silky, opalescent feathers of his magnificent wings as panic. But that was nonsense, he assured himself. It was just discomfiting to learn of her existence in such a manner, because there was no denying this young creature was one of Lahash's descendants. There was no way she could have come from one of his fallen brethren. Her eyes were the exact color of the wicked human female who had been the cause of his fall from grace.

Now those haunting eyes seemed to stare into his while a look of deep concentration crossed her face.

Although he was certain she couldn't possibly see him through his concealment, his eyes remained locked to hers until she finally turned her attention elsewhere. A feeling of foreboding passed through him. His and this female's path were linked in some manner. Armed with this knowledge, he would need to ensure this came to fruition on his terms.

Females were treacherous and emotional creatures whom he had little use for, but this one may be the exception.

He watched as she masterfully handled the distraught crowd of servants. She answered their concerns, but gave nothing away, all the while extracting information from them without seeming intrusive or untrusting.

Lahash enjoyed the calculating expression that crossed Inaya's face as she sorted through the information. Soon she came to the rightful conclusion that nothing could be gained from these insignificant beings.

His puppets would not be so careless as to bring

attention to themselves as they carried out their misdeeds. Capturing Levi had been a challenge for his soldiers, but had been possible with the element of surprise. Getting Marcelle to murder the king, that had been quite simple in comparison.

Marcelle had slipped soundlessly through the corridors of the royal family's wing of the palace. With Lahash's assistance, she easily went unnoticed by the soldiers on duty, and due to the late hour, the servants were tucked soundly in their beds. Thanks to Lahash's intervention, the king's chamber door was unlocked, giving her easy access.

Lahash watched in amusement as the devious female attempted one last try at gaining Vidar's favor.

Marcelle quietly pulled the door closed behind her and flipped the lock. Before she even made it through the king's receiving chamber into the sleeping quarters, she had already discarded the ill-fitting, tight, violet gown that had failed to acquire Vidar's attention earlier in the day. Carelessly, she left a trail of clothing in her wake as she approached the foot of Vidar's bed, naked.

Without a second thought, she crawled onto the bed, making her way over the sleeping body of the king.

The moment her weight shifted the bed, Vidar was startled awake. He quickly switched on the bedside light and reached for the blade he kept strapped to his head-

board. His hand stilled as he recognized Marcelle's fiery red hair in the dim light.

"What are you doing here?" he asked in confusion.

Marcelle sensuously rubbed her naked body against his as she pushed him back down to a prone position, his shock making him compliant.

"What does it look like?" she purred in her husky tone, brushing her lips against his as she settled her bottom firmly on Vidar's groin and rocked herself against him.

Coming out of his shock, Vidar placed his hands on her shoulders and pushed her up into a sitting position, exposing her breasts to his view. She took the opportunity to rub her hands down his chest, pulling the covers down as she went. When they reached his hips, he found the presence of mind to grab her wrists.

"Stop, Marcelle," he demanded firmly.

Undeterred, she lifted her knees off the bed and spread her legs wide, giving him a clear view of her sex.

"Don't fight this, Vidar. We both know this is what you want."

"No, it isn't," he denied as he released her and pushed himself to sit against the headboard. "You need to dress and exit my chamber."

Her body followed his forward, and she once again sat firmly astride his hips. Taking advantage of her breasts being directly in his view, just a few inches from his face, she caressed herself and pinched a hardened nipple for emphasis.

"You don't really want that," she said with a knowing smile as she watched his eyes follow her hands.

Before she could predict his intent, she found herself roughly pushed off him and onto the cold floor.

"Get out," came his growled response.

Unhurt but in a daze, she sat on the floor staring up at him.

"But—"

"But nothing, Marcelle. You've gone too far this time. I've put up with your behavior thus far because you are my wife's sister—"

"Your wife is dead!" she screeched.

Mindlessly, she reached for Levi's blade, which Lahash's soldier had given her and she had carelessly placed at the foot of the bed before climbing up.

"And you can join her," Marcelle vowed, and with a surge of adrenaline she lunged forward, slashing the blade across his throat.

Lahash had spectated this interaction with great amusement, but watching Marcelle stand frozen in fascination as Vidar's life's essence gushed from his wound, painting his torso and the surrounding area crimson, gave him cause for concern. A scream tore through the air, stirring Marcelle into action. Quickly, she threw on Vidar's robe and gathered her belongings. She slid the chamber door open and peeked into the empty hallway. All the commotion was coming from the corridor that housed Princess Amira's chambers.

With one final glance to verify she had left nothing

of herself behind, Marcelle hurried out and back to her room.

Thinking back on her detached state after murdering the man she had supposedly loved, and knowing at that exact moment she was upstairs in complete hysterics, Lahash had to wonder if she was losing touch with reality or if Marcelle was just that talented of an actress.

Coming back to the present, he watched Inaya take her leave to check on the princess's well-being. Yes, she would make a much more valuable asset, but unlike Marcelle, who had been a murderess long before his influence began, instinctually he knew Inaya could not be corrupted... but she could be manipulated.

SEVEN

 King Vidar's funeral came all too soon. His death still seemed unreal. Inaya had tried to fill the passing time with caring for Amira and keeping the palace organized, anything to prevent from having too much thinking time. If she could just remain busy enough, this pain inside wouldn't consume her and, hopefully, it would ease. She hurt so badly that at times it felt impossible to breathe.

"We're leaving now. Are you sure you don't want to come?" Murdock asked from the doorway.

Inaya looked up from where she was kneading biscuit dough for Vidar's memorial feast and took in her oldest brother, noticing the stress and grief etched in the worry lines on his face. Turning away, she nodded, but it took a moment before she could trust her voice to speak.

"Yes. I'm needed here. This feast won't prepare itself."

"Inaya, you—"

"I can't," she interrupted, finally meeting his sad eyes. "I can't face this. I can't watch as the only father I have ever known is burned to ash."

Murdock reached out to comfort her but backed off when she shied away. A sigh escaped his lips and she knew her rejection disappointed him, but she couldn't handle physical contact in that moment; she was just too vulnerable.

"I'm sorry," she whispered shamefully.

"Nothing to be sorry about, Inaya. I understand your reluctance to go, and so would Vidar. I just don't want you to have any regrets."

"I won't," she promised.

With a nod, he left her to her work.

Not sure how much time had passed, Inaya was pulled from her thoughts when a commotion in the courtyard drew her attention. She rushed to the window and immediately noticed the inner gates were open wide. Since the death of the king, the gates had been on lockdown. Movement to the right caught her eye. The sight made her breath catch in her throat. The courtyard was filled with soldiers, but not just any soldiers. These soldiers bore the seal of the territory of Ammon. These were Sorin's soldiers.

By the time she made it from the kitchen to the main hall, soldiers were swarming into the palace and rounding up the few workers who had volunteered to stay and help prepare. The chaos before her was overwhelming, and her body and mind froze. A cry of pain tore her from her stupor as one of the soldiers yanked a young maid across the room. Without thought, Inaya rushed him and, catching him by surprise, was able to break his hold on the female.

He reached back, preparing to strike her, but stayed his hand when he took in her attire and realized she was a lady.

"You will cease immediately," Inaya commanded with as much authority as she could muster.

"My lady—" he began, but was interrupted by a familiar voice coming from directly behind her.

"My soldiers do not take orders from filthy peasants."

Flinching at the insult, Inaya attempted to mask her reaction and hide her fear and self-doubt as she turned to face Sorin.

"Your soldiers have no authority here."

With a smirk, he ignored her completely and addressed the soldier behind her.

"This female is but a glorified servant and will be treated as such. She gets no special treatment simply because she wears the princess's hand-me-downs. In fact, lock her away with the other hostiles."

Inaya's words stuck in her throat as she watched

Sorin dismiss her from his thoughts and walk away. Besides, what could she say? Deep inside, she knew he was correct. With his words, all her doubts and insecurities were proven true.

"I see you're a liar," the soldier growled in her ear as he grabbed her arms and forced them behind her back.

The feeling of being restrained triggered a full-blown panic attack, and suddenly she couldn't breathe. Her lungs refused to take in enough air and her heart threatened to beat from her chest. Her vision turned black as flashes of her childhood returned. The soldier's hands were replaced with the feeling of the ropes that had bound her in the past.

She fought against it and struggled for her freedom, refusing to allow herself to be locked in that tiny room again. Momma wouldn't return for days, and Inaya would have nowhere to relieve herself and her belly would ache with hunger.

The primal instinct to protect herself took over. Her arms were released as she felt the back of her head smash against soft tissue. Blindly, she darted away from her captor. She only made it a few feet before something hard crashed into her from behind. She felt the brief sensation of falling and the intense pain of her head slamming into the floor, and then there was nothing.

~

The memorial service was a somber event, but Trevin couldn't allow himself to relax enough to actually mourn the passing of King Vidar. The knowledge that a murderer was hiding in their midst kept him hyper-vigilant. He scanned the crowd as they made their way back to the palace from the Meadow of Spirits.

Was the slaying of the king the danger he had been feeling, or was there still more to come? His gut tightened at the thought. The physical and environmental ramifications of this tragedy were still unknown. The protective shield around Cashile was showing signs of stress, and the occasional aftershock from the earthquake could be felt trembling the earth.

His eyes drifted to Princess Amira. There were dark circles under her eyes and her skin had a grayish tint. Both could be physical reactions to her grief, but Trevin wagered the burden of holding the blood bond securing the shield was also a factor. The bond was never meant to be supported by one as young and fragile as the princess.

His eyes drifted to the captain of the Royal Guard. Caeden hadn't left the princess's side all day. He seemed to be providing the distant support Amira needed to endure. Trevin found hope and reassurance in that fact. Perhaps Caeden was the solution. He was plenty strong enough to carry the bond and undeniably worthy. And there was no doubt Caeden adored Princess Amira.

Trevin noticed how Caeden's eyes continuously scanned the crowd for danger as well. They could trust no one; after all, there was physical evidence the murder could have been committed by one of their own. But although Levi's weapon had been used to slaughter the king, Trevin's gut instinct said it was impossible Levi was responsible.

Caeden's body became rigid, and Trevin followed the direction of his gaze, immediately realizing the cause of Caeden's alarm. The gates to the inner courtyard were open. Caeden signaled for the Guard to close in around the princess. Upon entering the courtyard, the soldiers of Ammon became visible.

Amira tried to push her way through the Royal Guard, but there was no way they would allow her to expose herself to danger, so she was forced to speak around them.

"What is the meaning of this?" she demanded.

The reply came from the bastard, Sorin, himself as he strolled from behind the wall of soldiers blocking their path to the palace. "Thank the heavens you are safe, my princess. I was so worried about your safety after hearing the terrible news."

The very sound of his sickeningly sweet voice made Trevin crave to commit violence. It was difficult to stand idle while the princess confronted their intruders. He waited anxiously for Caeden to give the signal for them to engage.

Amira's weariness and confusion were clear as she

asked, "Why are your armed soldiers in my courtyard, Sorin?"

Trevin didn't care what the reasoning was. He only cared about rectifying this situation and finally being able to take Sorin down.

"Why, for your protection of course." Sorin's face almost looked sincere as he said it, but his next words had Trevin nearly losing his self-control. "Your Guard has been compromised. Therefore, I take it upon myself as my duty to see to your protection. Secure the princess." Sorin addressed the last to his soldiers.

The enemy soldiers had the nerve to approach, and Trevin knew he wore a satisfied expression as he readied his weapon, anticipating the moment they were in striking distance. The crowd was eerily quiet, waiting to see what would happen.

"Stop!" Amira screamed into the quiet. "I appreciate your concern, Sorin, but I assure you this is not necessary. I already have my Guard, as you can see," she said, sounding panicked.

"Your Guard can no longer be trusted; surely even you can understand that. Was it not a member of your own Guard who killed our dear king?" Sorin couldn't hide his smugness at being able to deliver this news to the crowd. It seemed like everyone drew in a sharp breath at the same time. The crowd began to stir, and murmurs of Levi's absence could be heard.

Through his anger, Trevin missed the princess's answer, but he heard Sorin's next accusation clearly.

"Lie? Was it not your guard Levi's own weapon that killed our king? Where is Levi, by the way?"

Where had he obtained that confidential information? If possible, the Royal Guard tensed further. *Give the order to attack*, Trevin silently urged Caeden.

"The murderer has yet to be identified," Amira assured the crowd. "As for my guard's whereabouts, that is not your concern." Amira sounded calm, but Trevin noted her shaking hands partially hidden in the folds of her skirt. *Enough of this, give the order.*

"It is all of our concern, Princess. Your safety is vital to us all," Sorin countered before turning to address the crowd once again. "Our princess is in danger from her own Guard. This is unacceptable. While her loyalty is admirable, it is misplaced. Grief clouds her thinking. We cannot know how many of the Royal Guard were involved in the murder of our dearest king. We must insist on the princess's safety!"

In a frenzy, the crowd was now pushing and yelling. Pleas could be heard, along with outrage at the Guard. Things were quickly getting out of hand. Too many words had been spoken with too little action as recourse. Instinctually, Trevin took a step forward, ready to knock the teeth down that bastard's throat; see if he could continue to spew his lies then. Jaw clenched and without looking, Caeden lifted his hand in a halting motion. Trevin forced himself to stay in formation.

"All right, quiet, please," Amira yelled above the

noise of the crowd. "Please listen to me!" After a couple of seconds, the crowd began to still.

But in the silence, Sorin commanded, "Arrest the Royal Guard!"

"No!" Amira screamed, and in a shockingly quick move, pushed herself between Sorin's soldiers and the Royal Guard. "No one touches my Guard!"

In what Trevin could only believe was an attempt to calm the grieving and unstable crowd, Amira conceded, "Sorin, for my people's peace of mind, I will allow your soldiers' protection for the time being. That will free my Guard for the more important task of bringing my father's murderer to justice."

Trevin hoped Caeden would defy her wishes and give the order to attack. He knew that was exactly what his friend wished to do.

She turned to address the crowd. "Levi and the rest of my Guard are not responsible for the death of the king and will not be treated as such or punished in any way."

Sorin nodded once to his soldiers to stand down. "Come along, Princess," he commanded smugly, and Trevin eyed Caeden closely as Sorin approached the princess. They could end this all quickly—violently, but quickly.

"I will have a private word with my Guard before they are relieved of duty," Amira stated defiantly.

"I don't think—" Sorin began.

"That was not a request," Amira snapped,

completely out of patience. She pushed through the group, no one daring to get in her way, the Guard following her into a private chamber. Once inside, she pleaded with Caeden to leave her in Sorin's care so that the Guard would be able to hunt down the person responsible for her father's death.

EIGHT

Leaving the princess in the hands of Sorin was difficult for each member of the Royal Guard, but Caeden was barely able to contain his rage as they gathered in the soldiers' keep, putting Trevin on high alert.

"I'm going to kill him and be done with it," Caeden growled as he stormed in the direction of the main hall. It took Trevin and Osmond both to hold him back. Apparently, Murdock and Dalek approved of his intent because they made no move to help stop him. Once Trevin and Osmond had Caeden pinned against the wall, Trevin shot a look to the other two soldiers, and Dalek actually had the nerve to shrug in response.

"Now listen to me, boy," Osmond was saying, "you don't wanna do that."

"That's where you're wrong. I want to tear him

apart with my bare hands," Caeden answered through clenched teeth.

Osmond was probably the only person on earth who could get away with calling Caeden "boy." Being the oldest member of the Guard, that was just his way.

"I say we let him," Dalek chimed in.

Trevin shot him another look of annoyance, but told the group as a whole, "We have to play this smart."

"Trevin's right," Osmond agreed. "The people are scared stupid right now. They're going to be looking for someone to blame. They'll take your hide just as quickly as anyone else's," he told Caeden gruffly.

Caeden nodded in understanding, and seemed to have better control of this temper, so they released him, but Trevin stayed close just in case.

"Our competence has already been called into question with our failure to protect the king," Trevin said, stating what they already knew, but avoided voicing.

"Hell, they probably think were involved, considering Levi's disappearing act," Dalek said, finally understanding. He paused for a few seconds, looking to be in deep contemplation, before he added, "Maybe it would be best if we waited a couple hours, and then we killed the bastard."

Trevin groaned in frustration. Being second-in-command, it was time for him to take control, since Caeden was too emotionally involved to think clearly.

First order of business: "Dalek, you no longer get a vote."

"Fine," Dalek pouted in response.

"Murdock, you're being silent—"

"And unhelpful," Osmond interrupted.

"Hey, I'm up for whatever strategy gets this resolved quickest and me home to my pregnant wife," Murdock admitted.

With a glance, Trevin checked on Caeden before continuing. He was running his fingers through his hair in frustration, looking in danger of actually ripping some out, but otherwise, he was holding it together.

"So, it seems we have two main objectives: Finding King Vidar's killer and getting this kingdom back under our control." Trevin noticed Caeden nodding in agreement, so he continued. "To do the latter, we need to know how deep Sorin's control actually is and assess his manpower. We also need to consider the safety of our people."

Trevin's mind drifted to Inaya. He hadn't seen her when they escorted Amira into the palace. She was a strong female; surely she was safe.

"Sorin is a ruthless son of a bitch. There's no telling the harm caused when he seized control," Osmond stated matter-of-factly, which only seemed to agitate Caeden more.

Trevin shook his head at Osmond, letting him know he needed to keep those kind of statements to himself. Osmond immediately realized his mistake and took a step closer to Caeden just in case. The move did not go unnoticed, and Caeden turned his glare on Osmond.

Before Caeden could decide to release his anger on Osmond, a loud shuffling sound drew their attention. Trevin's body tensed as he drew his weapon, and he instinctually knew each of his brothers-at-arms had done the same. The noise was coming through both the front and the back exits. It seemed as though they were surrounded and had underestimated Sorin.

Caeden motioned Murdock, Dalek, and Osmond to the front door, and Trevin to join him at the back. Not one to wait for the fight to come to him, Caeden snatched the door open, immediately punching the closest soldier in the nose before throwing him out of the way in order to reach the next. If the situation were different, Trevin would have found the shocked expressions on the soldiers' faces hilarious.

Soldier after soldier came, and as much as they tried to prevent it, the soldiers were able to break through and enter the room. Trevin couldn't tell if the Guard members on the other side were faring any better or not. The vast size of the enemy was overwhelming. It seemed as though Sorin had not underestimated the Royal Guard and had actually sent a whole battalion against them.

~

Inaya's head was going to explode. And although the voices surrounding her were whispered, the noise bounced around in her brain, causing the throbbing to increase.

"...plans to make an example of any who challenge him."

"I'd like to see him try to make an example out of me!"

Inaya recognized that voice immediately. Francine was Osmond's wife, and truth be told, she might be more intimidating than her husband. Inaya wasn't sure what the conversation was regarding, but the idea of anyone trying to get the better of Francine was laughable.

"I'd give that boy a good thrashing, and then make him scrub his own blood from the floor," she continued.

Inaya peeked her eyes open, thankful to discover only dim lighting, and quickly scanned the room. It took her a moment to recognize she was lying on a couch in one if the palace's sitting rooms. There were only two other occupants: Francine and Endora. When Inaya pulled herself to a seated position, she gained their attention.

"Ah, you've decided to rejoin the land of the living, have you?" Francine asked as she made her way over to the couch. Kneeling down, she abruptly grabbed Inaya's chin and forced her head to the side. "The bleeding has ceased, but that's quite a knot you have there."

Inaya brought her hand to the right side of her face and winced when she came into contact with the enormous bump on the side of her head.

"Bet your head's aching something fierce."

Inaya tried to nod in response, but quickly discovered that wasn't a good idea as a sharp pain sliced through her brain.

"Oh, you poor dear," Endora cooed.

"Well, take your time getting yourself situated. Doesn't look like we're going anywhere anytime soon," Francine added.

Inaya closed her eyes again and tried to concentrate through the pain. "Why is that?"

"We're locked in," Endora explained hopelessly.

"Seems Sorin has deemed us a threat," Francine said with a snort.

Inaya scanned the room again, this time taking in the locked door that was barring their freedom.

"Okay, give me a moment," Inaya said on a slight groan, closing her eyes and resting her head against the back of the couch before continuing, "and then I'll have us out of here."

"But—"

A click drew their attention to the door. Now fully alert, Inaya's heart raced in anticipation. A sigh fell from her lips as her brother's head peeked around the door.

With a childish grin, Alyx's voice rang through the room. "Lookie here, my little sister actually staying where she's been put. I was unaware there was a lock ever made that could keep you in."

Inaya narrowed her eyes at him, but he was unfazed.

"We were just leaving," she assured him.

"Well, in that case, shall I escort you fine ladies to more hospitable accommodations?" he offered solicitously.

With a huff of irritation, Francine pushed past him into the hallway, Endora following closely behind. As Inaya approached, she watched his eyes narrow.

"What happened?" His voice was steel as took in her injury.

"I fell," she answered briefly, not trusting her brother's response to further details.

"Uh-huh." He clearly didn't believe her, but she was relieved he decided not to pursue the issue—that was, until he continued with, "We'll see what Murdock has to say about your clumsiness."

She gave him a dirty look before ignoring his last comment. "What's going on?" she questioned hesitantly, unsure she was ready for the answer.

"Let me get you somewhere safe before we get into that."

By safe, he meant Murdock's cottage on the western border of Velius. The sun was just rising in the east as they approached. Murdock's wife, Maryse, rushed out as fast as her pregnant belly would allow. The hope on her face vanished when she realized it was only Alyx, Inaya, and Francine. Endora had chosen to go elsewhere.

"Any news?" she asked sadly.

Alyx shook his head. "None of the Guard members have been seen."

"They'll show up eventually," Francine huffed as she pushed past Maryse to make her way inside.

"The Royal Guard is missing?" At her brother's nod, Inaya asked incredulously, "*All* of them?"

"Aye. We returned from the memorial ceremony to discover the palace had been taken by Ammon soldiers. There was a confrontation in the courtyard. Sorin actually endeavored to have the Guard taken into his custody to be charged for the murder of the king."

"No," Inaya gasped.

"That bastard," Maryse cursed.

"What happened?" Inaya urged Alyx to continue.

"The princess would have none of that, but she couldn't allow a battle to take place in the courtyard, so she dismissed her Guard and placed herself under Sorin's protection."

"Why would she do that?" Inaya tried to understand Amira's reasoning, but it made no sense.

"It was the only solution at the time," Alyx assured her.

"But then—"

"Patience, Inaya, I'm getting there," Alyx interrupted. "As the Guard went to confer with the princess, the Velius soldiers were rounded up to give instruction of our new duty under the command of Lord Sorin. Neither the Royal Guard nor Princess Amira have been seen since."

Inaya's mind raced with the different scenarios, but she refused to allow herself to panic. A thought occurred to her. "How did the soldiers of Ammon gain entry into Velius?"

"Excellent question," Alyx answered. "There is no way they could have arrived here from Ammon *after* hearing of the king's death, so they must have been close by, waiting."

Maryse drew in a sharp breath. "It was a setup! Someone from Ammon must be responsible for King Vidar's murder."

"Not someone," Inaya corrected, "Sorin."

"That's my conclusion too," Alyx agreed. "But what worries me the most is how little struggle there was to prevent Ammon's soldiers from entering and seizing control. In fact, someone had to open the gates to allow them entry."

"Maybe one of Sorin's men had stayed behind?" Maryse suggested.

With of a shake of his head, Alyx explained, "That's highly unlikely. After the king's death, the whole palace was put on lockdown and searched."

"So, it would have had to have been one of our own... most likely a soldier," Inaya concluded.

"Or a group of our soldiers," Alyx admitted.

The tension was heavy in the air. "Any idea who?" Inaya asked softly, as if speaking too loudly would bring the traitors crashing through the door.

Alyx shook his head in answer.

After a brief silence, Inaya asked, "Speaking of soldiers, how are you here? Why aren't you under orders?"

He puffed up his chest, and with a cocky grin, he announced, "Rules don't apply to some."

Inaya snorted at her brother's ego, despite the seriousness of the situation.

"Besides, someone had to look out for you ladies," he said with a smirk.

"So, what you mean is, with Murdock missing, you had to locate me so I could sort it all out for you?" Inaya teased, causing Maryse to giggle.

"Inaya, you will do no such thing," Alyx informed her sternly. "You three ladies will safely stay right here."

"While you what? Find the traitors, the Royal Guard, and Amira all on your own? Do you even have a plan?" Outside, the wind howled, echoing Inaya's frustration.

"Well...."

"That's what I thought. We'll work under the assumption the Guard is still within the kingdom. I know the palace better than anyone. I'll search there and check on Amira. You can search the soldiers' barracks and all the outlying buildings. Unless you're successful, meet me back here by morning."

"Inaya...." Alyx looked as if he were struggling with himself to find the right words to deny her. She raised an eyebrow, silently waiting. "I just got you out of there," he conceded on a frustrated groan.

"I guess you should have thought this through a little better. Would have saved us both some time."

"Just be careful."

"You as well. I know you're close with many of the other soldiers, but, Alyx, at least one of your brothers-at-arms is not who he seems. Be careful who you trust."

"At the moment, it's just you, little sister." He pulled her close for a hug. "I'll meet you here by morning," he said with a nod. As he turned away, Inaya heard him mumble, "Murdock is going to strangle me."

NINE

Sorin may have control of the palace, but Inaya knew its secrets better than anyone. Most of her life, she had straddled that tenuous line between servant class and honorary royalty. She'd had access to the royal family's private wing and the hidden passageways used by servants to go undetected. From the concealed entrance to the princess's chambers located in the closet, Inaya was able to spy on Sorin and Marcelle unnoticed.

"Why won't she awaken?" Sorin's frustration was clear in his tone.

"We knew she was not strong enough. What did you think would happen?" Marcelle replied sharply.

"So, are we to just let the delicate princess sleep while all of Cashile crumbles around her? This is just further proof that we are doing the right thing by taking control of the kingdom." By the ebb and flow of his voice, it sounded as if Sorin were pacing. "Reports are saying the ice storm in the east has continued to worsen, and the earthquakes in the south are threatening the integrity of the island."

"Which is proof we made a mistake!" Marcelle all but shrieked. "This is all your—" She ended with a yelp as Sorin cut her off.

"All my what?" he growled. When she didn't answer, he continued. "If I recall correctly, my darling pet, it was you who struck the killing blow, not I."

What was supposed to mean?

"I... I...." Inaya couldn't make out Marcelle's words through her thick sobs.

"Oh, quit sniveling and make yourself useful for once. Create some kind of elixir, or whatever it is the Supreme Healer is supposed to do, and fix the princess. We need her. In the meantime, I'm forced to make up for her weak disposition and take control of the situation. I could just let them all die, but as my first act as ruler, I shall show them mercy."

A knot formed in Inaya's stomach as she listened to Sorin ramble on in awe of his own imaginary grandeur. His narcissism knew no end, but, thankfully, a knock at the door interrupted his diatribe. The speaker was too far away for Inaya to hear who it was or what was said, but Sorin returned with good news: they would be leaving Amira's chamber.

"All right, my pet," he addressed Marcelle warmly, "I must meet with the future captain of the Velius army." The last was said with a chuckle, as if he'd amused himself.

"Can you trust him, my lord?"

"Of course not. He turned against his commanding officer with very little persuasion, and soon he will be rewarded in kind for his treachery, but for now, he is still of use to me until the rest of Velius's soldiers accept my command. While I'm occupied, make yourself useful as well, darling, and rouse the blasted princess," he demanded.

As Inaya heard them exit the chamber, she knew this was her opportunity to follow Sorin and discover who their traitor was, but it might also be her only chance to check on Amira. She struggled with the decision for only half a second. Her friend came first. Always.

With watchful eyes, Lahash perched in the corner of Princess Amira's bedchamber. Sorin and the redheaded she-devil were in a frenzy as they exited the chamber, leaving blessed silence in their wake. The weak little princess was unconscious and fading far faster than he had predicted. The bond tying her to the protective shield was proving to be unbearable.

Lahash entertained the idea of allowing the little princess to die, but the consequences of doing so remained unclear. The shield protecting Cashile could crash immediately, which might be enough to compromise the entire island and all its inhabitants, but in doing so, what would be the effects on the rest of the planet? The climate shift alone could have dire results. Although he had little regard for human life, extinguishing the Maker's beloved creation would not further his goal. Besides, he'd leave the downfall of man to the angels who had fallen with him; that seemed to be their new-found purpose after they had fallen from grace and abandoned their offspring.

No, if the shield fell, it must do so gradually so the rest of the world had time to adapt. Even now, he could feel the slight trembling of the earth as the shield's intensity fluctuated, and the drop in temperature caused the feathers of his magnificent wings to prickle.

Another risk he'd face at the princess's death would be the unlikely chance the blood bond found another worthy host. The angels responsible for its creation may have provided a failsafe. Even being of royal blood, he doubted it would fall to Marcelle, but there were other females with close ties to the royal family, such as the Lady Ferrara. She was a close enough relation that she had been granted rulership of the territory of Zefania. That might be enough for her to take full control. But soon Ferrara would no longer be a problem.

A noise from the closet gained his attention as a golden blonde head with bright turquoise eyes peeked out. A strange anticipation leaped in his chest at seeing

Inaya. It was ironic she would appear just as he had been considering likely contenders worthy to take control over the island. Cocking his head to the side, he examined her closely. There was no doubt she was clearly one of his descendants, but from whom? One of his offspring had been busy without his knowledge or consent. With there being only two of his progeny left in existence, not counting the girl before him, it would be easy to find out to whom she belonged. Throughout the centuries, he'd been certain to ensure his line had not been soiled by females. All female-born children had been extinguished immediately, and yet, this one had been created and allowed to flourish.

He watched curiously as the distraught female desperately attempted to wake the unconscious princess, but she failed just as Sorin and the Supreme Healer had. Unintentionally, he found himself being drawn closer until he stood at the edge of the bed. Inaya's anguished pleas intrigued him. This female was capable of true affection, which Lahash found to be a rare trait, and it was apparent the princess was of great value to her. The desire to help preserve and cherish that aspect of her personality conflicted with the idea of twisting that weakness for his own purposes. He detested the battle within himself, and it occurred to him that maybe he should just dispose of her immediately. In some indecipherable way, this small female was a risk to him, and that he could not allow.

With only a thought, he materialized beside her.

Decision made, he would make her death quick and painless. Lifting his arms, preparing to snap her neck, something suddenly gained her attention. As her head jerked in his direction, Lahash was given a clear view of her face for the first time since she entered the chamber. A cold fury washed through his entire being. Bruised. Her lovely face was marred with bruises. Someone had dared to lay a hand upon his child. Unacceptable. All of it was unacceptable.

But the most inexcusable part: he actually cared.

Leaving Amira lying helpless on the bed was one of the most difficult things Inaya had ever done. With one last look, she rushed from the room back to the closet that contained the hidden servants' passageway. Once inside, she leaned against the door, pressing her hand against her chest, feeling her pounding heart. She could barely breathe. Something had happened back in that room. It had felt as if all the air had been sucked out. Panic and fear had overwhelmed her, forcing her to flee.

From listening to Sorin and Marcelle before they had exited Amira's chamber, Inaya knew her friend was not in danger of direct harm from them at the moment. It seemed as if they were both truly concerned for her welfare and the Supreme Healer was doing all in her power to wake Amira.

No, standing in that room just now, Inaya sensed a very real threat, but it had seemed to be directed at her. She couldn't explain it, but she'd felt it. And so she fled, leaving her friend behind.

With her heart rate returning to normal, she realized her imagination had gotten the best of her and she had overreacted. The stress and worry were getting to her.

Knowing there was nothing she could do for Amira in that moment, Inaya mentally plotted her search route. Maybe there was still time to locate Sorin while he was meeting with the Velius traitor. She knew a great number of the higher-ranking soldiers, and while it was difficult for her to believe any of them would turn on the royal family or the Royal Guard, there was no denying the fact it had been one of the soldiers who was responsible for assisting Sorin to take over the palace. There was a good chance she would be able to identify who it was if she were to see him with Sorin.

It wasn't likely Sorin would lower himself by going to meet the soldier. Instead, he would make the soldier come to him, and fancying himself the new ruler, he would most likely take his audience in a room of importance. The king's study perhaps, or the throne room. *Hell, Sorin probably situated himself in the ballroom so more people could be present to marvel at his splendor and mercy.* Inaya snickered to herself.

As she snuck back through the servants' passageways, she also considered where Sorin could be keeping the Royal Guard. While it was not easy to picture him being able to best the Guard, surely something terrible had to have happened to them or else they would be here and Sorin would not. He had held Endora, Francine, and her in just a simple sitting room in the palace. Inaya couldn't see such a room holding the Guard. Given just a few minutes more for her to collect herself, and that sitting room wouldn't have been able to even hold her. It was unlikely any of the rooms within the palace would hold the Guard, but she still needed to check.

Inaya was surprised to discover the ballroom was, indeed, filled with people, but they were not there to raise Sorin's ego. They were frightened and seeking answers. The shield was failing, and while Velius was experiencing only mild effects, such as the earthquake and the temperature drops, the other territories of Cashile were not as lucky. People had begun to flee their homes to seek shelter elsewhere.

The tension in the room was overwhelming as the now homeless clutched their loved ones and their belongings. Apparently they had all been ushered into the ballroom and ordered to wait. For what? Inaya didn't know. From what she gathered from overheard snippets of conversations, neither did they.

She wanted to help them, but at this point, what could she do?

She had entered the room through a discreet door

hidden behind the bandstand. Sneaking around the back, she peered around the bandstand to observe the Ammon soldiers patrolling the crowd, attempting to keep the evacuees subdued through force and intimidation. Scanning the room, she found no sign of any Velius soldiers amongst the crowd. She was unsure if she should be grateful or worried by that fact.

She was terrified the traitor would be someone she knew and trusted, and she would be forced to turn them over to the Royal Guard—when she located them, of course. But not every Velius soldier found within the palace walls was a traitor, she reminded herself. Alyx had said Princess Amira had publicly turned herself over to Sorin's care, so it was only natural that the soldiers would follow his commands if given in the pretense of the princess's orders. That fact would make discovering the traitor's identity more difficult unless she caught him red-handed with Sorin.

With that thought in mind, she turned to slip away unnoticed, but her plan was derailed as the door to the main ballroom entrance was thrown open and Sorin appeared, Marcelle at his side and an entourage of soldiers behind him, this time both Ammon and Velius.

The crowd grew quiet as they made their way to the front of the room beside the bandstand. Their footsteps echoing on the hardwood floor matched the beat of Inaya's heart. She had escaped Sorin once before, but she was unsure if he would give her another chance. For unknown reasons, he had always despised her.

She crouched to make herself as small as possible as the soldiers continuously scanned the room. Were the Velius soldiers seeking to prevent a threat to Sorin, or were they possibly looking for something else? Could she safely reveal herself to them and seek their aid when Sorin wasn't around?

She searched their faces. A few she knew in passing, but none were close friends of her brothers, therefore not close to her. She couldn't risk it.

As Sorin grandly presented himself on the stage, a murmur passed through the crowd. They had been expecting their princess and were unsure what to make of her absence.

"Quiet." Sorin held his hand in the air as he demanded their obedience. As the crowd hushed, a transformation occurred within Sorin. His stance relaxed, and he had a welcoming, compassionate smile on his face. "I know you are frightened, but I'm glad you have come," he stated graciously.

This was not the person Inaya knew Sorin to be. She watched on in confusion as he continued.

"The princess deeply regrets that she is unable to attend to you at this time as she struggles with her grief at the loss of her father, but she has asked that I see to your needs."

Anyone who knew Amira personally would see his

words for what they were—lies. The princess would never disregard her duty to her people.

"It is my pleasure to serve as your humble servant," Sorin all but purred. "I will set up shelter for all in need as Lady Marcelle, our Supreme Healer, tends to any injuries. I will also be dispatching soldiers to the other territories to help where they are able. I assure you, you and your loved ones are safe within my keeping."

As Sorin turned to leave, the crowd, far from reassured, erupted into questions.

"What is happening?" and "Where's the princess?" were the two main concerns of the people, it seemed.

For a brief second, Sorin's façade slipped and his anger shone through. Apparently, he didn't like to be questioned. He quickly regained control. Although his stance remained rigid, his face once again displayed compassion.

"My people, now is not the time for hysteria. Now is the time for faith and action. I have promised to care for you. You must trust in me." His face grew hard as he continued. "But at the same time, I cannot abide disobedience or chaos at such a tenuous and dangerous time. Those who seek to cause trouble will be dealt with swiftly and firmly," he warned.

The crowd tensed but remained relatively quiet as they absorbed his words and took in the armed soldiers stationed throughout the room.

After giving them a moment to come to terms with

their new circumstances, Sorin continued. "I see we understand one another. Now, all who need medical attention, remain in this room. Everyone else will be escorted off the premises to the designated location of your temporary shelter, where you will assist one another in what must be done." Sorin paused as his eyes scanned the crowd. The Ammon soldiers readied, as if preparing for action, escalating the tension in the room.

"I trust there are no more questions or concerns," Sorin finally stated, eyes passing through the crowd one last time. "Good." He nodded once as he took his leave of the stage, his entourage in tow.

TEN

Lahash needed distance. He could not allow this new development to distract him from his goal. He had let a woman seduce him once before, and she had been his downfall. Now this girl, his child, was a threat to his ultimate goal.

Her injury should not be his concern, but it plagued his thoughts. His instincts demanded retribution, but logically, he knew the culprit was too valuable to him to dispose of at this point in time. Although Sorin, too, was his descendant, essentially his child as well, Lahash had no sentimental connection to him. Sorin was simply his puppet, a means to an end.

But this turquoise-eyed girl who bore a striking resemblance to the female who perpetrated his downfall, as well as exhibiting a great deal of himself—or who he used to be—she had managed to penetrate a part of him he had believed long dead.

Such a thing could not be tolerated. He forcibly pushed aside all feeling and allowed cold, calculating logic to overtake him. Sorin would pay for his mishandling of Inaya; Lahash's sense of duty would settle for nothing less, regardless of if he understood or agreed with it.

But in the meantime, he would leave this place and seek answers.

One of his male offspring had disobeyed him. He would discover whom, and they would suffer. Both of his living male descendants had purpose to him at this time, but, thankfully, death was not his preferred form of punishment.

ELEVEN

Getting out of the ballroom undetected was easy, but while searching the palace, Inaya wasn't as lucky.

Just as she exited the library, a hand sprung forward, clutching her arm and dragging her back inside. She barely contained the yelp that threatened to escape her lips. But just as quickly as she was snatched, she found herself free.

"Shh...."

Her eyes darted up to find a tall, muscular male peeking out into the hallway he had just pulled her from. After softly shutting the door, he turned to face her. Immediately, she recognized his handsome face and chestnut-colored eyes.

"Eldon," she greeted cautiously.

"Inaya, what are you doing here?"

"I'm... I'm...." She struggled with what to say, not

knowing if he was someone she could trust. She knew him fairly well since he was once a high-ranking soldier, and there was a time she might have even considered him a friend. For a brief period, before he was unexpectedly demoted, they seem to find themselves at the same location often, like fate was throwing them together. He'd always treated her with kindness and respect until one day he just wasn't around. She later discovered he was no longer an officer. It was unclear to her if it was his new duty that kept him away or his pride.

On a normal day, she would have no reason to doubt him, but nothing could be considered normal any longer. Not waiting for her reply, he grabbed her hand and pulled her away from the door and to the seating area in the far right corner.

"I have been searching everywhere for you," he said when he finally stopped. Holding her firmly, he turned her to face him, giving her a quick once-over. He frowned when his eyes encountered the bruising on her face. "When I heard Lord Sorin had locked you away, I tried to get to you, but I wasn't in time. I'm glad you made it out, but why have you returned?"

Instead of answering his question, she asked one of her own. "You came for me?"

She flinched as he tenderly trailed a finger down her injured face, more from the intimacy of the action than any pain or discomfort it caused.

"Of course, with Murdock—" There was a slight

hesitation before he continued. "—missing, I knew you needed someone to care for you. I would not have allowed for you to be held prisoner, but by the time I had discovered what had happened, you had vanished."

There was a lot wrong with what he just said, but she couldn't discount the sincerity in his voice.

"Do you know where my brother is? Or any of the Royal Guard for that matter?" she asked, addressing her top priority at the moment.

Strangely, all emotion left his face as he admitted, "I have not seen them."

"But you searched the palace looking for me, correct?" At his nod, she continued. "And you have found no sign of them?"

"They are not within the palace walls, but, Inaya, I am more concerned for you. You have somehow earned Lord Sorin's displeasure, and he is a dangerous male to cross. We must get you somewhere safe."

He once again grabbed her hand and tried to pull her along, but this time she refused to be moved.

"I have somewhere safe I can go." She jerked her hand from his grasp.

"Where?" he demanded. "To your brother's cottage?"

"No," she instinctively lied. "With the expectant arrival of their child, Maryse has traveled to Zefania to be close to her mother. I have been invited to stay with a few of the palace servants who have a home nearby."

"Nonsense, I can keep you safe."

"I am—"

"Eldon?" a deep voice interrupted her protest.

She found herself being practically thrown behind the sofa as Eldon rushed to hide her.

"Stay here, I'll return for you," he whispered before turning away. "Yes?" he answered, sounding completely unaffected as he made his way to the front.

"Lord Sorin is ready to see you now," the unknown male announced. "You need to hurry. He does not like to be kept waiting."

"Of course," Eldon responded, but he was too far away for Inaya to make out if he said anything else.

Why was he meeting with Sorin?

For long moments, she hid, debating her next course of action. She had already searched the majority of the palace and all the logical places within where the Royal Guard could possibly be held. She was fortunate that it had been Eldon who discovered her, and didn't think it was wise to continue her search. Besides, Eldon said the Royal Guard was not here, and she believed him.

But did she believe in him enough to still be here when he returned?

His desire to help her seemed genuine, but could she convince him to help her in the ways she needed most?

She needed someone to guard Princess Amira until she was awake and well enough to be moved. She also needed help to locate the Royal Guard. But most of all, Sorin needed to be stopped. She considered that for a moment. It was clear Eldon had access to Sorin, but could she convince him to take that risk? Was he even capable? With the number of soldiers Sorin surrounded himself with, she doubted Eldon's chances of success. But if he were able, what happened next? With Amira being incapacitated and the Royal Guard missing, who would lead the people?

Inaya's head throbbed from all the what-if scenarios playing through her mind. There was just too much to consider. She needed to focus on the smaller picture for now and decide what she would do next.

Eldon's loyalty seemed to lie with her, but he was obviously following Sorin's command to some degree, or else he wouldn't be meeting with him. Also, there was no guarantee he wouldn't force her into hiding "for her own good." There was far too much that needed to be accomplished for her to allow that to happen. With her mind made up, she peeked around the sofa to verify the way was clear. It was time to get out of there.

They had been bested.

Trevin had only felt this type of defeat once before in his lifetime, and he had not let it destroy him, as he would not allow it this time either. The Royal Guard had been greatly outnumbered and overwhelmed. Sorin's soldiers could have killed them all, but they hadn't. Instead, he and his brothers had been thrown in this dark hole, chained, and beaten. But they remained alive. Therefore, Sorin must need them for something, but what, he didn't know.

Trevin sure as hell planned to use Sorin's mistake to his advantage though. As long as there was breath in him, Trevin would continue to fight, and he knew his brothers would as well.

Looking around the damp cellar, he took stock of his surroundings. The cellar was two-room, underground storage with a small supply closet in the rear of the main room. To his knowledge, the cellar was no longer in use. The Royal Guard, excluding Caeden, were being held in the smaller of the two rooms.

Iron chains had been bolted to the floor and allowed limited movement. A soldier stood guard just on the other side of the locked, solid wood door. A small window had been cut into the door to allow him to watch his captives.

Now that Trevin's eyes had fully adjusted to the darkened room, only illuminated by the light peeking in from the soldier's lone candle, he assessed his brothers. Murdock sat on the floor across from him, arms resting on his bent knees, eyes sharp and alert. Osmond was stretched out to his left, loudly snoring while he napped, as if he hadn't a care in the world.

Dalek was at the far back wall, seeing to an unconscious Levi.

Finding Levi in this cellar was both a surprise and a relief. He had remained unconscious since they had been captured. The extent of his injury was still unknown, but it was obvious he had been severely beaten and most likely drugged.

It was also clear he had been kept here since his disappearance, so how was it he hadn't been discovered when they had searched the kingdom?

"Eldon and Isaac were responsible for searching this area," Murdock said, as if reading his mind.

He turned his gaze to find Murdock staring intently at him. He nodded his acknowledgment. Trevin, Murdock, and Eldon had a complex history. Eldon was a good soldier and a born leader in his own right, but he wasn't the best. In fact, he'd contended to be a member of the Royal Guard during the last recruitment but was not successful in earning his place. But his skills had not gone unnoticed, and Caeden had promoted him to an officer.

That position afforded him a place of respect and greater responsibility. At times he was known to overstep his bounds, which tended to happen when dealing with dominant males in an adrenaline-filled environment. But the real problem occurred when Eldon had attempted to court Inaya.

Trevin had not gotten in the way of Eldon's pursuit, at least not much anyway. He may have taken every opportunity to steal her attention anytime Eldon was near, but he didn't physically stop Eldon or forbid him.

It had been before her maturity, when she still openly accepted and embraced her feelings toward Trevin, before he had hurt her and she closed herself off to him. Eldon had pursued her with intense determination, but he had been unable to win her favor. Despite the fact that Inaya had repeatedly refused his advances, Eldon had gone to Murdock to request her hand in marriage.

Murdock had not answered his plea with care. In fact, Murdock had laughed in his face. Trevin had, thankfully, not been present during this encounter, but Alyx had, and word spread quickly.

If Trevin had been present, things would have ended much differently. He would have done much worse than just crushing the male's ego with laughter. Eldon was not right for Inaya, and he would have made that clear in the most persuasive and brutal way.

Thankfully, after his denied request, Eldon had ended his courtship. But their troubles with him had escalated. It had come to a head when Eldon defied Trevin's orders and outright challenged him. With the princess being in attendance at that time, Trevin had swiftly handled the situation, but due to their history, he may have used more force than necessary—although even now, he couldn't find it within himself to regret his actions.

With minimal effort, Trevin taught Eldon the lesson he desperately needed to learn, and afterward, Caeden stripped him of his command.

From then on, Eldon had not been in a position to cause them any trouble—until now, it seemed.

Trevin cared about Inaya, a little too much in fact, and he wanted her to be happy. If Eldon had been her chosen mate, Trevin would have stepped aside and allowed it to happen; at least that's what he'd told himself at the time. But looking back, he knew that to be a lie. Trevin had no delusions of what type of person he was or what he was capable of, and although he didn't want Inaya for himself, couldn't have her for himself, he didn't think he could allow her to be with another. She was special—kindhearted, brave, loyal, and a bit wild—she needed someone who could nurture her free spirit and keep her safe. He didn't trust another male to that task, so he would take on that duty from a distance, just as he always had.

But since the night of her maturity celebration, when Inaya had confessed her feelings for him instead of allowing it to be an unspoken fact between them, things were different. He had been fighting his changing thoughts and feelings toward her for years now. Their relationship was so much easier when she was just the tomboy, sister-like kid who followed the soldiers around. But when she became a woman, he couldn't help but notice her in a new way, just as many of the other soldiers had. Thankfully, Murdock and

Alyx did a good job keeping them away from their sister, so that was one less worry for Trevin. And when his brave little hellion sought him out and confronted him about claiming her, their relationship had been forever changed. Not only could he no longer put her in the category of a little sister, but he had also hurt her by rejecting her. He didn't know if that was something they could ever get past.

"They were both stationed at the gate during the king's memorial as well," Murdock added quietly, bringing Trevin back to the present. Somehow, his mind always drifted to Inaya. Thoughts of her were getting in the way of his duty. He would need to find a way to repair their relationship and return it back to the way it once was, so that he could focus on what was important.

Again, Trevin nodded. "Then we have our traitor."

And when they were free, Trevin would handle this matter personally.

TWELVE

"Malcolm...."

Lahash's singsong tone echoed through the room. The beautiful sound could enchant even the most hardened disbelievers, but that was not the intended purpose of this visit. A spike of adrenaline ran through him as he watched his prey tense. Malcolm wanted to run; Lahash could see it in the way his eyes darted to the exit. A part of him wished he would. He yearned for the release it would bring, the opportunity to smite his enemy. However, he knew Malcolm would present no real challenge, and in the end, Lahash would be left unsatisfied and just as empty as he was before. Besides, Malcolm would never run. As much as he desired to do so, he was conditioned to know it would prove fruitless.

"My lord, you have returned," Malcolm greeted with a deep bow.

"Indeed." Lahash circled him slowly, invading Malcolm's personal space, but careful to ensure his wings in no way brushed against him.

"M-my lord, how may I be of service to you?"

Lahash enjoyed his fear, but the stuttering was annoying. Coming to a standstill before him, Lahash cocked his head and examined the male closely. Dark brown hair from Malcolm's bowed head filled his gaze, but he knew he would be met with dark brown eyes as well, if the male were ever brave enough to meet his eye.

Neither Malcolm nor Sorin shared the golden-blonde hair or turquoise eyes of Inaya. In fact, in all his existence, he'd only encountered one other with that shade of eye color before. They had enchanted him from the moment they first gazed upon him in wonder. And the moment that wonder turned to love, he knew he'd give up forever to absorb that feeling and freely return it to her.

But when that look of love turned to pity and disdain, he realized his fatal error. By then, it had been too late.

His gleaming opalescent wings caught his attention from his peripheral vision, bringing him back to the present. He tucked the abominations securely behind his back before continuing with his task.

"As my offspring, you have been graced with my protection and my guidance. Over the centuries, I have demanded little in return from your fathers and your descendant. For the grandness I have bestowed upon you, I require blind obedience, nothing more. And yet, you have failed me."

"My lord?" Malcolm's head jerked up in shock.

"The female, Inaya, she is yours, is she not?"

"Fe-female? My lord, I do not understand. I am wed to the female of your choosing."

"That is not the female of whom I speak. Your mate is of no consequence. The child is of whom I speak."

Malcolm's body froze. "Child?"

Lahash's eyes narrowed. He did not appreciate being questioned nor dealing with ignorance, but he needed to understand if he was encountering blatant disregard or simple foolishness. Neither were acceptable, but the answer would determine how he would proceed.

"In the last century, I have given you much freedom as I have attended to your son. It seems you have taken advantage of my inattention. A quarter-century past, a female was born unto you."

Malcolm's entire body quaked with his fear. "My lord, that child is no more. You have decreed that no female shall exist of your blood. I vowed to honor you in all ways. The child was extinguished."

"By your hand?"

"N-no, by her mother."

Lahash was quiet for a moment while he watched Malcolm squirm. "And what of the mother?" he finally inquired.

"She is dead, my lord, by her own hand." His voice broke at the end. He cleared his throat and wiped the sweat from his brow before he continued. "She had a delicate mind, and the strain from disposing of the child was too much for her to bear. She hanged herself."

"Indeed?" Lahash lazily circled the trembling male once again.

"Of course, my lord, I would never—"

"Cease with your excuses. The child remains in existence. Therefore, I require a more detailed explanation. Begin with the mother."

Malcolm looked as if he wanted to faint, but he swallowed audibly and began his tale instead. "Lorelei was my true mate. I stumbled upon her quite by accident. It seems she did not have the fortitude to await her true mate, and she had married another. They lived in a cottage on the border of Ammon and Zefania. She bore him two sons, but they had grown and moved away by the time we had found one another."

Lahash recognized the glazed look in Malcolm's eyes, and he knew the male was lost in reliving the past.

"Lorelei was exquisite—beautiful blonde hair, emerald green eyes, and a smile that rivaled the stars in their beauty. Of course, I could not allow another to hold what was clearly meant for me. I dispatched of her husband quickly. It took some convincing, but she came to understand I did it to claim her in the only way I was able and to declare my love."

Love; what a treacherous, deadly concept.

"As my duty is to you and the life you have granted me here, my lord, I never considered abandoning my hand-chosen mate or my son, but I could not allow her to be with another. I gave her what time and attention I could offer, and I admit, it wasn't much. She longed for companionship and proof of our love and allowed herself to become with child. Were the babe male, I would have allowed her to keep it—with your permission, of course, my lord."

Lahash didn't lower himself to respond, but instead studied Malcolm closely as he fidgeted, before once more continuing his tale.

"The child was female and, therefore, needed to be disposed of. Lorelei begged for one day alone with the child and promised to dispense with it after. Out of love, I foolishly granted this favor. For over a decade, the child was not mentioned again. But through the years, Lorelei's glory began to fade as her reasoning deteriorated. With you requiring less and less of me, I granted her more of my attention in hopes of mending what was broken within her, but it only made it worse."

Malcolm's fists clenched, and his pale complexion was replaced with red fury.

"The female child lived. Lorelei had caused me to

unknowingly break my vow to you. She had hidden the child away—restraining her and locking her within a small storage room during my every visit. For days at a time, the child would remain that way."

"And with the increased frequency of your visits, the more often this would occur," Lahash added.

Outwardly, Lahash knew his appearance remained as stoic as ever, but he was forced to conceal his own clenched fists behind his back, as on the inside, he felt ready to erupt.

"Y-yes."

"Continue."

"The child's existence was finally revealed to me when she escaped her bonds during one of my visits. My anger overrode my reasoning, and I did not take into account Lorelei's fragile mental state. As punishment, I demanded she correct her mistake. But in doing so, I pushed too hard and broke her completely."

"And you did not remain to ensure she followed through with her task?"

"No," Malcolm confessed, "in my anger and arrogance, I wrongly assumed she would not disobey me again. As an additional punishment, I implied she'd lost my favor and I would not return for her. Her body was later discovered hanging from the rafters. Since our relationship was a secret and I could not allow anyone to discover I was the father of the child, I did not further investigate her death or that of the child."

"No one knows she is your descendant?" Lahash questioned, an idea formulating in his mind. At Malcolm's hesitation, he knew that to be untrue. "Who else knows?"

"My son, Sorin."

Thirteen

The agonizing screams reached Inaya's ears moments before her hand touched the handle of Maryse's front door. Her heart pounded a wild rhythm as she threw the door open and rushed inside. In shock, she glanced around the empty living room. Where was the danger?

"Maryse?" she called cautiously.

An angry shriek had her clutching her chest and flying in the direction of Maryse and Murdock's room.

"Oh, quit your bellyaching. It doesn't hurt that bad."

"Francine," Maryse's voice came out as a growl, "I'm going to get out of this bed and strangle you."

A sweaty and obviously in pain Maryse was lying on the bed, clutching her stomach as she glared at Francine. Belying Francine's harsh tone, her hands were gentle as she wiped the sweat from the pregnant woman's brow.

"I'm looking forward to it, dearie, but first you need to toughen up and push this baby out."

"The baby's coming?" Inaya asked as she came fully into the room.

The women's heads snapped in her direction. Maryse sat up as much as she was able, anxiously peeking around Inaya. Francine only looked mildly curious before she went about her task.

"Murdock?"

Maryse sounded so desperate that the denial became trapped in Inaya's throat. As she shook her head, Maryse's face crumpled, but before the tears could fall, another contraction hit, causing her body to tense.

"Breathe through it, girl." Francine motioned Inaya forward.

"You breathe, old woman." Maryse's demonic growl had Inaya stopping in her tracks, but Francine only chuckled.

"Don't be frightened, Inaya. This silly female doesn't have the strength to leave this bed, even if she wanted to." Francine paused to glare down at Maryse before meeting Inaya's eyes once more. That's when she recognized the fear in Francine's eyes. The old woman hid it well behind her callous façade, but for a brief moment, it was clear. "The foolish female has depleted her strength by trying to fight nature."

"I have to hold off. I need to give Murdock time to get here," Maryse cried. The desperation in her voice shot a pain directly into Inaya's heart.

"Don't be—"

Maryse didn't let Francine finish. "Murdock needs to be here."

"Babies wait for no one," Francine huffed before sending Inaya an imploring look.

Another contraction must have hit, because the color drained from Maryse's face and an unintelligible, animalistic growl rose from her throat.

Inaya rushed forward, grabbing Maryse's hand, and tried not to wince at the pain when Maryse squeezed her back. Movement on the other side of the bed caught Inaya's attention.

"Reason with her," Francine murmured before moving toward the end of the bed and lifting the blanket to check on the progress of the baby.

When the pain seemed to ease and the grip on her hand loosened, Inaya took the cloth from the bedside table and wiped Maryse's brow. It took her a moment to find the words, but she finally confessed, "I searched the entire palace, but there was no sign of my brother or any of the Royal Guard."

Maryse whimpered at the news, but Inaya pressed forward. "I don't know where they are, but I do know, if it were possible, Murdock would have already checked in with you." Inaya swallowed the lump in her throat and met Maryse's eyes before continuing. "He's not going to make it. I understand you need him here, but you fighting this only puts you and the baby in danger." Maryse let out another broken sob. "Murdock wouldn't want that."

A look of determination crossed Maryse's face, and she nodded once before another contraction hit and her face twisted in agony.

"Bear down and push," Francine coached from the end of the bed.

"I-I can't," Maryse panted.

"Yes, you can," Inaya encouraged. "You have to be strong for you and Murdock and bring this baby into the world so he can meet his daddy when he comes home. You can do this."

Maryse looked defeated as she whispered, "I'm not sure I have the strength left."

"You *do*," Inaya said confidently.

The next two hours were the most frightening of Inaya's life. For a while there, she was sure neither mother or child would survive. But finally it was over, and both mother and son were resting peacefully. Uselessly, Inaya tried to wipe the tears from her cheeks as Francine collapsed in the seat next to her.

"You all right, girl?"

Without thought, she blurted the first thing that came to mind. "I'm never having children."

With an amused huff, Francine sent her a half smile. "Your time will come."

Inaya shook her head adamantly in denial.

"Mark my words, that Trevin is a strong, virile male. I've no doubt he's capable of creating his own little army with you."

"Trev—"

"Oh, save your breath, dearie. That stubborn one over there has already worn me out." Francine pointed over at Maryse.

Inaya's mouth snapped closed and they sat in silence for a moment.

Without looking in her direction, Francine quietly asked, "So there was no sign of them?"

"None," Inaya answered just as quietly.

After a moment, Francine nodded once, wiped her hands on her apron, and heaved herself out of the chair. "Time to check on the new mom."

Sighing, Inaya pushed herself from the chair and joined the other women. She was exhausted and couldn't begin to imagine how Maryse must feel.

As they approached the bed, Maryse's eyes popped open and a radiant smile crossed her face. "Isn't he perfect?"

"So, what's the child's name to be?" Francine questioned.

Maryse's smile dimmed a bit. "Well, Murdock and I had planned to decide after the birth."

"Seeing as he's not here, and the child can't go

nameless, looks like you need to decide," Francine said in her brisk manner.

Maryse looked thoughtful for a moment, and then she looked up. "His middle name will be Jacob after Murdock's father. I'd like your help in deciding his first name." She looked up them expectantly.

"Oh no, I'll help bring him into the world, but I'll leave the naming and rearing to you," Francine protested.

Maryse turned to Inaya. "How about you? Will you stand in for your brother and help name your nephew?"

Only one name came to mind. The name that, to her, embodied bravery and selflessness. A name that honored a boy she had never met.

Elijah.

Fourteen

The moment he returned to Velius, Lahash was drawn to Inaya. From what he'd learned of her past and what he'd gleaned of her impulsive temperament, the girl needed a keeper, at least until he fully determined her usefulness.

Fully camouflaged, he perched upon the table beside the sofa and stared down at her as she cuddled the tiny infant to her chest. The other females had long since fallen asleep, but Inaya remained awake to care for the child.

Lahash had encountered a strange feeling in his gut when he had located her within the small cottage. The feeling had been somewhat similar to that of relief. When last he'd seen her, she had been within the walls of the castle and in close proximity to Sorin. Lahash now understood the cause of Sorin's hatred for Inaya. So surely if the feeling were relief, it was only because she had done nothing to distract her half-brother from his purpose while Lahash was away. It had nothing to do with her well-being; demons cared nothing for the well-being of others, especially one of the insufferable Nephilim.

Another surprise had been witnessing the birth of the child. In Lahash's long lifetime, he had never borne witness to such an event. The pain and torture a female endured while bearing a child appeared excruciating, and yet afterward, the female became besotted with the cause of her torment. It made little sense.

Persis, the arbiter of his disgrace, had already forsaken him by the time their child had been ready to join this world. He wondered if she had suffered such agony. Had she endured it alone, or had she found the comfort of friends to help her through it such as this new mother had? He had never considered it before and had no idea why he should care now. But he couldn't help but wonder if Persis had loved their child as much as this child before him was clearly loved.

Inaya gently rocked the infant as she murmured words of love, hope, and strength. Earlier, she had told the older female that she would not bear any young, but it was clear that her maternal instincts emerged naturally. The older woman had mentioned a male by the name of Trevin with whom Inaya would create offspring. Lahash would make it a priority to determine if this Trevin was a good match for his daughter.

Not that they would have long together, he

reminded himself, because soon his plan would come to fruition and the Nephilim would be wiped from existence, but in the meantime, Inaya would not spend her time with one who was unsuitable.

"Sweet boy," Inaya cooed to the infant, "I have no doubt you will grow to be as brave and strong as the boy you were named after. You see, the previous Elijah lived many, many years ago, before even I was born, but his legend lives on. The oldest of the Royal Guard, Osmond, shared his tale with me, and now I shall share it with you. It all started with a mean ruler named Malcolm who lived in a territory not far from here."

Suddenly, Inaya's words caught Lahash's complete attention. He wondered how much she knew of Malcolm and which of his misdeeds she would recount.

"Malcolm's heart was filled with greed, and he was not satisfied with ruling the territory of Ammon. Instead, he wanted the entire island of Cashile! He planned to amass a great army, but he was not a wise man. As a way of finding the strongest and bravest soldiers, he set up what he called 'the game.' All males were forced to participate in the game. A huge arena was erected for spectators to watch and cheer on their favorites. The participants were dragged into the center of the arena and were made to fight one another for a certain length of time, and anyone left standing at the end was deemed worthy, but forced to fight again. The most worthy of all Malcolm's fighters were the mighty warriors Levi and Trevin. Neither were willing participants, and together they secretly saved the lives of hundreds of young males."

Lahash recalled the timespan in which Malcolm had entertained "the games." Lahash had deemed it a ridiculous idea to try to raise an army by slaughtering your potential soldiers. But he had allowed it to continue because it kept Malcolm focused elsewhere while he molded Sorin to his needs, and as far as he was concerned, it was just less Nephilim to destroy in the end. Plus, the results had been favorable to his cause. Malcolm had become all but obsolete, and the repercussions of "the games" removed Malcolm from power and put Sorin one step closer to where Lahash needed him to be. Now he wished he had paid better attention to these great warriors she spoke of, Trevin and Levi.

"Sweet baby boy, I know what you're thinking: 'Aunt Inaya, if Levi and Trevin saved everyone, then why was I named after Elijah?' Well, young man, I'm getting to that part. You see, Levi and Trevin came up with a plan to stop the twisted ruler once and for all, and they never could have done it without Elijah. He sacrificed himself so the king and queen could be made aware of what was happening in Ammon. Trevin and Levi's plan had Trevin sneaking out past the guarded borders of Ammon and riding swiftly to Velius while Levi stayed behind to protect as many people as possible. But while Trevin was away, Malcolm the Meanie declared there was to be a special tournament, in which both Trevin and Levi would have to perform. So instead of Elijah risking discovery that Trevin was gone, he donned his armor and took his place in the fight. You see, Elijah was Trevin's little brother, and although he was not a skilled fighter like Trevin, he looked similar enough to be mistaken for Trevin at a distance. Because of this brave decision, Trevin was successful in bringing the Royal Guard and the soldiers of Velius into Ammon and seizing power from Malcolm, effectively ending the game for good. Sadly, Elijah did not survive his brief time in the arena, and that is why we have honored his sacrifice by passing his name to you, sweet boy."

Lahash was unsure of what to make of this tale of bravery. Still trying to make sense of the conflicting emotions inside of him, he watched the older female approach and take the infant from Inaya.

"Don't you think that was a little morbid of a tale to be sharing with this little one on his first day on this earth?"

"I suppose you're right," Inaya answered with a giggle. "Perhaps he won't remember, and I haven't caused too much damage."

"Off to bed with you, girl. It's my turn with this little angel." Francine shooed her away, and Lahash took note of the exhaustion in his daughter's eyes.

FIFTEEN

Alyx hadn't shown up the next morning. Inaya waited until the sun rose high in the sky. The minutes passed as hours. She couldn't lose someone else; she wouldn't. More determined than ever, she pushed her fear aside and made her way to the palace and snuck into Amira's sitting room.

Not knowing what to expect, she pushed the servants' entry door open as carefully as possible, and yet the noise seemed to echo throughout the small room. Slamming her eyes shut, she held her breath and waited. When no one came rushing in, she slowly edged closer to the connecting door leading into Amira's bedchamber.

Relief flooded her system when she recognized Amira's voice, but it was quickly replaced by shock and dread as the conversation unfolded.

"What have you done with them?" Amira demanded.

When Inaya heard the response come from Sorin, the blood rushed through her head so fast that she missed part of what he said, but there was no mistaking his words when he boasted, "Your Guard are currently my... guests, until they can be punished for their part in the murder of King Vidar."

How dare he!

When he continued, Inaya fought the impulse to either vomit on the pretty pink rug or storm in there and force Sorin to reveal the Royal Guard's location. She did neither.

"My dear, you should be thrilled I am bringing justice to your father's murderers; I know the people of Cashile will be. But you're too selfish to care about the people, aren't you? They are suffering, and you lie here thinking about yourself and your wants and refuse to do the one thing that will save the people. If the people don't matter to you, how about I trade you for what does matter to you? How about I give you the life of your captain? I can't give you them all—someone must be punished—but I would be willing to exile the captain in place of the death sentence, for your cooperation in the binding ceremony."

Anger, like she had never known, surged through Inaya at Sorin's words. She didn't have the strength to defeat Sorin and the army of Ammon on her own, but by the angels, she would find a way to free the Royal Guard and she would take pleasure in watching them take Sorin down. He had made a grave error in bragging about holding the people she loved prisoner. First, she would free Amira.

Thankfully, Marcelle chose that moment to interrupt, and she and Sorin left to prepare for the binding ceremony he had spoken of.

When Inaya poked her head inside the bedchamber and saw Amira pale and helpless lying on the bed, the tears finally broke through and she found herself frozen in place. When Amira held out her arms to Inaya, she wasted no time rushing to the princess's bedside. The crushing relief stole her breath, and she found herself sobbing in her best friend's arms. For once, it was Amira who provided the comfort and reassurance. She was also the voice of reason when she brought the focus back to what was most important.

"Shh... it's okay, but we don't have much time. Marcelle drugged the tea she gave me, and I'll soon be asleep, so this will have to be quick. Did you hear what Sorin said about the Guard?"

Anger clogged Inaya's throat, forcing her to nod her answer.

"Is it true? Have you heard from Murdock or any of the Guard?"

"There is no sign of them. My brother Alyx is the only soldier I have been in any contact with, and he says no one knows anything about their whereabouts, but they have scouts out searching. Maryse had her baby last night. Murdock wouldn't have been absent for that unless he had no choice." Her voice cracked.

"Okay, then we assume it's true; Sorin has the Guard locked up."

"That son of a bitch!" Inaya said through clenched teeth, silently vowing to make him pay.

"Inaya, I need to know if everything else he said was true. Is the shield really failing? Have there really been extreme changes to the island?"

The color had completely drained from the princess's face, and Inaya wished she could save her from the truth. She looked at her lap and answered, "Yes... it's bad."

"What is being done?" Amira's voice was barely a whisper.

Since she had left the palace and the servants had been removed as well, Inaya didn't have many answers. She explained that, then added, "Our army was sent out yesterday morning when most of the devastation was reported. It's too soon to know all of the details, but we do know Velius has been affected the least. I guess that is because you are here. Refugees from the other territories are making their way here, but are getting little help and are not even permitted within the palace walls. Sorin has the palace locked down with his soldiers. They are spreading rumors of your death." Her tears were now flowing freely again.

It was obvious the princess was trying to be brave as she assured Inaya she was fine and that her aunt had a plan to save her, even though it was clear Marcelle was in league with Sorin to take control of Amira's kingdom. They couldn't trust Marcelle or her plan, but what choice did they have? Even if Inaya could somehow safely remove Amira from the palace, the blood bond connecting her to the shield around Cashile was slowly killing her.

Terror and guilt crushed Inaya's chest as she realized she would have to leave her friend behind, but she promised herself and Amira that she would locate the Royal Guard and send help for the princess.

Inaya discovered following Sorin around the palace undetected was easier than she had expected. With the servants removed and their replacements minimal, the palace was practically barren. Most of Velius's soldiers had been dispatched to the other territories, leaving Ammon's soldiers busy handling the refugees who were flocking to the palace for aid. Although it was easier to stalk Sorin, it was also uneventful and discouraging—that was until he decided to take a trip to the produce cellar located at the rear of the palace.

His demeanor shifted as he approached the door, suddenly appearing nervous, darting glances around him. He lost his usual cocky swagger as he opened the door and began to descend the stairs. Inaya was just able to squeeze in behind him unnoticed.

His breathing became harsher the further he went, and through the dim light of the lantern he carried, she could see the glistening of sweat dripping down his neck. She tried to step lightly as she followed behind him at a distance, staying in the shadows, but she hit a loose board wrong and a loud creak echoed through the stairwell. Sorin swung around, nearly tumbling down the stairs in his haste, but caught himself on the wall. Inaya started to panic as he held his light forward and scanned the area. She held her breath, sending up a quick prayer to whomever might be listening. And by some miracle, he didn't spot her.

Sorin raised his chin and seemed to gather his courage before turning and continuing his descent into the dark cellar. She slowly released her pent-up breath and took a moment to slow her rapidly pounding heart. When she felt steady, she snuck forward. The closer to the bottom she got, the stronger the pungent smell became. She barely restrained her gag reflex as she identified the scent of human waste and body odor.

Her attention was diverted from the possible horrors that awaited her as Sorin began conversing with the guard stationed at the bottom of the steps. Careful to remain hidden, Inaya listened as the soldier gave his report that all was "quiet" and the prisoners were "subdued." The words hit her hard. She had done it! She had found where Sorin was keeping the Royal Guard.

Red-hot anger flared at the soldier's words, but it was nothing compared to what she felt at Sorin's response of "Yes, well I can imagine being kept in the dark with little food for days would subdue any weak male."

The blood rushing through her system echoed in her ears, and her hands shook violently with the need to rip him limb from limb and then maybe fling the pieces around for a while. She had never felt this desperate need to cause harm before, but this male was directly responsible for hurting everyone she loved, and she wanted to make him pay.

"I will speak to the former captain alone," Sorin said. Panic flooded Inaya's system as the soldier nodded and turned to leave. She glanced up the staircase, preparing to flee, but Sorin spoke quickly, halting both Inaya and the soldier. "You will wait at the bottom of the stairs and leave your light with me."

Short-lived relief eased Inaya's flight instinct as the soldier fumbled through the dark while Sorin selfishly took the light and headed to the other side of the cellar. He stepped just out of Inaya's sight, but she was able to still hear him. Her hands balled into fists as she listened to him taunting Caeden, saying vile things about Amira. Her worry escalated at his words, not because she believed them, but because she knew there was no way Caeden would ever allow anyone to speak of the princess in such a manner, and yet he did nothing to stop Sorin. But then Sorin's words were cut off by the sound of chains rattling, and he let out a sharp yelp. A deep voice murmured something too low for her to distinguish, but whatever Caeden said, it left Sorin looking shaken as he quickly made his way back to the stairs.

Fear warred with the anger inside her. She wanted nothing more than to rush down there and free the Royal Guard, but that just wasn't an option. Sorin and his soldier would grab her the moment she stepped into the light.

Not wanting to come face-to-face with Sorin just yet, Inaya began easing her way back toward the door. She'd need to slip out before Sorin ascended. But just as she was exiting, his command registered in her ears.

"You'll stay on duty for another shift," he instructed his soldier.

"But, my lord, I've already served a twelve-hour duty without food or rest," the soldier complained.

"Then you'll serve another twelve." Sorin's words were cold and uncaring.

And suddenly, Inaya knew how she would free the Royal Guard.

~

It took little to no time for Inaya to sneak into the palace kitchen and grab what she needed. Before she knew it, she was almost back to the cellar. Just when she started to believe she could pull off her rescue mission, a hand covered her mouth, an unyielding arm banned around her waist, and she was lifted off the ground and pulled into the shadows beside the palace. Fear alone had her clenching her grip on the heavy tray of food she carried. She twisted from side to side, frantically fighting for release.

"Inaya, stop!" a harsh voice whispered in her ear.

She froze as soon as she realized who that voice belonged to, and when she did, the hand on her mouth dropped and she was released. She spun around and glared at her brother.

"Alyx, what are you doing here? Why didn't you meet me this morning?"

"Shh, keep your voice down," he scolded, while glancing around to make sure they hadn't been spotted. "I couldn't meet earlier. I'm being dispatched, along with the remainder of Velius's soldiers. My unit is scheduled to depart at any moment. We're all being watched; I couldn't risk leading Sorin's men to you and Maryse to let you know. What are you doing here?"

"I've found them! I found the Guard!"

"Really? Where are they?" Alyx looked around again, as if the Royal Guard would suddenly pop out of the bushes.

"They're being held prisoner by Sorin. I was just on my way to release them."

"Like hell you are. Where are they? You get to safety and I'll free the Guard."

"Alyx, you just said you were being watched and about to leave. If you don't, they'll come looking for you and ruin the opportunity to free them." Alyx looked like he was about to argue with her, so she continued. "Don't worry, I have a plan."

"You have a plan," he scoffed. "Why do I not find that comforting?"

If her hands weren't full with the tray of food, she would have knocked her brother upside his head. "Yes, I have a plan, and you can help." That seemed to get her brother on board. His shoulders squared, and he cocked his head to the side as he listened. "The Guard will need our soldiers if they have any chance at defeating Sorin and regaining control of the palace. I need you to bring them back."

"I can't just command our soldiers to defy a direct order from Lord Sorin and march them back into the palace walls."

This was true, but it only took Inaya a moment to find a solution. "Tell them the command is from the captain of the Royal Guard on behalf of Princess Amira—"

"Is it?"

She ignored Alyx's question. "Have them assemble

at the southern crest; that will keep them out of Sorin's sight."

"Then what?"

"Then you wait for further instructions from the Guard."

Alyx stared at her silently for a moment, looking as if he wanted to argue, but eventually, he nodded in agreement. "Are you sure you can free them on your own?"

"I told you, I have a plan. You just get everyone ready."

"Okay. You be careful."

With an awkward hug, considering her hands were still full, Alyx rushed off to rejoin his unit. Inaya waited in the shadows, making sure he was gone before she made her way to the cellar. The last thing she needed was Alyx deciding she needed help and drawing attention to her inadvertently.

If it were possible, Inaya was more frightened heading into the cellar this time than she was the first time. So much rode upon her success. Balancing the tray and gripping a lantern, she descended the steps. She didn't need to keep her presence hidden this time; she just needed to convince the soldier on duty that she belonged there.

He was at the foot of the stairs just as before, but jumped to his feet when he spotted her, instantly on guard. Being a soldier from Ammon, there was little risk that he would recognize Inaya, but just in case, she bowed her head in what she hoped was a shy, respectful fashion.

"This area has been restricted. You need to leave," he barked.

"I-I was ordered to bring you your evening meal, sir," she forced out. Her palms were so sweaty she feared she would lose the grip on her tray.

"On whose authority?" he demanded.

She'd finally made it to the bottom, and she didn't miss the way his hand tightened on his weapon as she approached. She hesitated for a second but didn't stop. If her plan was going to work, she needed to get closer.

"Lord Sorin's of course." Given what she knew of the male ego, she added, "I was informed you are one of his most valuable soldiers and that you deserved a warm meal."

Inaya barely contained her laughter as he puffed out his chest and smirked. She kept her concentration centered on the male in front of her. If she allowed herself to think about Trevin and Murdock and the other Guard members being held against their will only a couple feet away and all the things that could have been done to them, she'd never be able to pull this off.

"Where may I serve you, sir?"

"There will be fine." He indicated to a small table just a few steps away.

"Would you mind holding my lantern?" she asked,

giving him a bashful smile. She needed to time this right; she'd only get one chance to catch him off guard.

"Sure." He took it from her, freeing her hand to unload the food off the heavy tray. "Seems you brought enough food to feed an army," he remarked with a crooked grin.

Or a group of underfed prisoners.

"Hope you're hungry," she replied nervously as the reality of what she was about to do set in. She'd never intentionally set out to hurt anyone before, but here she was, waiting for the opportune moment. She shifted the now empty, but still quite heavy, tray in her hands as she wiped her sweaty palms on her clothes.

"What's your name, girl?"

"Inaya." She winced, realizing honesty was probably not the best idea.

"Well, Inaya,"—the way he dragged out her name, as if savoring it, made her skin crawl—"my shift ends in eleven hours. How about, after I get some sleep, I come find you? We can keep each other company." He placed her lantern at the edge of the table and took his seat, but his focus remained on her.

"I, um... that sounds nice," she forced herself to say. "Enjoy your dinner. I'll keep you company while you eat. You must get terribly lonely down here all by yourself."

The soldier actually paused to think through his answer, apparently taking his duty seriously. Or maybe not, because he smiled and sat back in his chair before patting his lap. "By all means, let's get to know each other."

Inaya swallowed hard. It was now or never. As she moved forward, closing the distance between them, she bumped the table with her hip, causing the lantern to tumble to the floor.

"Oh no," she gasped.

"No problem, dollface."

As he bent to retrieve it, she struck. Lifting the heavy tray high into the air, she brought it crashing down on the back of his skull as hard as she could. The fear and anger she had tightly bottled inside herself finally found an outlet. A primal scream ripped from her throat as she lifted the tray again and again.

She seemed to lose herself for a moment, and by the time she came back to the present, her throat was raw, her arms were shaky, the soldier was unmoving on the floor, and she was on her knees beside him. It was only just then that she realized she didn't even know his name.

What had she done? She sat back on her heels and stared at the prone body in front of her, and only when she saw his chest rise and fall did she allow herself to breathe easy. Her guilt only slightly lessened, but her mind raced at the consequences of her actions. Nephilim were impervious to disease and lived longer and healed faster than humans, but they weren't invincible. Had she left permanent damage?

She must have been in shock because it took a

while to realize someone was yelling her name. The sound of her brother's voice brought her back to the present and reminded her of her purpose. When it all clicked into place, she sprang into action, snatching the keys off the disabled soldier's belt and racing to the makeshift cell that held her brother and the rest of the Royal Guard.

Sixteen

Hearing Inaya's screams was the scariest part. Trevin's heart had lodged in his throat as the first one echoed throughout the cellar. He'd never experienced such helplessness before as he was forced to listen to the commotion in the other room. The not knowing was killing him. It had started with hearing Inaya peacefully conversing with the soldier in the next room. Then out of nowhere came a loud, repetitive banging accompanied by her shouts.

Futilely, he yanked against his restraints, heedless of the tearing of flesh and the blood trickling down his arms. His mind raced with the possibilities of what could be happening just on the other side of that door, and none of them were good.

Then there was silence that seemed to stretch for an eternity. Trevin closed his eyes and stilled as he strained to hear any indication that she was all right.

The breath rushed from his lungs at the first sound of Inaya's broken sobs. Relief overwhelmed him, but at the same time, his heart broke.

What had happened? She was alive, but was she injured? There was no sound coming from the soldier. What had she been forced to do?

Trevin renewed his struggle, determined to get to her somehow. It was Murdock who had the sense to call out to her and break her out of her despair. Typically, Trevin was the voice of reason, the calculating one, the one who acted out of logic and necessity. But in this instance, he was not that man.

Murdock's calm voice as he coached Inaya into action also brought a semblance of reason back to Trevin as well. He buried the fear and the panic, but let his anger simmer and mix with his determination. Soon he would be free, and then he would do what was needed—just do the next right thing. That was his motto, that was what kept him focused and on the right path.

As he heard the lock click in the door, he forced his mind to concentrate on what must be done and in which order.

But at the first sight of her, his mind went blank. She pushed open the heavy door and tentatively stepped inside. Her golden hair was a tangled mess around her shoulders, and her face was red and blotchy from her tears. Seeing her shoulders hunched in fear and the trembling of her hands brought Trevin's anger from a simmer to a boil. Someone was going to pay. As if hearing his thoughts, Inaya's eyes locked onto his in that moment.

She's okay, he assured himself. She was in a dark cellar, singlehandedly rescuing the Royal Guard, and looking a little worse for wear, but she was okay.

"Inaya, sweetheart, bring the keys to me." Murdock interrupted their moment, prompting her into action once again.

When she looked away, Trevin took a deep breath and released it slowly. As second-in-command, he was in charge here—at least until Caeden was freed. It was time he started to behave as such.

Murdock quickly unfastened his chains then threw the keys to Trevin before pulling his sister into his arms. "You foolish girl, what have you gotten yourself into now?" Trevin heard Murdock mutter as he freed himself.

Not wasting any time, Trevin strode to the door. As he passed Osmond, who was sitting on the floor with his back to the wall, he dropped the keys in Osmond's waiting hands. The urge to go to Inaya and assure himself she was unharmed rode him hard, but instead, he forced himself to do his duty.

As he cautiously peeked around the doorframe and accessed the situation, pride and horror mixed at the sight before him. There, on the ground, lay the soldier, and beside him lay a dented and misshapen serving tray.

Foolish indeed! Inaya had faced off with an enemy soldier twice her size armed only with kitchenware?

Trevin's eyes shot to her and he found her studying him. He sent her a hard look to let her know that they would be having words. Then he turned his attention to the Guard.

"Murdock, Osmond, get Levi up and prepared to leave. Dalek, free Caeden."

Trusting his orders would be followed, he turned to do the next right thing—ensuring the soldier who had kept them imprisoned never got a second chance to do so again. He completed his task quickly and efficiently before the others gathered in the main room with him.

Hearing them enter, his eyes locked on his target and he stalked up to Inaya. As he approached, he noticed something he hadn't seen before. Her face held bruises—bruises too colorful to be fresh. What had happened? Who had done this to her?

As if sensing his attention, she turned from her brother and watched Trevin wearily. "I brought food." She motioned to where Osmond sat at a small table and helped himself to the meal. Levi was propped up on the wall beside him, still unconscious.

"Are you insane?" Trevin couldn't help but snap.

"Obviously," Murdock answered for her. Apparently, he had gotten over his relief that she was safe, and the reality of her actions were starting to set in.

"What were you thinking? A serving tray?" Trevin

asked, part angry, part incredulous, part impressed. "Out of all your options, your choice of weapon was a serving tray?"

"I-I—"

"What! Inaya, please tell me you didn't," Murdock interrupted.

"Balls of steel, that one," Osmond mumbled, mouth full of food.

"Shut up," Trevin and Murdock said in unison, neither taking their eyes off her.

She held her hands up in a placating manner and turned to her brother. "Stop yelling at me so I can tell you that you have a son, Murdock." Then she turned to Trevin and shouted, "I should have left you chained to the wall!"

Trevin's anger erupted. He lowered his voice and promised, "When this is over, I'm going to give you the spanking you deserve."

Apparently looking for an ally, she glanced at her brother and then to Caeden, who was striding up to them. "Are you going to let him say that to me?"

Trevin eyed the males, daring them to intervene. By the goofy grin on Murdock's face, Trevin knew he wouldn't be getting any objections from him, and the determined look on Caeden's face told him that their leader had far more pressing issues on his mind. Trevin turned back to Inaya and found her glaring at him.

"I have a son!" Murdock announced excitedly.

"And you can meet him after we have escaped and

Sorin is dead," Caeden informed him. Murdock's expression turned serious, and Trevin once again forced himself to push aside all feeling and focus on his duty.

"Tell me everything," Caeden commanded Inaya.

She closed her eyes and took a deep breath, obviously trying to rein in her temper. It must have worked, because when she opened her eyes, she appeared calmer, but her gaze remained locked on Caeden.

"All right, but as I do so, please eat something." She indicated the food once more.

Caeden looked as if he were going to argue, but surprisingly, he conceded. Trevin took that moment to gesture to Dalek, instructing him to discreetly relocate the body of the soldier to the other room. As Dalek did so, Trevin angled himself to block Inaya's view; he thought it best if she not see. But if he were honest, he'd admit he didn't like the idea of her knowing what he'd done. He knew dispatching the male that had beaten and kept prisoner him and the rest of the Royal Guard was a necessity, else it would just be delaying an inevitable confrontation at a later time, but he took no pleasure in the task. It was at least a quick and painless death, he assured himself.

Dalek returned just as Inaya began explaining how Sorin and the soldiers of Ammon entered the gates during the king's memorial. She was thorough as she detailed the happenings of the last few days, but as she reached the end of her tale, it was clear she was leaving out a few details.

"I have just one question," Trevin said when she grew quiet, and the rest of the Guard appeared to be digesting all that had occurred.

"What's that?" she asked, returning her attention to Trevin for the first time since she began her story.

"The bruises on your face, who gave them to you?"

Her hand shot up to cover the offending mark, and her eyes darted away, as if she believed she had something to be ashamed of.

"I...." She faltered.

"The truth, Inaya," Murdock insisted. Trevin recognized the banked rage in his eyes.

Squaring her shoulders and lifting her head, she confided, "Sorin." She didn't expand on her answer, but she didn't need to. The male's fate had already been determined; now it was just an issue of which one of the Royal Guard would get the privilege of tearing him to pieces.

Trevin knew that was one death he might actually take pleasure in.

It was decided that Murdock would escort Inaya and Levi to the safety of his home while the rest of the Royal Guard would go after Princess Amira and Sorin.

Seventeen

The cold detachment around Lahash's heart matched the freezing temperatures of the southwest border of Cashile. With the instability of the protective shield around the island, the environment had become unstable as well, leaving areas such as this uninhabitable. The drastic climate shift had occurred suddenly, giving the residents here no opportunity to save themselves.

His eyes were drawn to the Velius soldiers methodically searching the rubble of the fallen city, desperately seeking survivors. It was a hopeless endeavor. Those who had managed to live through the earthquakes and the collapse of the buildings had already abandoned this hopeless place, leaving the dead behind.

The fruits of his labor were before him. Lahash's plans were becoming reality. Little by little, the Nephilim were being destroyed. The protective shields continued to weaken, and when Sorin merged with Amira and his evil corrupted the bond, it would only be a matter of time before all of Cashile fell to ruin.

Where was the elation that should come with his success? Instead, Lahash felt hollow, empty. His redemption was at hand, and yet something was amiss.

The tensing of his opalescent wings as they contracted closer against his body was the only acknowledgment he gave to the being who suddenly appeared at his side. Moments of silence ticked by, one after another, but time had no real meaning to creatures such as they.

"You've made quite the mess," the former recipient of God's grace said as he used the toe of his large brown boot to scoot away the arm of the deceased Nephilim who lay at their feet.

Lahash turned his full attention to his past companion. "Why are you here, Gusion?"

"As I have spoken, you have made quite the mess."

"You and the others care not for the fate of our offspring," Lahash reminded him.

"True, but did you not consider the ramifications of your actions? Destruction of such epic proportion affects us all, as we share the same planet."

"I care not one way or another for the fate of Earth, as you are aware. But I am curious as to why you've come to me. The ramifications of my actions should suit your purpose and that of our fallen brothers. The downfall of humanity is your goal, is it not?"

"Indeed." Gusion turned away from Lahash and surveyed the destruction surrounding them. "You mistake my intention. This has set in motion a chain of events that are far bigger than your drive for vengeance." Gusion's fathomless black eyes locked on to Lahash's. "I once again ask that you join us, brother."

The imploring tone caught Lahash off guard. It had been centuries since he had seen any of his fallen comrades, seeing as they had different purposes, but he'd always been closer with Gusion than with the others.

Before they had stolen the free will that had not been granted to them as angels, Gusion had been a mighty servant blessed with the gift to see the past, present, and future. But before the fall, his vision of the future began to become hazy, until it became unclear altogether.

"Has foresight returned to you?" Lahash questioned, a feeling much like hope burning in his chest.

Gusion's eyes dropped back to the corpse at their feet as he shook his head. "The future remains mercurial, shifting and swaying with the tide. But one fact remains consistent." His eyes bored into Lahash once more. "Your role is crucial in the outcome. We must unite as one to succeed."

"Our objective has never been the same—"

"Give the word," Gusion interrupted. "Give the

word and I shall smite these abominations on your behalf and free you of this burden."

"No. Grace cannot be obtained through dishonor."

"There is no grace to be had, Lahash! Why can you not see this? The Creator has turned his back on us. Why would you desire his favor anyhow? Why bow down and beg when you were meant for so much more?"

"That ideology is what led to our disgrace in the first place, Gusion." A feeling much like anger flooded his veins, and he barely remembered to keep his presence concealed from the unsuspecting Nephilim around them as his voice rose. "I was not meant for *this*! I was glorious. I was magnificent in my purpose. Now I am nothing."

"It doesn't have to be that way."

"True." Lahash lowered his voice as he continued. "I will complete my task and rectify my mistake—all of our mistakes. You shall see."

"I may no longer have perfect insight into what shall be, but I do know you strive for nothing. You cannot succeed in this endeavor, brother. But if you feel this is a path you must traverse, then I shall leave you to it."

Lahash reached for his previously cold detachment but found it unobtainable. Instead, he was filled with these recently emerging emotions that had begun to plague him. He strived to put a name to the uncomfortable weight in his chest but was unable.

Gusion had turned as if to walk away, but he stopped and peered over his shoulder. "Remember, it only takes one word to be free. Your hands will remain clean." Gusion paused with a sigh as Lahash shook his head. "So it shall be." He looked into the darkening sky. "The tide has shifted. You will be forced to choose, Lahash. Be prepared."

And with that, Gusion was gone.

His fallen brother's words echoed in his head, and not for the first time of late, he began to reconsider the plan he had set into motion. Redeeming himself had been his motivation, his sole purpose for being, for so long now that it had become all that he could see. By breeding with humans, he and the other fallen had broken divine will and altered the Maker's plan. Because of that, the others now doubted the glory and the power of the Creator. They believed it to be proof of the Maker's fallibility and weakness, so they sought to destroy the divine plan altogether by corrupting the precious humans.

For Lahash, this entire situation created more questions than answers.

A commotion brought his attention back to the here and now as a small contingent of soldiers came barreling into the ruins of the city. Lahash recognized the leader of the group. He was the young male who was often with Inaya, her half sibling. Alyx, he believed his name was.

Lahash's curiosity was piqued as the others gathered around Alyx, listening intently. Lahash was too far to hear what was being said, but it was clear that the soldiers argued amongst themselves, but in the end, it appeared Alyx was able to convince the others to do his bidding, as they all rushed to depart, heading in the direction of Velius.

Interesting. What has occurred to cause such urgency?

And then he felt it. Electricity sizzled in the air and the ground shifted beneath his feet. Lahash closed his eyes and opened his senses. A smile stretched across his lips as excitement flared inside him.

Sorin had done it. He was now connected to the bond that protected Cashile and the Nephilim. He had succeeded in binding himself to the princess and was now in place to seize control. Power corrupted, but what happened if the one to come into power was already corrupt? Lahash's smile spread wider.

The purity of the blood bond forged by the angels to protect the Nephilim would never survive the evil taint inside of Sorin. The very thing that was meant to save them would become what destroyed them all.

Lahash's earlier doubt flashed in his mind. It was too late to reconsider now. The plan had been set in motion, and that couldn't be undone. It was only a matter of time before their world imploded and the abominations were wiped from the earth.

An array of emotions followed that last thought, and if a bit of guilt and fear were mixed in, well then, Lahash would just have to squash that weakness and refocus on his ultimate goal.

His female descendant could no longer be a distraction or a consideration for him. Sorin, his deliverer of retribution, required his full attention.

EIGHTEEN

Inaya paced the floor of her brother's cottage. She had complete faith that the Royal Guard would rescue Amira from the palace safely, but the wait was excruciating, combined with the guilt she felt for leaving the princess alone and helpless in the first place.

But even after they arrive, Amira's life will still be in danger.

Inaya shut down that train of thought immediately, refusing to entertain her fears. The Royal Guard would find a way to help her friend.

"You'll wear a hole straight through the floor if you keep that up, girl," Francine grumbled. "Don't you have something to do?"

That was the problem, there was nothing left to be done. Food was prepared, the cottage was clean, and Francine had already seen to Levi. He seemed to be resting peacefully while his body worked to heal itself. Francine sat calmly by his bedside, knitting some form of garment for the baby. Murdock was with Maryse, getting acquainted with his long-awaited infant.

Inaya's mind wandered back to what was happening at the palace. It had been hours, and they still hadn't arrived. Had something happened to them? Had Sorin's soldiers captured them again? Was it Amira? Was she still too unwell to travel? Her panic rose with each unanswerable question.

"Maybe I should go after them, make sure everything is all right?" Inaya suggested.

"You're just looking for trouble, aren't you? Won't be happy until you get that fool neck of yours broken."

Francine's words unintentionally brought to mind the creak of a rope as it swung from a rafter, weighted down by the dead weight of a body. Suddenly, that was all Inaya could see—that and the lifeless eyes of her mother staring back at her.

Inaya couldn't breathe; the air had been sucked from her chest, replaced by a burning sensation as her lungs struggled for oxygen. Black dots danced in her vision as her heart slammed against her ribs in a furious rhythm. She was going to die... just like her mother.

"Head down, deep breath," a deep voice rumbled next to her ear as a large hand pushed her head forward.

Compelled to obey the voice, she drew in a shaky breath.

"Good. Take another deep breath, Inaya, and let it out slowly."

The tension eased as the hand glided down the length of her spine, bringing comfort, and the panic receded and the burning in her chest lessened.

"Now come here." She found herself pressed against a warm, firm chest, and strong arms wrapped around her. She tucked her face in the crook of his neck and inhaled deeply. His familiar scent comforted her as nothing else could.

Trevin.

Trevin held her in his arms.

She should pull away. She should fight against this comfort, this need of him. Prove that she was strong on her own. Instead, she wrapped her arms around him, clutching him tighter as she was reassured by the steady beat of his heart.

"What happened to her?"

Inaya shivered as she felt the words rumble through Trevin's chest. In response, his hand caressed the back of her head and through her hair, holding her more firmly to him.

"I'm not sure. One moment she was pacing the floor, the next she was unresponsive and struggling to breathe," Francine answered, a frown creasing her forehead.

"Panic attack," Murdock's deep voice rumbled from nearby.

"Does this happen often?" Trevin asked, and Inaya

couldn't find the energy to be angry about them discussing her as if she weren't in the room.

"Not that I know of," Murdock answered, sounding confused.

"She had them when we were younger," a soft female voice added.

That voice was enough to break through Inaya's daze.

Amira.

Inaya's head popped up, eyes scanning the room until they locked on her friend. Without thought, she tore out of Trevin's hold and rushed to where Amira was standing by the door. The two women embraced as if it had been years since they had been together, instead of mere hours.

Pulling back, Inaya gave the princess a once-over, searching for injuries, but thankfully not finding any. "Are you okay?" She failed to hide the fear in her voice. The last time she'd seen Amira, she was clearly unwell and nearly unconscious. Guilt at leaving her unprotected in the palace with the enemy consumed Inaya once more.

"Thanks to you, I'm safe. I knew you could do it!" Amira pulled her back into her arms and squeezed until Inaya couldn't breathe.

"You've both been through a lot. Why don't you take a seat?" Trevin suggested.

Only then did Inaya notice he had followed her across the room and was standing just to her left. As she pulled out of Amira's embrace, his hand settled on the small of her back, and he guided her to the nearby couch.

"How are you feeling?" he murmured so low that only she could hear.

She took a moment to consider her answer. "Better."

His only response was a brief nod. Once she was settled, he took up post standing beside the arm of the couch. His nearness unnerved her, so she turned her focus to Amira's retelling of what she'd been through. Sorin and Marcelle had forced a blood bond on her that now connected Sorin not only to the princess but to Cashile as well, putting all Nephilim in danger. Inaya couldn't begin to comprehend the consequences, but she had to admit that, regardless of being forced against her will, Amira's health seemed to no longer be declining as quickly.

A shrill cry broke Inaya out of her musings, and only then did she realized her mind had wandered. She looked up just in time to see Maryse and Murdock share a proud-parent smile before turning their attention back to the baby.

"Calm now, Elijah," Murdock murmured.

"Elijah?" Trevin repeated.

"Yes, Inaya suggested it. I think it fits him," Maryse said, beaming proudly.

"A fine name," Murdock agreed before bending to kiss both mother and son on the forehead.

Inaya felt Trevin's eyes boring into her, but she refused to look his way. Instead, she focused on her brother. She had never seen him so happy. He hadn't left his wife's side since they had arrived. When Maryse yawned and Murdock immediately pulled her closer, Inaya's chest tightened as she recalled what it had felt like to be held in Trevin's arms.

She ached for it again as emptiness enveloped her. She wanted his comfort, his strength.

That thought, along with the still vivid image of her dead mother, was enough to shake her back into reality. What Murdock and Maryse had, and what Caeden and Amira were developing were anomalies, not the norm. As the malevolent voice in her head liked to remind her, there was no love, no safety in someone else—at least not for her.

Inaya glanced around the room at all the tired faces. They had all been through so much in the last few days. Amira looked as if she were ready to drop, and Maryse struggled to keep her eyes open. As for the males, Inaya couldn't imagine how they felt after being held captive, but each of them had dark circles under their eyes.

"Why doesn't everyone get some rest?" she suggested.

The question sprang Maryse into motion. "Oh! We only have three bedrooms, but there's also the office and the living room. I'll grab some blankets—"

"Maryse," Inaya interrupted, "I know where everything is. I'll get everyone settled. You just go rest."

"Are you sure?" she asked around another yawn.

"Absolutely," Inaya assured her.

"I'll help," Amira offered. She attempted to pull away from Caeden but wasn't having much luck with his arm wrapped around her.

"You need rest," Caeden murmured.

When Amira opened her mouth to argue, Inaya intervened. "The captain's right. You've been unwell and need to rebuild your strength. You take the third bedroom. Francine is watching over Levi in the second."

Surprisingly, Amira didn't protest, which was a clear indication that she still wasn't feeling well. Instead, she turned and whispered something into Caeden's ear. He nodded before they both rose to their feet.

"Seems like you have it handled," Maryse said as she came to hug Inaya. "I'll see you in the morning." As Maryse turned to her husband, Inaya noticed the males were deep in discussion.

"I'll take the first watch and await Osmond and Dalek's return," Trevin assured them.

Murdock clapped him on the back. "Have Osmond take second watch. The old buzzard spent the last two days napping. He should be well rested." Then he turned to pull Inaya into a tight hug. "Thank you, for everything," he whispered in her ear.

"I love you, brother. Get some rest," she answered.

"Love you too." He turned and led his family to their bedroom.

Caeden and Amira said good night, and Inaya was slightly shocked to see Caeden lead her into the back bedroom. When Inaya realized she had been left alone in the room with just Trevin, she sprang into action.

"I'll set up pallets in the office for the three of you. With you on duty tonight, and Osmond and Dalek coming in late, I'm sure you'll want to sleep in. I'll just take the couch."

His hand shot out and clutched her arm as she tried to rush past.

"We need to talk."

She hated those words—everyone hated those words.

Trevin wasn't sure where to begin, but his anger had subsided, and he was thinking a bit clearer.

"I don't—" she began as she tried to pull away, but he wasn't having that.

"How are you feeling?"

That must not have been what she expected him to say, because she froze. He waited patiently as she watched him.

"I-I'm okay," she hedged.

"It took a lot of courage to do what you did. You saved us. You saved the princess. Thank you."

She seemed flustered by his praise. "I-I just did what needed to be done."

Trevin smiled at how her motivation so clearly matched his own way of thinking. Perhaps she was more mature than he gave her credit for.

"It was very brave of you."

"You said it was foolish," she mumbled, pouting.

"Well, it was that too." Inaya's back straightened, and she appeared to be gearing up for an argument, so he rushed on. "But out of everyone at the palace—the soldiers, the servants, the residents—you were the one who fought for us."

When his hand cupped her cheek, she didn't pull away, giving him a glimmer of hope that he could one day mend what he had broken between them.

"So, Inaya, let me be there for you now. Tell me how you feel. Tell me about the panic attack. Do you have them often?"

Her eyes darted away from him. He thought he saw embarrassment and possibly fear in her expression, but he said nothing. He remained quiet and let her decide what she was willing to share. He slid his hands to her shoulders and began kneading some of the tension away. Her shoulders relaxed, and she shifted a bit closer.

"I...," she began, but changed what she was about

to say. "Amira was right. I used to have panic attacks when I was younger, but I haven't in a long while."

"What triggers them?"

"When I was younger, locked doors, being alone, certain sounds, the nightmare...."

"The nightmare? As in a specific dream?"

"Yes. It's always the same."

"How often do you have it?"

"Every night when I first moved to the palace, but as I got older, it became less frequent until it finally went away... until a few months ago."

"Is that why you've looked so tired lately?" She shrugged instead of answering, so Trevin took that as a yes. "I see. Do you want to tell me about your dream?"

"No." Her response was instantaneous, and he felt her shoulders tense again. When she stepped back, he let her pull away from him.

"Shouldn't you be patrolling the grounds or something?"

Trevin recognized her attempt to change the subject and gave her that space for now. As far as he knew, not even Princess Amira knew the details of Inaya's life before coming to live at the palace. To her brothers' worry and frustration, she had never shared it with them either.

"I will, but we should be safe at the moment. I just have one more question. You gave your nephew my brother's name, why?"

She froze and looked even more uncomfortable

than she had when discussing her own past. Until that moment, he hadn't known she was aware of his brutal past. Feeling unclean by the reminder of his past sins, he stepped away from her, unconsciously slipping his hands behind his back. He was about to walk away when her eyes shot up to meet his, freezing him in place.

"It's a fine name, and your brother's sacrifice should be remembered, but more than that, it was to honor three males who showed us all what bravery and courage really mean."

Her words humbled him like nothing before. Words escaped him, so he nodded once in acknowledgment of her praise. After a moment of silence, he said, "When you're ready to confront your past, I'll be here for you."

"And I'll do the same for you."

Her response surprised him. Yes, Inaya was far more intuitive and mature than he had given her credit for. "Thank you. Rest easy tonight, Inaya. I'll keep you safe."

Body aching, mind exhausted, he turned away to do just that. He couldn't relieve her of her bad dreams, but for tonight, he could provide her the security and safety she deserved.

~

Inaya wasn't the only one who had nightmares, Trevin discovered later that night. The entire household had been alerted to Princess Amira's distress as she cried out in terror—well, everyone except Levi and Inaya. Levi was showing signs of improvement but had yet to awaken. As for Inaya, she had managed to stay awake until Osmond and Dalek had returned from the palace, but soon after she had them settled into her brother's home, Trevin found her fast asleep at the kitchen table.

He couldn't imagine what the last few days had been like for her, but apparently, it was all catching up to her. She didn't even stir when he lifted her into his arms, carried her to the living room, and settled her onto the sofa.

Once Osmond had taken over the watch, Trevin had tried to get some rest himself, but he kept waking with the need to check on Inaya. After witnessing her panic attack and her confession of having nightmares, he hated the idea of her facing them alone.

After the princess was settled from her bad dream, Trevin gave up attempting to sleep in the office. Instead, he grabbed a blanket and made himself as comfortable as possible in the chair across from the sofa. It wasn't ideal, but even in the uncomfortable position, he slept better just being in the same room as her.

A hand landing on his shoulder had him jerking away and instantly awake.

Murdock took a step back and silently motioned toward the doorway before turning on his heel and walking away, expecting Trevin to follow. Trevin's eyes darted to the sofa. The light of the sun was just peeking through the curtains, highlighting Inaya's messy hair in a golden shimmer. She was the most beautiful sight he'd ever seen. Seeing her like this, resting peacefully, completely unguarded, felt right. Contentment washed over him, yet at the same time, his heart felt heavy.

With a sigh, he turned toward the door, only to find Murdock studying him. Trevin expected to see anger, or maybe a hint of irritation in his eyes, considering how protective Murdock was of his sister. Instead, he recognized only curiosity as he met Murdock in the doorway to the office. When Murdock didn't show any sign of moving, Trevin stopped in front of him and arched his eyebrow in question.

"Watching over my sister?"

"Someone needs to."

Murdock's back straightened and anger flared in his eyes. "She's not going to cause any trouble. She's more—"

Trevin didn't like having to explain himself, but this was Inaya's brother, so he made an exception. "Princess Amira isn't the only one who has nightmares."

That statement shut Murdock up. He looked as if

someone had slapped him, and his eyes darted to Inaya. "Did she have one last night?"

"Not that I could tell."

Murdock nodded, appearing deep in thought as he stared at his sister. Trevin gave him time to sort his thoughts.

"She's been through a lot," Murdock finally murmured.

"The last couple of days have been difficult—"

"No," Murdock interrupted, his brown eyes locking on to Trevin's, the pain in them clear. "Before that. Before she came to the palace."

"I asked her about that. She didn't say much."

"She won't talk about it. I've tried as well." Murdock shook his head, looking defeated. "I'd hoped the wounds of the past had healed, but if she's still having nightmares...."

"She's stronger than we've given her credit for. She saved us all yesterday."

Murdock smirked proudly. "Yeah, she did."

"You ladies plan to gab all day?" Osmond grumbled. Trevin turned to see Osmond, Dalek, and Caeden watching them from within the office. "We have a princess to heal and an enemy who won't defeat himself."

"Are you sure about that?" Dalek questioned. "Sorin doesn't seem like the type to be winning any awards for intelligence."

"He was able to take command of the palace," Osmond countered.

"But he won't keep it," Caeden vowed. "Now everyone grab a journal. The answer has to be here somewhere."

After an afternoon of scouring Supreme Healer Marcelle's journals, they were no closer to discovering how to free Princess Amira from her twisted bond with Sorin, but a few unwelcome facts about the deaths of her parents had been uncovered. Trevin was surprised at how well Amira was dealing with this discovery.

Unfortunately, it appeared Inaya wasn't handling their situation quite as well. As he paused in the kitchen entryway, watching Inaya cleaning the dishes from their afternoon meal, he noted her stiff posture, tense shoulders, and the slight trembling of her hands. She'd been quiet lately, and he noticed she hadn't eaten much. He knew he should probably give her some space, but instead, he found himself seeking her out once again.

"Need some help?"

With a gasp, Inaya spun around. The wooden bowl she had been holding slipped from her fingers and bounced along the floor as her hands flew to cover her heart in freight.

"Hey, it's okay." He was tempted to pull her into his embrace, but settled for resting his hand on her shoulder for comfort.

She took a deep breath, steadying herself. "Sorry, I was lost in thought. And you move awfully quiet for such a big man, tiptoeing around like you do." She smirked at him, obviously trying to distract him.

He retrieved the bowl and placed it back in the sink. "I'll wash, you dry."

"That's not necessary. I—"

"Let me help," he interrupted. She opened her mouth to say something, but he shot her a disapproving look, and she wisely decided not to argue. "You're safe here, you know," he offered after a few moments of silence.

Her shoulders tensed even more. "None of us are safe." Her voice was so low, he almost missed it. In a clearer voice, she continued. "Our location was discovered today. It's just a matter of time before Ammon soldiers stumble across us."

"Jericho and his family are loyal to the royal family. They would never reveal Amira's location." They had all been surprised that afternoon when Velius's long-time stablemaster, Jericho, had arrived, along with his daughter, Sadie, and William, the stable hand. They had intentionally sought out Murdock's cottage after hearing rumors that the princess had gone missing and had possibly been murdered. Although having visitors had been unexpected and unwelcome, Jericho was able to provide valuable information that would help the Royal Guard defeat Sorin, and he had offered his help in organizing the evacuation of the civilians still within the palace walls. "Besides, Murdock's cottage is well secluded and not likely to be stumbled across."

"How can you be sure?"

He turned to meet her gaze. "You're right, things don't look good right now, and Sorin has bested us once before, but now we know what we're up against, and Princess Amira can use his bond against him to know if he's coming for us. We're prepared, and we *can* keep you safe. I would give my life to protect you."

Her eyes welled with tears. "That's what I'm afraid of." When her chin quivered, he didn't hesitate to pull her into his arms. "I don't want anyone else I love to die," she sobbed.

With everything else that had happened, he hadn't considered how the king's death was affecting her. She was grieving the only father she had ever known. Wrapping his arms around her, he offered her comfort the only way he knew how. He pressed a kiss to her hair, her temple, her cheek, and when she tilted her face toward his, he brushed his lips against hers. She responded hesitantly at first, but then her lips parted, and she eagerly kissed him back.

His blood rushed through his veins and his heart pounded. This kiss was no longer about providing comfort; it was about passion and need. Tangling his fingers in her hair, he angled her head to deepen the kiss. Her curvy body pressed against his as she clutched him tightly.

When a soft moan passed from her lips to his, Trevin was sure he'd lose his mind. His hunger for her threatened to overcome his logic and self-control. He couldn't allow that. Now was not the time to claim her body, he'd be taking advantage of her fear and desperation. It took all his willpower, but he forced himself to break their kiss.

Reality slammed into him, and he jumped back, breaking all contact. What had he done? This was Inaya, Murdock's little sister. Hell, she should be like a little sister to him as well... but she wasn't. She hadn't been for a very long time. He'd been fooling himself all this time, thinking he could keep her at arm's length and keep pretending she was the same little girl she used to be.

Taking a deep breath, he looked at Inaya, but she refused to meet his eyes. Instead, she stared at the wall beside his head. It was apparent that reality had returned to her as well. Her posture was closed off, and she wore an expression of indifference. The person standing before him was not the female who had just returned his kiss with a fiery passion. No, this was the female he had rejected on one of the most important nights of her young life. This was the hardened female she had become... or tried to become. With that kiss, he knew that girl who had once stared at him with adoration was still in there, she was just a bit wiser and tougher. Good.

But he would need time to consider the best course of action. This was Inaya, she was too important, and he had already made too many mistakes with her.

"I'm leaving in a few hours. I should probably rest while I can, but if you need anything before I go...." He let his statement trail off. Caeden had ordered him to take command of their army gathered at the southern crest a half a day's ride from Velius. Trevin intentionally left out the part of the plan where he and Caeden were headed back to the palace that night before Trevin joined up with the army. According to Jericho, Sorin was planning something, and the Guard needed to know what it was. Sorin had secured himself within the palace and had made himself an inaccessible target. However unlikely a possibility, Trevin secretly hoped they'd be able to gain access to wherever Sorin had hidden himself; he'd end this once and for all. But he didn't want to get Inaya's hopes up, or give her something else to worry about, so he kept the detail of tonight's mission to himself.

"I won't," she rushed to say, but then she hesitated. He was fascinated by the emotions that flickered in her expression and wondered what she was thinking. "When do you leave?" she finally asked. He was so enchanted by her flushed cheeks and kiss-swollen lips, he almost missed her question.

"After dark."

"Who will be riding with you?"

"The others will remain to guard the princess and evacuate the remaining civilians within the palace walls."

"But what about the traitor?" she protested. "One of our own has been working with Sorin. There is no other explanation as to how the soldiers of Ammon gained access to the palace."

"I can handle the traitor," he assured her.

"Alone? There is no telling how many are working against us, and you've already been captured once."

It was the truth, but hearing her say it and her lack of faith in him bruised his ego and triggered his anger. "I *will* handle the traitor," he repeated through clenched teeth. He would make sure Eldon paid for causing Inaya to doubt him, along with all his other sins.

"I'll go with you."

"You will stay here where it is safe," he declared. Trevin struggled to control his anger as he watched her wrestle with fear and frustration.

"Nowhere is safe any longer, and I can be of help to you," she argued.

"How?" He knew that was the wrong thing to say as soon as it slipped off his tongue, but he couldn't take it back. A dejected look crossed her features before her mask of indifference returned.

They stared at one another in silence. Finally, she nodded. "I trust you to take care of yourself."

Her words soothed his anger, and he couldn't take the distance between them a moment longer. Ignoring the way her body tensed at his approach, he stepped toward her and ran his fingers through her hair, resting his hand at the nape of her neck before pressing a kiss to her forehead. "I trust you to do the same." He met her eyes. "No reckless heroic feats while I'm away." He was only half joking. With Inaya, he never knew quite what to expect.

"I make no promises," she said, smiling for the first time in days. He could only chuckle and shake his head. At least she was honest.

Nineteen

Inaya couldn't shake her sense of unease. She'd spent all day trying to distract herself from the possibility of soldiers bursting through the door to drag them all away. And although Trevin had meant for their conversation earlier to be encouraging, it had only given her something else to worry about. She hated the idea of him going alone. And that kiss....

"Darling, you keep frowning like that, I'm gonna start believing I'm not as pretty as I once was."

This unexpected statement had her nearly tumbling out of her seat. "Levi, you're awake!"

"How could I possibly sleep with such a beautiful woman keeping vigil at my sickbed? Plus, it's hard to rest with all your grumbling about 'hardheaded males.'"

Inaya's face flamed with embarrassment. She hadn't realized she'd spoken her frustration aloud.

"How do you feel? Can I get you anything?" she asked quickly to change the subject. "Caeden and Trevin are gone, but shall I wake the others?"

Levi had briefly regained consciousness before, but never when it was her turn to sit with him. He had opened his eyes and spoken to Osmond earlier that day, but then he had drifted back to sleep quickly. But he seemed perfectly alert now.

"Something to drink would be nice," he requested, "but let the others rest."

"Of course." Inaya rushed through the quiet house. Dalek was on patrol outside, but everyone else seemed to be asleep—well, except for Trevin and Caeden. Trevin had left shortly before dusk, as he said he would, and Caeden had disappeared around the same time. No one spoke of his whereabouts, and Amira had already retired to her room for the evening, still not having regained her full strength, so Inaya had no one to ask. She could try talking with her brother or Maryse, but everyone had been treating her differently after witnessing her panic attack, as if she were fragile instead of the strong female who had singlehandedly freed the Guard from the cellar. She couldn't stand the way they watched her, as if she would fall apart at any moment, so she had decided to just avoid them until they forgot about her moment of weakness and things went back to normal.

When she returned, she found Levi sitting up in bed, his chest bare as the covers pooled at his hips. She almost stumbled over her own feet. Despite everything he'd been through, the male was still gorgeous. Levi gave her a knowing grin.

Pretending she hadn't momentarily been struck stupid by the sight of him, she concentrated on her feet as she brought him his drink and resumed her seat beside his bed. After downing nearly the entire glass of water, Levi turned his attention to her.

"So, tell me which 'hardheaded male' has you worked up this time."

"You don't need to worry about that. You just need to rest and get better."

"No, what I need is to know what's going on," he replied, showing that steely edge that was always just under the surface, hidden by Levi's charming façade. He may have acted like the careless womanizer, but there was a reason he was part of the Royal Guard—he was deadly.

Osmond had given Levi the abridged version of everything that had occurred since his disappearance, but Inaya was able to fill in a little more detail. Pain flashed in his eyes when they discussed the king's murder, only to be replaced with fury when they touched on the unnatural bond Sorin had forced upon the princess. At one point, she feared he would leap from the bed and try to take on Sorin and his army singlehandedly. But thankfully he was able to control himself. With noticeable effort, his carefree façade slipped into place.

"And this 'hardheaded male'? Don't tell me your brother dared to forbid you from conducting some reckless idea you've concocted," he teased with mock outrage.

"Of course not." Inaya fought her embarrassment, but felt her cheeks heating.

"Of course not. How silly of me," he said with a wink. "That wouldn't make you angry. That would just make you even more determined."

"I—" He cut her off before she could defend herself, which was just as well, considering he was right.

"Don't get riled, sweetheart. That's one of the qualities I like best about you. You're strongminded and free-spirited." She couldn't help smiling over his assessment... until he continued. "So, it must be Trevin." Her smile faded. Levi was entirely too observant. "You'll have to be patient with him, love. I've tried to advise him on how to court a lady, but I fear it is a lost cause."

For a moment, her heart stilled at his endearment. Levi's charm could be lethal, but she understood he didn't mean anything by it.

"Yes, well, his courting tactics are not the issue at hand." Or not completely. But she wasn't willing to discuss the kiss, or Trevin's behavior afterward, the way he had pushed her away and pretended it never happened. "His arrogance and lack of self-preservation are the problem." At Levi's arched eyebrow, she continued. "He's gone to assemble our troops."

"Is that not his duty?"

"But he's gone alone, and the traitors are still out there."

Offering comfort, Levi held her hand, and his voice was soft when he spoke. "Trevin has earned his arrogance. He is more than qualified to perform his duty. Have faith in your man. He can handle Eldon."

"What? What does Eldon have to do with anything?" She didn't even bother to address Levi's "your man" comment. She knew there was no reasoning with him, and the more she denied it, the more he would persist.

His hand tightened on hers. "He's the traitor, sweetheart. He's the one who attacked me."

Inaya jumped to her feet and paced the small confines of the room. "That bastard! How could he? And then to act concerned about my welfare and pretend he wanted to help."

"Shh, darling, didn't you say the others were sleeping?"

Only then did she realize her voice had risen. Taking a deep breath, she marched back over to the bed. "Why would he turn against us?" Her voice was much softer.

"I don't know." His voice was just as soft as hers.

"Trevin doesn't know. Someone needs to warn him."

Levi grabbed her hand as she tried to turn away. "I'm sure the Guard has figured it out by now."

"But—"

"Trevin can handle himself, Inaya."

"I know, but I don't like him being alone and at a disadvantage."

"We're the Royal Guard, darling, we're never at a disadvantage." He playfully winked at her.

Since he was trying to make her feel better, she didn't point out the fact that he'd been unconscious for days. She squeezed his hand. "I'm glad you're feeling better. I'll let you get some rest." Besides, she had somewhere else to be.

"Inaya." His voice stopped her when she reached the door. Looking over her shoulder, she took in his serious expression. "Stay safe."

Did he know what she was planning? Judging by the hard glint in his eyes, she'd bet he did, but he wasn't going to stop her. She nodded and headed out the door.

The horrified expression on Levi's face instantly filled Trevin with trepidation, stealing the joy he felt at seeing his fallen brother conscious and active. The two males stopped at opposite ends of the hallway in Murdock's cottage and stared at one another—Trevin in confusion and Levi in what looked like fear.

"What the hell are you doing here?"

Well, those were not the first words he expected to hear when Levi finally awakened. He and Levi had a complicated history that should have brought them closer; instead, it built walls between them. Trevin had forgiven his friend long ago but feared Levi would never forgive himself for his part in Elijah's death. But despite all that, there had never been hostility between them.

Trevin raised an eyebrow in response and waited patiently.

Levi's head fell forward, and he quietly said, "She went after you."

Trevin didn't need clarification of who. Before he made the decision to move, he found himself in Levi's face. "When?"

"Hours ago." As Trevin turned to leave, Levi grabbed his arm. "I thought you'd be there to protect her."

Trevin nodded in understanding. He knew it was near impossible to stop Inaya when her mind was made up.

"I will be."

~

The silence was deafening, a stark contrast to the once vibrant trade town that bordered Velius. Although Inaya knew the town had only been deserted because of the erratic storms that came with the weakening bond that protected the island, she couldn't help but feel as if the town had been tainted by a malevolent presence. Her body tense, she held her breath, waiting for the shadows to come alive and attack.

"This is ridiculous," she told Knight, patting the stallion on his silky neck. "Everything is fine." But it was clear by her whispered reassurance that even she didn't believe it.

Velius's soldiers were gathered less than a mile outside of town. Inaya knew much of her anxiety was due to the upcoming confrontation with Trevin. He wasn't going to be pleased with her arrival, to say the least, but with the vital information she had, he'd remain alive and the traitor would meet justice. Anger flared inside her at the thought of Eldon's betrayal. When she'd last seen him at the palace, he'd seemed genuinely concerned for her, and she'd believed she had an ally at a time when she'd needed one most.

Inaya had learned early on not to give her trust easily but living at the palace and being around truly honorable men such as the Royal Guard had broken through her defenses. Once again, her faith had been shaken, her sense of security ripped away.

The island of Cashile had been created to protect the Nephilim from the evils of man, but now it seemed they were a danger to themselves. Humankind were not the only ones to fall victim to cardinal sins, which shouldn't be a surprise since the Nephilim were a blend of humans and fallen angels.

Inaya's mind wandered, contemplating the traits passed down through their heritage, but before she knew it, her thoughts returned to the one topic she had been trying to avoid.... Why would he kiss her? Trevin had made it clear that he was not interested in a relationship with her, had stated as much to her in the past, but his actions told a different story. Perhaps he didn't know what he wanted. That seemed the most likely truth. Trevin wasn't the type of male to play games.

But how did she feel? Did she want someone who had failed to choose her in the past, someone who didn't know if she was worth the effort now?

Her love for Trevin had been pure. There had been no doubt in her mind that they were meant to be together. Perhaps those were just childish dreams; after all, there was no "meant to be." Right?

After her maturity celebration, she had decided to grow up and let go of the silly dream of a soul-deep love between her and Trevin. Since then, she had almost managed to accomplish that feat, but now... she didn't know. Trevin may not intentionally be playing games with her, but his actions were toying with her emotions and confusing her mind. She couldn't allow that to continue.

Pushing aside her emotional turmoil, she looked around and realized they had made it to the town's border. Tall trees and shrubs covered the outlying hills, making the silence seem normal and not so eerie. The tension eased from her shoulders as she relaxed. Knight seemed to relax as well.

In the distance, lightning danced in a mesmerizing display of power. With her eyes locked on the sky, she didn't see the attack coming, but she felt the sharp, burning pain as something pierced through her right side, sending her tumbling from her mount. The air was forced from her lungs as she collided with the unforgiving ground, her head bouncing against the stone trail. Then there was nothing.

TWENTY

Lahash's eyes were once again drawn to the wilted leaves of the potted plant next to the window. There was something disturbing about the way they drooped, their color shifting from a vibrant green to yellow and brown. It occurred to him, with just a little nurture, this plant could survive—no, not survive. It would thrive and produce beautiful pink and red flowers the size of his fist. He held his hand in front of him, palm up, fingers splayed.

One hand, given the right directive, held so much power. It could save this fragile plant, or he could rip it from its soil and end its pathetic existence.

So much power... and yet... Lahash's gaze went to the window. Lightning flashed across the sky as an angry storm brewed in the distance. The flicker of multiple campfires just outside the palace walls stole his attention. From this viewpoint in the castle, he watched them huddle for warmth. Homeless, unused to this cold weather, they mourned the death of their loved ones and life as they knew it.

The bite of his nails digging into his palms drew his eyes to his now clenched fist.

So much power....

Without thought, he flung his arm and sent the dying plant crashing to the ground.

"Wh-who's there?" Sorin's unsteady voice asked as a light filled the room.

Oh, you should be afraid.

Lahash burned to reveal himself but knew it was not yet the time. But there were other ways he could make his presence known. He gathered all the newly released emotions inside himself and projected them into Sorin—sharing the rage, guilt, self-doubt... helplessness.

Sorin was now just as much to blame. He deserved this burden just as much as Lahash.

Twenty-One

Cheers greeted Trevin as he rode into the soldiers' camp. It was well into the night, but many of the soldiers were still awake, and those who weren't were disturbed by the noise and stumbled from their tents. Trevin scanned the growing crowd but didn't catch a glimpse of Inaya's honey-blonde hair.

Alyx pushed his way through the crowd and clasped Trevin on the shoulder. "It's good to see you well, friend."

Nodding distractedly, Trevin asked the only thing that mattered to him. "Where is she?"

The smile slowly slid from Alyx's lips. "Where is who?" But from the fear in his eyes, Trevin knew Alyx was well aware of who he was referring to.

Greetings and questions were still being thrown at him from all directions, but his attention stayed on

Inaya's brother. An expletive slipped from Alyx's lips before he bellowed, "Why would Inaya be here?"

"You know your sister" was the only answer he could give. Trevin scanned the crowd again, this time searching for a new target, but again coming up empty. Fury exploded within him.

"Sir?" Erid, one of the senior officers, stepped forward, seeking direction.

"Gather the officers for debriefing," Trevin ordered. Then he raised his voice to address the crowd. "Lady Inaya is missing. She was on her way here, but never arrived. Alyx will organize the search party. I want her found."

As Alyx rushed to do as ordered and the crowd started to back up, Erid and the officers returned.

"I did not see Eldon or Isaac. Where are they?" Trevin asked quietly.

The officers looked to one another, each shaking his head before Erid answered. "They were here earlier, sir."

"Blane, Phyn, you will find them and bring them to me," Trevin tasked.

Trevin paced the small confines of the makeshift command tent that had been set up at the base of the camp. Nearly an hour had passed since he'd arrived, and still there had been no word of Inaya or the traitors. Trevin needed to be out searching for them, but duty demanded he remain at camp to debrief the officers and put Caeden's plan into motion.

"So, over the upcoming days, the rest of the Guard will sneak the civilians out of the palace walls while we sneak in and, one by one, take out Sorin's soldiers?" Erid clarified.

"Yes," Trevin confirmed, doing his best to focus, but failing. With both Inaya and Eldon missing, there was no doubt in his mind that they were together. But how was Eldon able to get to her so fast... and what was he doing to her? The possible scenarios flashed through his mind, playing out in graphic detail. Clenching his fists, he struggled to push the disturbing thoughts away. Letting his imagination torment him would solve nothing.

"I like it. Simple, but effective," Erid added. "What do we know about the execution and the hostages?"

During Trevin and Caeden's mission to the palace earlier that night, they had discovered that Jericho was correct, Sorin was planning something, but it was far worse than they had imagined. After discovering the princess's escape from the palace, Sorin devised a plan to force Amira to return to him. He had imprisoned eight innocent people and accused them of murdering the princess. Their public execution was set for three days' time... unless, of course, Amira proved herself alive by returning to the palace. There was no doubt in Trevin's mind that Princess Amira would sacrifice herself to save those people, but they couldn't allow her to do that. While Caeden and Trevin had come up with a plan to stop the execution and trap Sorin, Trevin was unsure how Caeden would prevent Amira from intervening.

"Sorin plans for the execution to be a public spectacle. The hostages are men, women, and children." Just the thought of those innocents being falsely imprisoned and what they must be going through made Trevin sick to his stomach and anger race through his veins.

"That goddammed monster. Sorin is pure evil," Erid spat, followed by agreement and similar statements from the other officers. Trevin felt the same, and regretted not being able to get to Sorin while he was at the palace this evening and end this all before it could go any further.

"We begin after sunset tomorrow," Trevin announced, bringing the focus back to the solution. "But first we—"

"Excuse me," a soldier interrupted, popping his head into the tent and scanning the room. Trevin believed his name was Roland but couldn't be sure. "Is Alyx here?"

"He hasn't returned from his search," Erid answered.

Roland nodded but looked disappointed as he started to turn away. Instinct had Trevin stepping in. "Did you have something to report?"

"No, sir, we still have yet to locate Lady Inaya. But we did find Alyx's stallion. That mean bastard won't let anyone near him."

"Where?" Trevin barked, and the smirk slid off Roland's face.

"Just ou-outside of the market village. Not far from the main path."

"Take me there."

No one dared question his order or his decision to leave camp; instead, they responded to his urgency.

Knight was a mean bastard, but he was loyal, at least to two people—Alyx and Inaya.

Fire pulsed in Inaya's side and spread throughout her abdomen as reality abruptly returned to her. Ignoring the pain, she lurched to a sitting position and took in the unfamiliar surroundings. She was lying in a bed in a dark room, but before she could determine more than that, a shadow moved toward her.

Her gasp originated from surprise but continued from the sharp pain in her flank. She was unsure what kind of injury she had, but the more pressing threat was the person coming her way.

"Hold still, don't move," a deep voice commanded.

She froze, not because she was commanded to but because she knew that voice. He was at the top of her list of people she didn't want to run into. *Eldon.*

Before she could decide how to handle the situation, he spoke again. "You fell from that beast you call a horse. You're hurt, but the wound has stopped bleeding, and I'll take care of you."

There was more to that story. Something had struck her; she hadn't just fallen off her horse. Eldon sat beside her on the bed and grasped her hand. His touch sent a chill down her spine, but she sat locked in fear and indecision.

"Why...?" She paused to lick her dry lips before trying to ask her question again. "Why are we in the dark? And where are we?"

"Why were you traveling these roads alone in the middle of the night?" he countered as he lit a candle and placed it on the bedside table.

How could she answer that? She couldn't tell him that she was coming to warn Trevin about *him*. Inspiration struck. "I was afraid to be at home alone—I mean, with all the strange soldiers from Ammon and Sorin's dislike of me—so I came to find my brother." When his body stiffened, she added, "My brother Alyx." She didn't want him to think Murdock was at the soldiers' camp. She hoped her helpless act would satisfy him until she could figure out how to get herself out of this.

"Well, it is wise of you to seek protection, but a soldiers' camp is no place for a lady. Once you're healed, I'll take you somewhere safe where I can look after you. I had told you to stay in the library and wait for me last time we were together, and look where your hardheadedness got you." He waved a hand to indicate her injured body. "You'll know better next time, I'm sure. It's a good thing I found you."

"How did you find me? And where exactly are we?" she asked again.

"We're not far from the soldiers' camp. I was out doing recon."

"That's great." She hoped her cheerful tone hid her true feelings from him and her disbelief in his explanation. "Then you can escort me to my brother. With your help, I know I'll get there safely."

Eldon's chest puffed out with pride at her flattery. "Of course you're safe with me."

"So, you'll take me to my brother?"

"Ummm... no, as I said, that is no place for a lady."

Panic clawed at her, causing her next words to come out high-pitched and louder than she intended. "I need to see my brother. He's expecting me."

"I'll—"

"Keep it down!" Isaac rushed into the room. Inaya was familiar with him but didn't really know him. "They're back," he said in a harsh whisper, and Eldon lurched off the bed and flew to the window, peeking around the curtain. The first light of day was just beginning to brighten the sky.

"Dammit," he hissed before turning to Isaac. "There are more this time. Did you recognize any of the Guard?"

"The Guard is out there?" Hope flared in Inaya's chest, until a fist slammed into the side of her jaw, sending her reeling back onto the bed.

"Quiet," Isaac snarled.

Tears blurred her vision, and the world spun. Dizzy and face throbbing, she moved quickly, rolling off the side of the bed and away from Isaac. Her eyes locked on the men. Before she knew what was happening, Eldon had Isaac pinned to the wall by a fist wrapped around his throat. Isaac's eyes bulged out of his face, and Eldon was growling something in his ear, but with the blood rushing in her head, Inaya couldn't make out the words. A stabbing pain lanced up her side, but she ignored it, her mind registering the fact that this might be her only chance to get free.

Adrenaline fueled her speed as she raced through the bedroom door. In the unfamiliar surroundings, she was forced to pause and search for the exit. Her focus centered on the door, she dashed forward, arm extended. The Royal Guard and her freedom were just on the other side, only feet from her. A heavy weight slammed into her back and tackled her to the floor, knocking the air from her lungs.

"Leave her!" Isaac hissed.

"She comes with us!" Eldon declared as his body lifted from hers. Even with his weight gone, air refused to return to her lungs. Panic overtook her. Clawing at her throat, her clothes, gasping for air, she rolled to the side, making it to her knees. In a jerking motion, Eldon pulled her to her feet, pressed his shoulder to her abdomen, and stood. Air rushed back into her lungs as he carried her toward the back of the house. Her relief at being able to breathe lasted only long enough for her to realize she was once again being held captive.

"We still have time," Eldon said as the men paused in what looked like the kitchen. Inaya jerked, trying to free herself, but Eldon's hold tightened, reminding her that she must have reinjured the wound on her side when she rolled off the bed earlier. The pain pulsing through her body froze her movements. "If the Guard hasn't returned, then they can't know what we've done. We continue with the plan."

"What about her?" Isaac questioned, his tone sounding more accusing than curious.

"I'll stash her somewhere while you find out why the soldiers are patrolling here. Get rid of them and continue to watch for whatever Guard member comes. Take him out immediately. He can't be allowed to reach the soldiers' camp."

"They'll send someone else," Isaac argued. "Let's just return to the palace and join Sorin's soldiers."

"And tell him we allowed the Royal Guard to take back command of their army? Do you honestly think he will allow you to live after that?"

"This was your idea. I never should have gone along. Sorin cannot win this!" Inaya couldn't see Isaac's face, but the fear was clear in his voice.

"He has already won, you idiot! He has taken the

palace and will bond with the princess. Sorin couldn't have done this without us. He won't forget that. Because of me, you will be richly rewarded. And don't forget it was you who messed up and mistook a female for a Royal Guard member. I should kill you myself for hurting her. If I hadn't stopped you, you would have killed Inaya."

Hanging upside down over Eldon's shoulder had the blood rushing to her head, but she had a feeling her dizziness and nausea was more than that. "I'm going to be sick," she murmured as loud as she could, but it still came out whisper soft. The men ignored her and continued their argument.

"So get out there and do your job," Eldon commanded.

"Let's just kill her and be done with it," Isaac argued. "Sorin despises her, and she's in the way."

"She has been promised as my wife," Eldon growled. "But you, on the other hand, are becoming dispensable. We have no time for—"

Unable to control it, vomit flew from her mouth and down Eldon's backside. She found herself uncere-moniously dropped to the floor, where she dry-heaved until nothing was left in her stomach. When she looked up, Isaac was nowhere in sight, and Eldon was kneeling at her side, holding her hair from her face. His once white shirt was stained scarlet. It took her confused mind a moment to realize he was covered in blood. Her eyes darted to her side. She was covered in blood as well.

"Dammit, your wound has reopened," he told her unnecessarily, but his words were muffled, and her vision turned black. She thought she heard a crash, followed by an inhuman roar, but that wasn't enough to free her from the darkness that overtook her.

Twenty-Two

The sight of Inaya unconscious on the floor, covered in blood, while Eldon stood over her was a vision that would haunt Trevin for the rest of his life. As fear, desperation, and rage consumed him, he didn't even stop to think through his actions. He just charged. As if time somehow lapsed, he found himself being pulled off a bloody and unconscious male. Eldon's face was damn near unrecognizable. Trevin had no memory of attacking him. As his foggy brain cleared, he rushed to Inaya's side, where some of the others had already begun assessing her condition.

Trevin pushed one of the soldiers away and knelt beside her, taking in her pale skin and the swelling bruise on her face. His gaze traveled lower to the unfamiliar men's shirt she was wearing, which had been pulled up to expose her torso. A blood-soaked bandage was secured to her side. Ian, a field medic for the Velius army, carefully pulled it off to assess her wound, revealing a large gash in her side.

"Nothing vital seems to have been punctured by whatever caused this, but I can't know for sure until I clean out the wound. Bring my satchel in," Ian requested as he re-covered the wound and held pressure to slow the bleeding. A random soldier ran to do his bidding; Trevin was unsure of who as his focus remained on Inaya. Time slid into slow motion, and helplessness threatened to suffocate him as he watched Ian tend to Inaya. Nephilim were much stronger and could heal faster than humans, but that didn't mean they couldn't die. Logic told him that her wounds were not life-threatening, Ian had assured him as well, but that didn't ease his fear.

Only after Ian had patched up her wound and they were preparing to move her into the bedroom to make her comfortable did Trevin even remember Eldon and Isaac's existence. He was almost certain he hadn't beaten Eldon to death, and when he looked around, the traitor was nowhere to be found. "Where are they?" he demanded.

Erid stepped forward. "Eldon has been taken into custody. He's been taken back to camp. Isaac wasn't here when we arrived. We have soldiers out scouting the area for him."

Trevin's head and heart battled over what his next move would be. Logic told him he needed to return to camp to interrogate the traitor, but his heart said he needed to remain with Inaya. She needed him. Duty had always come first, and because of that, Inaya was lying unconscious after being injured and nearly bleeding to death. If he hadn't remained in camp, if he had been out searching for her instead of sending others, could he have prevented this? If he had put her first, could he have saved her from this? The what-ifs swirled in his brain, creating a tornado of regret, self-doubt, and anger.

"Interrogate him. Find out everything," Trevin commanded. Erid's expression was a mixture of shock, determination, and pride. Clearly, he hadn't been expecting such an important task.

Hours had passed while he waited helplessly at her bedside, but when her beautiful turquoise eyes finally opened, it was like the heavens opened as well, returning life back to his existence. It started with just a flutter, as if it were a struggle to keep her eyes open.

"Inaya, baby, can you hear me?" She nuzzled into the hand he had cupping the side of her face but didn't respond. "You're going to be okay." As she struggled to regain consciousness, he spoke softly, reassuring her of her safety and his presence, speaking more in that time than he could remember doing in the last several years.

It took her a while to come to fully, and it was clear how weak she was. It would take her time to regain her strength after so much blood loss and the trauma to her body, but Ian had assured him she would survive.

"Where am I?" she asked weakly. "Why does my entire body hurt?"

He would give anything to take her pain away. "You're safe," he assured her again. "We're at a cottage near the traders' village." Her body tensed, and her eyes seemed more focused. "You've been injured, but you'll heal within a few days' time."

"Eldon...."

"He's in our custody. Do you remember what happened?" Trevin asked when she didn't continue.

"I was coming to warn you about the traitor. I had discovered their identity, but I was struck by something and thrown from my horse." Knight was not hers; she had stolen the wild beast from her brother, but now was not the time to remind her of that detail. In the past, he would have warned her against riding such an unpredictable animal, but now he was grateful for her thievery. "I think Eldon and Isaac attacked me thinking I was you."

Rage boiled inside him, but he forced it down. "Yes, Alyx had informed all the soldiers that the Royal Guard would meet them at the crest. In an attempt to prevent that from happening, Eldon and Isaac set a trap, which you just happened to stumble into."

During the interrogation, Eldon had stayed true to his character and betrayed Sorin and Isaac with little effort on Erid's part. It was a shame he hadn't made it more difficult so Trevin would have been forced to intervene and beat the information out of him.

"So, you know they are the traitors who kidnapped Levi and framed him for murdering the king, and they also allowed Ammon's soldiers into the palace walls?" she asked in confusion.

"Yes, we had already figured that out."

"Why didn't you tell me that?" Her statement sounded like an accusation.

"Why would I?" She looked as if he had just slapped her. "What would you have done with the information?" She opened her mouth to answer, but he cut her off. "Would you have gone after him yourself, determined to bring him to justice?" Her mouth snapped shut and she looked away, confirming that might have been her plan. "Inaya, that is not your place," he finished gently.

"I saved you and the entire Royal Guard," she argued stubbornly.

"You did, and we all appreciate your bravery, but it's not always necessary for you to take those kinds of risks. Like last night. You were needlessly injured by trying to follow me here."

"If I hadn't, you would have fallen into that trap and possibly have been killed."

"So be it! My life is not a suitable exchange for yours. That was my risk to take. You are far more valuable than that." Frustration forced him into action. He launched himself from the chair beside the bed and paced across the room, fingers tangling in his hair. "Why can't you see that? Why must you impulsively risk yourself for others?"

"I am nothing!" Her outburst startled him. He froze midpace, his head jerking in her direction. She was sitting up in bed with a furious expression on her face. "I have never been what the world sees in me... what Vidar saw in me." Her chin quivered, but she visibly steeled herself. "But I try. By putting others first, I earn my place as Lady Inaya. Don't you see that?"

"That's—" She didn't let him continue.

"Yes, I'm impulsive and reckless at times, but there is more to me than that." She turned her face from him, trying to compose herself.

Within a few steps, he was back at her side. "I'm sorry. I didn't mean to upset you, you've been through so much. Inaya...." She continued to stare at the opposite wall. "Inaya, look at me." It took a few seconds, but she finally turned back to him. "You've become a brave, honorable, amazing woman, I see that, but I don't think you do. You don't have to earn your place. You don't have to sacrifice your needs, and especially not your life, for others. King Vidar would have never wanted that for you, and no one else expects that from you." A single tear slipped down her cheek, breaking his heart.

"I had no right blaming last night on you," he continued. "You were only trying to help. I'm sorry I didn't get to you before you were injured, and I'm sorry it took so long to find you."

"It's not your fault."

"If I had—"

"No, you're not to blame. You've always taken care of me and gotten me out of trouble. I finally understand what you meant a few days ago when you said you can't trust me. You can't trust my reactions, and you need that. You deserve that. I'll change. I'll do better."

"I don't want you to change. You keep me and everyone else on our toes. I like that. I want you to be you. I just want you to be safe." She nodded in understanding.

And in that moment, Trevin gave up. He gave up fighting. Inaya was his. She always had been.

As if drawn to her by a gravitational pull, he leaned in to taste her lips, but before he could touch her, her head turned away. "No." Her voice sounded shaky and lacked conviction. "You can't kiss me again."

Trevin leaned back to search her expression, thankful not to find a look of indifference on her face. Instead, she looked torn. He knew the feeling. Now that he had decided to stop fighting his feelings for her, he wanted to tell her, to show her. His rejection had hurt her in the past, and he was sure his actions of late were confusing to her. Hell, they had been confusing him as well, but not any longer. He loved Inaya, always had. His love for her had taken many forms throughout their relationship. It had grown into a passionate, forever kind of love. She felt it too, but he had to re-earn her trust. And to do that, he'd need to take this slow.

A knock sounded at the door, startling Inaya. Her body jerked, and she hissed in pain at her quick movement.

"Careful. Are you all right?"

She lifted the edge of the shirt she was wearing to expose the clean bandage on her side. "I don't think I reopened the wound."

Trevin nodded. "I'll send Ian in to check on it just in case." Another knock sounded on the door. "Enter."

Erid stepped inside. "Sir, it's time to head out. Alyx and the scouting unit departed half an hour ago."

"Head out? Where are you going?" Inaya asked.

"The army is returning to Velius. You'll be unable to travel for at least another day or so...."

Inaya must have read the indecision on his face, because she said, "Go, do your duty. I'll be fine here."

"Eldon is in custody, but Isaac is still out there...."

"I'm sure he's far from here by now. Was it just the two of them working with Sorin?"

Trevin nodded. "From what we've learned from Eldon, yes, but he can't be trusted. I'll leave soldiers here to protect you, along with Ian who can treat your wound." He still didn't feel good about leaving her behind. "Please, do as he says."

"I'll be fine," she repeated. "Go."

He leaned forward and kissed her forehead once before making his way to the door. He hated leaving her, but perhaps time apart was what they both needed at the moment. She had been through so much lately, and she needed time to heal. And he needed time to come up with a plan and figure out how to make things work between them.

When Erid exited, Trevin turned back to her. "And, Inaya"—she looked up at him, giving him a weak smile—"don't follow me this time."

TWENTY-THREE

The days passed like minutes when you were facing an eternity, and for Lahash, the future would be bleak if he failed at his task. Ridding the world of the Nephilim was his only chance at salvation, and regaining the Creator's grace was worth any sacrifice. At least, that's what he'd told himself for the last two days as he stared out the window, counting down the moments, avoiding the turmoil creating tornados with his thoughts.

Sorin was adjusting to the spiritual bond that intertwined his soul to the princess's, and thus connected him to all Nephilim and the very island that kept them safe. He was on a euphoric high, feeding off the exquisite emotions Amira felt, her goodness lighting the darkness that filled his soul and becoming a drug that Sorin would never get enough of. Sorin wasn't capable of that range of emotion. He would never know love of anything but himself, and compassion, humility, generosity, and even simple kindness were foreign to him. And during this time of adjustment and pleasure, Lahash kept his distance, allowing Sorin to savor what he could never truly obtain. Experiencing the beauty of a pure soul would only magnify Sorin's own desolation when all that goodness was ripped away, and it would be. The unnatural bond Marcelle had forced between Sorin and Amira would soon fail, but not before Sorin's evil tainted it, and the safeguards left behind by the angels would collapse and destroy the island and all its inhabitants. A massive storm was already brewing in the distance, just waiting for the chance to wreak havoc.

A pained gasp stole Lahash's attention, and he turned to find Sorin collapsed onto the floor. Just then, the wind outside picked up momentum, howling to the heavens, spreading a message of despair. The sky turned black, and large pieces of ice plummeted from the sky. Cocking his head and narrowing his eyes, Lahash sent out his senses, searching for the change in the atmosphere, and then the knowledge slammed into him, leaving confusion in its wake. The princess had left the island and crossed through the barrier that protected them all. Lahash would not have predicted this turn of events, the princess abandoning her people, but what else could be her reasoning for escaping?

And although her defection was unplanned, it

would only serve to further his purpose, for Sorin now had complete control of the sacred blood bond that protected the island. The storm outside ceased as quickly as it had begun, serving as only a warning of what was to come.

A tickle of awareness danced down his spine, and Lahash tucked his opalescent wings closer to his body before shifting to address his former companion. "Gusion."

"It appears your lapdog has fallen and can't get up," Gusion returned by way of greeting. "Perhaps you should invest in Life Alert." Lahash arched a brow in confusion. "It's a human—you know what, never mind."

"Why have you returned?" Lahash felt no need for small talk of trivial matters, nor did he care about some such human contraption.

"As I said before, your actions have global effects, and this latest event tore a ripple through the atmosphere... something that will draw out the light bearers."

"You've seen this?" Something close to foreboding settled in his chest. Lahash hadn't considered angelic involvement into his plan. Angels suffered far too many rules to be able to step in and save the Nephilim, and why would they lower themselves to care anyway. The Nephilim were not of divine plan; they were mistakes and challenged the Creator's original design.

"Yes, but the vision remains unclear."

"Will I succeed?" Lahash despised the weakness in his question.

"I have advised you from the beginning that this is a foolish endeavor. There is no retribution or forgiveness to be had, and yet you remain on this course."

"My plan has reached its conclusion. A reckoning is at hand," Lahash defended.

"Brother," Gusion's voice took on a sympathetic tone, "you speak of a minor skirmish, ignoring the massive battle."

"Back to that again? I care not for the fate of mankind. The only human whom I ever deemed worthy of my consideration proved false and has long since paid for her sins."

"Because you cannot see the bigger picture. Come with me. Speak to *him*. You will see. As angels, we were mighty, but with our appropriated free will, we have broken the bonds of servitude and can become so much more. *He* has a plan for us."

"If Lucifer's plan was so great, why has it not come to fruition? Why are you still the unseen outcasts? Why come to me for help at all?"

"Lahash, you better than most know the value of biding one's time and cultivating the perfect environment to blossom change... speaking of... what is that you are holding?"

Lahash looked down in confusion and then back up, meeting Gusion's eye, daring him to say something adverse. "It's a plant."

"It's a dead plant."

"So?"

"So why are you carrying around a dead plant?"

"I have decided it shall live," Lahash declared.

"So, you're carrying it around so that it will live?" Gusion's confusion was evident.

"Yes."

"Have you tried Miracle Grow?"

"What is Miracle Grow?"

Gusion shook his head and gave up on the discussion. "If you will not abandon this foolish mission, what shall you do when the light bearer arrives?" Lahash's stomach tightened at this possibility. He did not have any desire to battle against one of his former brothers, no matter if he was no longer worthy of being amongst one of their ranks.

"Light shall meet the darkness. What more can I do?" Gusion opened his mouth to answer, but Lahash cut him off. "Besides forsaking all that I have worked for and becoming a champion for your cause?"

"Nothing," Gusion admitted. "And I cannot intervene when it occurs, brother. None of us will. Lucifer forbids it."

"I did not ask you to, nor will I. Our paths diverged long ago. I do not seek your assistance or interference."

"But you will come to us once this has reached its conclusion?"

"You are the seer of the future. You tell me," Lahash challenged.

Gusion's body stilled and his eyes went vacant. Snapping out of his trance, he shook his head. "Your path is not yet clear."

"Then there is hope for my success."

Gusion didn't acknowledge his statement. Instead, he stated, "You know how to find us. *He* will be awaiting your arrival." And then he was gone.

Lahash looked down at the plant he held in the red clay pot. "He shall have a long wait," he mumbled to the plant, having heard that speaking to a plant would benefit its growth.

Twenty-Four

Trevin had hated leaving Inaya, especially in her weakened state, but he had no other option. The Royal Guard and Velius soldiers had spent the last two days moving all civilians away from the palace, and slowly, one by one, they'd systematically taken out each and every one of Sorin's patrol units and exterior guards, replacing them with their own soldiers. The only Ammon soldiers left in play were the soldiers on duty within the palace, where Sorin had secluded himself.

The execution was just hours away. Sorin planned to snuff out the lives of eight innocent people in an attempt to get Princess Amira to return to him, but he and the Royal guard were not about to allow that to happen.

At the sound of approaching footsteps, Trevin

turned his attention from his conversation with Dalek. Looking over his right shoulder, he took in a grim-faced Murdock approaching. Since he'd returned with the army, there had been little time for discussion. By the time he had arrived, Alyx had already informed Murdock of Inaya's injury, and by the dirty looks Murdock had been sending his way, it was apparent Murdock laid the blame at his feet. Trevin didn't blame him.

"It's time we had a talk," Murdock said by way of greeting.

"Yes, yes it is," Dalek added, crossing his arms over his chest, trying to look firm. Turning to Murdock, he asked, "So, what are we discussing?"

"Not now, Dalek," Murdock answered, sounding unamused.

"But you just said it was time," Dalek pointed out.

Great, just what Trevin needed, Dalek aggravating Murdock more before the conversation even started. "We'll finish our discussion later," Trevin told him in dismissal.

"I agree. What Murdock has to say seems way more exciting."

Murdock looked like his head was going to explode. "Leave us," he growled.

"Wow, no need to get snippy. If you wanted privacy, all you had to do was say so. You know, next time I'll—"

"Dalek." The warning was clear in Trevin's voice.

"Fine, but if he attacks, I—" Murdock let out an inhuman growl, and Dalek shuffled off without another word.

"Someday he's going to push someone too far," Murdock murmured as he watched Dalek's retreat.

"Good thing he can hold his own in a fight; otherwise I'd worry for him."

Murdock nodded his agreement before turning back to Trevin. His expression turned from thoughtful to stone-cold. "What are your intentions toward my sister?"

Trevin had known this conversation was coming, and yet he still wasn't prepared. Murdock took the overprotective brother role to a whole new level, and as much as he'd appreciate and value Murdock's blessing, it wasn't a requirement, even if that meant ruining their friendship and causing strife within the Royal Guard. "I'm in love with her and plan to make her mine."

"And what does she think of this?" Murdock's expression remained unreadable.

"She doesn't know yet, but when last we spoke, she didn't seem too fond of the idea," Trevin admitted.

A slow grin was not the reaction Trevin was expecting. "Okay. I wish you luck." Murdock slapped him on the shoulder and turned to walk away.

"Wait. That's it? That's all you have to say?"

· · ·

Murdock turned to face him once again. "I've waited a while for you to come to your senses, and it seems like you have, so yeah, that's all I have to say."

"But she's your sister." Trevin wasn't sure why he was pushing this and prolonging the conversation, but it was a bit shocking that Murdock hadn't threatened him at least once.

"Yeah, and you know what that means." Trevin was sure the brotherly warning would come now, but again he was surprised. "She's headstrong and impulsive and has a wild streak that she has been unable to tame, so you'll have your hands full with her, but I wouldn't trust anyone else with the job. She's loved you almost her whole life, and it's about damn time you pulled your head out of your ass, because I was afraid I was going to have to do it for you."

That comment sparked a memory of Murdock reminding Trevin how Inaya was his responsibility. In the past, Trevin had interpreted that as a demand to back down and leave his sister's care to Murdock, but Trevin was now seeing it for what it really was—a challenge to Trevin. Murdock had known all along that Trevin had been fighting his feelings for Inaya, and he had been pushing him to step up and be the man Inaya needed him to be.

Before Trevin could figure out how to respond to that, Murdock was walking away. Not wanting to spend too much time in his own thoughts, Trevin decided to check on Caeden. While Trevin was gathering the army and looking after Inaya, Princess Amira had left for the human world, along with Levi and Osmond, hoping to seek out Kearney, the Nephilim scout. Today was an important day for them. If all went well, they would defeat Sorin and regain control of the palace. If things did not go as planned, many lives could be lost. Caeden needed to be 100 percent present, and in the fight, and as second-in-command and Caeden's closest friend, it was Trevin's job to see that that happened.

Most of the soldiers were disguised as Ammon soldiers and patrolling the area surrounding the palace, keeping up pretenses, but also ensuring no civilians would be caught in the crossfire when things went down with Sorin. Caeden stood at the edge of the tree line, his eyes locked on the palace. Trevin stepped up beside him, not saying a word. He'd allow Caeden to steer the conversation, giving him the best insight as to Caeden's mindset. It didn't take long.

"I'm ready to kill that son of a bitch." There was no anger in his tone, just pure determination, and that was all Trevin needed to hear.

"It will soon be over."

Caeden nodded once. "Let's move out."

Sorin had erected a grand platform in the middle of the courtyard to serve as his stage as he killed eight falsely accused prisoners of a bogus crime. From the rear of the platform, the Royal Guard watched as Sorin strutted out of the palace and onto the stage, surrounded by his hostages, even going so far as to hold one of the children in his arms. There was no room for anger, so Trevin pushed all feelings aside. Each soldier had been assigned a task; his and the captain's was taking down Sorin while the others rescued the hostages and contained the remaining Ammon soldiers.

Sorin's arrogance and delusions knew no bounds as he took center stage and gave an egotistical speech about being a just and fair ruler. He even went so far as to claim his actions were in the name of justice. Trevin's attention stayed focused on Caeden, waiting for the signal to attack, and when Caeden lifted his arm and circled his hand in the air, Trevin sprang into motion, adrenaline coursing through his veins, his complete attention on the sadistic male who had hijacked their kingdom. Locked in shock, Sorin stood immobile as the fighting broke out around him, and just as he regained his senses and turned to flee, Trevin kicked his feet from beneath him, sending him to his knees. He was met with Caeden's sword pressed to his throat as Trevin held him in place.

"You were correct, there will be justice today,"

clearly envision the person in her mind. He was tall, surely pushing seven feet in height, and his body seemed to consist of nothing but lean muscle. In the fading light of day, his hair appeared to be a sandy blond, just long enough to fall into his dark, piercing eyes, which seemed to bore into her soul as they stared at her intently. Just the thought had a chill running up her spine. Strong legs braced far apart and arms crossed over his chest, he had stood menacingly, eyes locked on her. And if her imagination wasn't insane enough, it had gifted this being beautiful opalescent wings.

Inaya opened her eyes and peered back toward the cellar, finding nothing out of the ordinary this time. But a heaviness filled the air, carrying a sense of danger and malice. In an attempt to dislodge these crazy thoughts, Inaya shook her head and focused on the path in front of her. Not much longer and she would find herself back in her own bed and catching up on some much-needed rest.

"Wait for my assistance," Alyx cautioned as they approached the stable. It was a command Inaya was more than willing to comply with. The journey to Velius had not been easy, and her right flank throbbed with pain. Picking up on her discomfort, Alyx had done his best to distract her by basically reenacting Sorin's capture from the day before. His description of Sorin wetting himself and begging for his life as snot ran down his chin didn't really match with what Inaya knew of the arrogant bastard's personality, and of course Alyx's version of the events had him singlehand-edly defeating hundreds of enemy soldiers. Yes, it appeared her brother believed himself to be an army all to himself. She snickered at the thought, causing a sharp pain to lance up her side.

"Still in pain?" a deep voice rumbled, and she spotted Trevin approaching from the stable doors. Before she could respond, he was at her side and gently lifting her from her horse and to the ground, where he continued to hold her until she was steady on her feet. Without intent, she breathed in his familiar scent as he bent forward to press a kiss to her forehead, the tension easing from her shoulders. Only when he leaned away and stared at her questioningly did she remember he'd asked a question.

"Barely at all," she lied.

Trevin shot her a disbelieving look before staring over her shoulder and commanding, "Report," bringing her attention to Ian's presence.

"The wound is healing but remains tender. She'll need rest as she is still weak from the blood loss. I'll recheck the injury when she is settled, but perhaps one of the local healers should look in after her as well."

"That has already been arranged," Trevin assured him.

It didn't bother Inaya that they spoke around her as if she weren't present. Her attention was on the oppressive sensation of malice that had returned and seemed to be increasing by the moment. Heart racing, she glanced around for any sign of danger but found nothing. Instinctually, she shifted closer to Trevin and didn't complain when his arm slipped around her shoulders and pulled her closer.

She was only vaguely aware of Erid's approach and the topic of conversation shifting to Eldon's transport back to Velius for imprisonment until Amira returned and a sentence for justice could be determined, and punishment could be dealt. Isaac was still at large, but was actively being tracked.

Inaya missed whatever else was said, but rejoined the conversation when Trevin turned to her and asked, "Can you walk, or will you permit me to carry you?"

"I'm fine on my own, thank you."

He appeared displeased by her decision, but he accepted it. "Then I shall accompany you inside so that you can rest."

While they had been talking, their horses were taken inside and were already being cared for, so with nothing else to look after besides herself, she accepted Trevin's offer, but pulled away to put proper distance between them. With all that had happened in the last few weeks, it really put her relationship with Trevin into perspective. She could no longer hold on to the petty anger and resentment over his rejection. He was a kind and honorable male, one who had always been there for her. Their relationship was not how she had originally envisioned it, but she was lucky to have such a caring friend. Being stuck on bedrest for the last few days had given her time to consider how to proceed with their relationship, and she had decided she would no longer attempt to push him away, but she would need to continue to use caution so that she would not be swept away by her unrequited love once again.

Twenty-Five

Inaya's presence had been missing from Velius for days. Lahash had not let himself seek her out, but instead hoped that she had found a place to be safe and happy until this was all over, until Cashile and all Nephilim ceased to be... including Inaya. But feeling her return, he was drawn to her. Sparing one last glance at Sorin as he huddled in the corner of the cellar, pouting, Lahash transported himself outside. He had only intended to gaze upon her briefly and then return to the task at hand—feeding Sorin's fears and delusions, driving him to the brink of self-destruction. With the deterioration of Sorin's mind came the deterioration of the blood bond—but just as she had once before, she seemed to stare right at him. And just as before, a sense of foreboding passed through him, reminding him that somehow his fate was tied to hers.

Instead of triggering anger, he now only felt acceptance.

As she turned away and continued on, something in her posture, in the way she carried herself, seemed to be different. Cocking his head, he studied every nuance, but only when she giggled and immediately tensed, clutching her right side, did he realize she was injured. Without thought, he found himself at the stables, watching as the dark-haired soldier approached his child and tended to her needs.

Since hearing of Inaya's interest in Trevin, Lahash had given special attention to the male, determining him strong, even-tempered, and principled, but this was the first time Lahash had seen him with Inaya. His hands were gentle, and even as he held conversation with others, it was clear his focus remained on her, sensitive to her needs. Perhaps Trevin would suit, and if ever a time came that he didn't, Lahash would step in and remove him from the equation.

And while Inaya's chosen mate was deemed satisfactory, the content of their conversation was not. Inaya had once again been injured, and considering the rate of Nephilim healing and the fact that her injuries were taking so long to mend, he could only conclude the wound had been critical. White-hot rage flared inside him. His child should not have been made to suffer, and those who were responsible would pay. The males spoke of due process before justice, but Lahash was a fallen angel, and therefore not restricted by such paltry nonsense.

As an angel, he'd had an inherent duty to uphold right from wrong, at least until his disgrace. And unlike the other fallen, Lahash liked to believe he still carried a sense of integrity, so to him, enacting swift justice was not wrong, it was a part of his duty... and if he enjoyed it, all the better.

With his daughter safely resting, he transported to the palace prison. With night upon them, most of the inhabitants were sleeping. Lahash made his way past rows and rows of cells containing Ammon soldiers, seeking just one individual. Conveniently, Eldon, being the only Velius captive, occupied the very last cell all to himself.

Unseen, Lahash peered through the bars at the sleeping form on the cot, watching his chest rise and fall in peaceful slumber. Needing answers, he couldn't do as he desired and end this pathetic being. No, he'd have to contain himself... for now. Deep breath in and slow exhale. He was ready. With just a thought, he was inside the cell, looming over one of the males responsible for harming his child. Perhaps feeling his ominous presence, Eldon shifted in his sleep, his facial features becoming clear.

Lahash knew this person. He was one of Sorin's

spies within the Velius army; therefore, he was one of Lahash's assets as well. Anger and something more, possibly guilt, surged through him before he squashed it down—well, he squashed some of it down. His foot slammed into the side of the bed, lifting it a foot into the air and sending it crashing into the wall. Eldon surged up in bed, fist clutching his chest, panic widening his eyes as he scanned the area. When his eyes locked on to Lahash, he stilled, face going deathly pale.

Lahash spread his mighty wings, making it abundantly clear just who this moron was dealing with. Trembling, Eldon fell to his knees before him, mouth opening and closing like a fish, but no words emerged, which was fine with Lahash. He had no patience for platitudes or endless questions about the Creator, which never failed to come once an angel revealed themselves.

"Eldon of Velius, you have been found guilty of treason and the harming of innocents." That should be all that was needed to be stated before he distributed justice, but again he reminded himself he needed answers. "What say you?"

"I... I...."

"You shall only have one opportunity to explain. I suggest you do not waste it," Lahash advised.

"I did only as directed, glorious one."

The accolade clawed at his nerves. Of course this insignificant, ignorant being would think him glorious. He would not see Lahash's wings for the abhorrent disfigurement that they were. He would have no knowledge that true angels bore magnificent obsidian wings, not these pearly white monstrosities that exposed him to the world.

Lahash did not need to ask who had given him his orders, but he wanted to be clear regarding the orders. "Sorin ordered you to harm innocents?"

"He said to make an example of all who opposed him. But it was all in the name of doing what is right by our people. The Nephilim require strong leadership. I simply played a role in reconstructing our leadership, for the good of all."

It seemed as if Eldon believed the propaganda he spouted, and why wouldn't he? Lahash had trained Sorin to be conniving and manipulative. There was just one more thing he needed to know. "And Inaya? Did he specifically order you to harm her?"

"In-Inaya?" Eldon hesitated, as if he knew the importance of this question. "Not me specifically, but it is no secret that he despises her. I fought for her. I negotiated a trade, my service to his cause for Inaya. He gave her to me, on the condition I keep her far from him. I tried to protect her."

Gave her to him? As if she were a pet. Disgust left an acidic taste in the back of his throat. "You failed to protect her. She was injured while in your care, is that not right?"

"Isaac... it was a mistake, and when he tried to kill her, I defended her."

Lahash's body tensed with anger, causing Eldon to shrink further away.

"Where is Isaac now?"

"I don't know." Lahash took a menacing step forward, and Eldon changed his answer. "His sister has a home on the border of Ammon. He'd go there." Almost as an afterthought, he added, "I thought angels were supposed to be kind and majestic."

"Apparently, you haven't met many angels." Lahash closed the distance between them, placing his hands upon Eldon's cheeks. "Besides, I'm offering you a kindness—" He snapped Eldon's neck and allowed his body to fall to the stone floor. "—one Isaac will not receive."

True to his word, Isaac's death was not peaceful or quick. Lahash took his time, making sure he was punished properly and understood the full extent of his crime, especially after his damning revelation— Sorin had ordered Inaya's execution. He never intended to fulfill his promise of marriage to Eldon; instead, he'd wanted her dead, sooner rather than later. Apparently, Isaac had only hesitated due to Eldon's presence, but fully intended to carry out the task.

Logically, Lahash knew he was reacting irrationally. It was out of character for him to care about another, much less one of the Nephilim—they were abominations, a disease he needed to cut out—and yet he couldn't stop himself. Somewhere, his focus had shifted. Not knowing what this meant for his future, and not caring at the moment, he let emotion guide him.

Manifesting inside Sorin's cell within the cellar, he studied Sorin's meditative form. Sorin had mastered the art of connecting with the princess through their bond as she slept. He tortured the princess much like Lahash tortured him, small mental attacks meant to break one down slowly. But Lahash was finished with games. It was time Sorin knew the puppeteer who pulled his strings. Time he learned his true place in this world.

When Sorin's eyes popped open, Lahash was waiting. Leaping up in shock, Sorin stumbled over his own feet, landing hard. He scooted away until his back hit the wall. Sorin was no fool; he was under no delusion that Lahash was a majestic and benevolent creature. Perhaps it was instinct, or maybe it was the way Lahash's dark eyes flared crimson with his anger, but either way, he saw Lahash for what he was.

"Greetings, child."

TWENTY-SIX

Life in Velius was supposed to return to normal after Sorin's defeat, but it was no shock to Trevin that life didn't always turn out how it was expected. Instead, they awoke before sunrise to the news of a dead body and a storm brewing on the horizon. Eldon was discovered dead in his cell, the night guards having no knowledge as to how his death occurred, and the previous night's bloodred moon had served as an omen of the storm yet to come. With a biting wind, the temperature continued to drop, and the gray thunderclouds threatened to bring a massive storm, the size of which Cashile had never before seen.

The people of Velius had been through so much in the last few weeks; they didn't need more adding to their nightmare. There was already so much else to worry about. The local residents were returning to their homes, and the refugees who came to Velius for shelter and safety were being provided for as best they could.

"How could this happen?" Murdock questioned, standing over the body occupying the last prison cell.

Caeden met Trevin's eye before answering, "Perhaps Sorin has someone else working with him."

"But why would they go after Eldon? He was on his side," Dalek questioned.

"Eldon was on his own side. He had loyalty to no one else. He turned on Sorin just as quickly as he turned on us," Trevin reminded him.

"Perhaps it was one of our own soldiers seeking retribution?" Murdock suggested.

"Or maybe it was an accident." Dalek studied the body, looking for evidence.

"What, he stubbed his toe on the edge of the bed, fell down, and broke his neck?" Murdock scoffed.

"It could happen... right?" Dalek looked to his friends hopefully. No one wanted to believe there was a murderer among them on top of everything else, but they needed to explore every option.

While Murdock and Dalek argued the theory of an accidental death, a shimmery white object lying near the foot of the bed caught Trevin's attention. Upon closer inspection, it appeared to be a small feather, but it was unlike any other he had ever seen— stronger yet softer, and the color a beautiful opalescent.

"Did you find something?" Caeden bent down beside him to have a look.

"Nothing helpful, but quite unusual." Trevin showed him the feather.

"Where did this come from?" Caeden scanned the area.

"No idea," Trevin admitted, but strangely, his gut told him it was important. Before he could give it more thought, Murdock interrupted.

"So what now?"

"Let's go see if Sorin has any answers."

The Guard had spent the previous day trying to discover what Sorin knew about reversing the bond between him and Amira, but either he didn't know, or he wasn't telling, so there was no guarantee he'd be more helpful today.

Strangely, the cellar was completely dark. They normally left a light on at all times. Sorin had a fear of the darkness, and although he was a prisoner, they had no intention of using psychological torture on him by playing on his fears. As Trevin followed Caeden into the room, it became apparent that something else wasn't right. The day before, Sorin complained nonstop, throwing fits and spouting his delusions of grandeur. But now the room was not only dark, but it was also silent as well.

Trevin held up his lantern and scanned the makeshift prison, finding Sorin huddled on the floor, a vacant expression in his eyes.

"Sorin," Caeden barked, but received no response. Caeden repeated his name once again, but it was as if Sorin couldn't hear him.

Murdock knelt beside their prisoner. "Careful!" Dalek warned, causing Murdock to leap backward out of his crouch and fall on his ass. Grinning stupidly, Dalek added, "I hear he bites." Now was not the time for laughter, but Trevin's lips twitched in amusement anyway.

Murdock shot Dalek a scathing look. "Ass." Then he turned back to Sorin, waving his hand close to his face. Still nothing, he remained in a trancelike state.

"Shall I go get a stick to poke him with?" Dalek offered. No one bothered to answer.

"I don't think he's faking." Caeden looked to Trevin.

Trevin bent down beside Murdock, using the lantern to check for pupil dilation. "Doesn't appear so," Trevin agreed. "Perhaps one of the local healers can help."

"I'm not sure what they can do, but it's worth a try." Caeden's voice was gruff, his frustration bleeding through. "We need answers. We have a possible murder, a storm on the horizon, and now an incapacitated prisoner."

"Bet Sorin regrets murdering the Supreme Healer.

She was probably the only person on this island who could help him," Dalek remarked.

"The irony." Murdock smirked, clearly having no sympathy for their prisoner.

Trevin despised Sorin as well, they all did, but with his connection to the princess, they needed him alive. Caeden's expression told Trevin that his thoughts were traveling the same course. Trevin pressed his fingers to Sorin's neck, feeling his pulse beating strong, before he stood and clapped Caeden on the shoulder. "He doesn't appear to be in any physical danger."

"At least there's that," Caeden agreed. "Trevin, I'm placing you in charge of finding out what happened to Eldon."

Trevin nodded his agreement. "I'll start by re-questioning the soldiers on duty last night and the prisoners in the surrounding cells." His hand was drawn to the feather he had stashed in his coat pocket. Hopefully, he'd solve that mystery as well.

As Trevin turned to leave, Dalek announced, "I think I like him better this way," earning him a slap to the back of his head, courtesy of Murdock. Even in such a grim situation, Trevin exited the musky cellar with a grin on his face.

Inaya had been naive to believe life would go back to normal once they had captured Sorin. Too much had changed, and they still faced danger. The very island itself felt unsettled, with ice storms to the south and the occasional earthquake. The shield protecting Cashile was obviously unstable. She could only hope it would get better when Amira returned, which should be any day now. Until then, she focused her attention on something she could control, something she was familiar with—running the palace. Sorin had only occupied the castle for a short time, but his filthy presence could be felt throughout.

Unable to find peace due to unrelenting nightmares, Inaya had risen before dawn and come up with a plan to decontaminate the palace. Every room would be cleaned from top to bottom until there was no sign of the enemy, which turned out to be more difficult than she had expected, Ammon soldiers apparently lived like pigs. Making it even more difficult were the constant interruptions from servants needing direction and concerned citizens looking for reassurance. Inaya tried to be patient, knowing that they had all been through so much, but more than anything, she just wanted to lose herself in a physical task so the worry in her own head would cease.

That's how she found herself in the rear courtyard draping rugs over the clothesline, planning to beat the debris from them. Just as she pulled the paddle back, preparing to swing, a voice called out.

"Lady Inaya?"

Lowering the paddle, she turned to find one of the

local carpenters swiftly approaching. "Gordon, what can I do for you?"

"Sorry to be a bother, but I was wondering after our princess."

"What about her?" Inaya prompted when he didn't continue.

"Is she... is she still alive?" Before Inaya could answer, Gordon rushed on. "The Royal Guard said she was, but... but you know all that happened just after the king died, and then the Guard and the princess disappeared, and we didn't know what to believe from Sorin, but I know I can trust you. So, is the princess really alive?"

Gordon had rambled on so quickly, it took Inaya a moment to sort through everything he said, or what she thought he said. Part of her wanted to be offended that he would doubt the Royal Guard's integrity, but she understood his words stemmed from fear.

"I assure you, Sorin lied about Amira's death, and many other things. I was with our princess just days ago, and she was alive and well."

"Is it true then? She's left the island and abandoned us?"

"No, never. Amira would never abandon her people. It is true that she left the island, but only to seek help. She is scheduled to return any day." Inaya wasn't comfortable with general physical affection, especially with someone she barely knew, but it was obvious he needed that reassurance, so Inaya placed her hand on his shoulder and gave it a squeeze. Unfortunately, Gordon took it as an invitation, and before she knew what was happening, he yanked her to him and wrapped her in a tight embrace. Her body tensed, and panic threatened to take over. Thankfully, a voice interrupted them before her fight-or-flight response could pick a side.

"There you are, Gordon. I've been looking everywhere for you."

Looking guilty, Gordon released her and jumped back. "Trevin, wh-what is it that you need?"

"We're constructing temporary shelters for the evacuees, and we could use someone of your talent." Trevin stepped up next to Inaya, placing his hand on the small of her back and gently rubbing, and suddenly it was no longer difficult to breathe and her panic receded. Just then, it occurred to her that this wasn't the first time Trevin's touch had soothed her. She found pleasure and comfort in his physical affection, whereas even a hug from her brothers was uncomfortable.

Gordon's chest puffed out with pride, and he finally looked up to meet Trevin's eye. "I'd be glad to offer my services."

Trevin nodded. "Meet up with Murdock at the palace gate. He'll assign you to where you'll be the most useful."

"Thank you, sir."

They watched as Gordon rushed off, and only

when he turned the corner and was out of sight did Trevin turn to Inaya. "Are you all right?"

The intensity in his eyes sent a thrill racing through her body, and her heart leaped in her chest. "Yes, of course," she answered, taking a step back.

Looking displeased, he allowed her to retreat, but he didn't allow her to placate him with her words. "Is it a certain physical attribute that sets you off? Or just males in general?"

"I—"

"Don't lie to me." He cut her off, knowing her too well. "I'm not judging you. I want to help."

Inaya considered his words for a moment and then decided to go with the truth. She trusted Trevin. "It's not just males. It happens when females touch me too. There is nothing you can do to help me."

"It seems to be more severe with males though," he stated, ignoring her last comment.

"Not all males."

"That's right." His voice had lowered, and he grabbed her hand, rubbing small circles into her skin with his thumb. "My touch doesn't bother you... at least not in that way."

"You're different," she admitted.

"Damn right I am." His other arm slipped around her back and he pulled her against him.

Her hand flattened against his chest, and she leaned away. "But that doesn't mean you have touch privileges."

"Do you dislike my touch?" he asked, not letting her go, but not pushing for more.

"Well, no, but...." His shoulders relaxed at her words, and only then did she realize he had tensed.

"We'll take this slow, as slow as you need." That intense look had returned to his eyes.

"Take what slow?" His touch must be addling her brain because she wasn't keeping up with this conversation.

"Us."

"There is no us, remember?"

"There has always been an us in one way or another, but it's time we developed into something more."

"Trevin, no. I can't." She pulled out of his arms, her gaze drifting to the ground.

"You can. I hurt you in the past, and I'm sorry for that, but let me make it up to you."

She had thought that she had forgiven him before, but now it felt as if a weight had lifted from her chest. But she wasn't ready to let him back into her heart. She had just come to terms with being friends, and that was where they needed to stay.

She looked up and met his eyes before speaking. "I can't," she repeated.

With a deep sigh, he nodded, and her treacherous heart dropped in her chest, thinking he had given up, but then he spoke. "Like I said, we'll take it slow. You can have all the time you need, and when you're ready, let me know."

Her mind and heart were at war. "And if I'm never ready?"

"Then I'll continue to wait," he said matter-of-factly. "In the meantime, I've been looking for you. Shouldn't you be resting?"

"I thought you were looking for Gordon?" she asked, ignoring his question.

"No, I just said that because you were uncomfortable with his presence, but it wasn't a lie, we really could use his help."

She was floored by his ability to read her and his thoughtfulness. "Thank you."

"You look tired. Are you still not sleeping well? Nightmares?"

"Yeah." There was no point in lying to him since he already knew about her bad dreams.

"Anything I can do?"

"I don't think so," she said with a shake of her head.

"If you ever need me, or just don't want to be alone, come to me. I'm always here for you."

Emotion clogged her throat, so she just nodded her acknowledgment. She swallowed hard and asked, "So why were you looking for me?" ready to change the subject.

All emotion left his face and he announced, "Eldon is dead."

"What? How? I thought he was being held prisoner until Amira returned."

"We're unsure how it happened. He was found dead in his cell this morning, his neck broken. I've spent all morning questioning the guards on duty last night and the other prisoners, but no one knows anything, or no one is talking."

"Do you think it was one of our soldiers?" That was just another thing that had changed for Inaya. Her faith had been shaken in those around her. There were few people in her world that she could trust anymore, but the male in front of her was at the top of her list.

"I don't want to believe so, but we can't be sure," Trevin admitted, sounding like his faith had been shaken too. "But until we figure it out, just be careful."

"I will."

Trevin's body tensed, and his head jerked to the left, but then his muscles relaxed. Inaya followed his line of vision and saw Caeden approaching.

"Sorry to interrupt, but can I speak with you for a moment, Inaya?" Caeden asked.

"Sure."

"I'll just—" Trevin began, but Caeden stopped him.

"No, you can stay." He turned back you Inaya. "I have a favor to ask of you."

"Okay...."

"The people are scared and confused. We've all been through so much lately, and they don't know what to believe. Amira's absence is making it even harder for them to adjust."

"I've noticed," Inaya shared. "I've had people approaching me all morning with questions and looking for reassurance."

Caeden nodded. "They need a member of the royal family to guide them. They need leadership in this difficult time."

"What do we do?" Inaya asked in confusion. "Amira is the only one left, and she's not here."

"That's not true." Caeden shook his head. "They have you."

"Me? I'm not of royal blood," Inaya argued.

"No, but you are a part of the royal family, and they trust you," Caeden replied.

"And as you said," Trevin joined in, "they are already looking to you for guidance and support."

"Yes, but I can't lead them."

"Inaya." Caeden placed his hand on her shoulder, and she forced herself not to back away, knowing he meant it as a reassuring gesture. "You've been running the palace practically singlehandedly for years. The people of Velius respect you, and they will listen to you. In every way that matters, you are a part of the royal family." His hand gave a gentle squeeze and then released her.

Inaya looked from Caeden to Trevin. Trevin nodded his agreement, and Inaya took a deep breath. "Okay, what would you like me to do?"

"I met with the local healers this morning. They are forming a committee to carry out the Supreme Healer's duties for the time being. I've released Marcelle's journals to them. I believe Amira would agree that it is time to share that knowledge with the other healers. Along with that, they will be searching for a way to break the bond between Sorin and Amira, as well as planning Amira's upcoming coronation. I have advised them to seek you out for guidance," Caeden informed her.

Okay, that wasn't so bad. Inaya could handle that task, but before she could commit herself, Caeden continued.

"We also need to address the people as a whole and answer any questions they have. It'll be easier to do it all at once. We need to give them the truth and reassure them."

"So you want me to give a speech?" she clarified, a weight settling in her chest.

"Yes, and I'll be there with you to help answer questions."

Some of her fear eased with that knowledge. "All right. When would you like to do this?"

"The sooner the better."

"I'll set it up for this evening then," she informed him, sounding more confident than she felt. Trevin's hand gave hers a reassuring squeeze, and only then did she realize she had reached for him sometime during her conversation with Caeden.

TWENTY-SEVEN

Sorin had become a sniveling mess, cowering in his own mind, attempting to block out Lahash, but it wouldn't work. Lahash would break him.

He paced the small confines of the cellar, soaking up that chaotic energy surrounding him. Having been an angel, the angel-created shield surrounding the island and protecting the Nephilim was a living, breathing entity to him. He could feel its distress, and instead of filling him with joy, it was a weight on his soul. How could that be? He was so close to accomplishing his goal, but all he felt was dread.

A commotion above ground caught his attention, and desiring the distraction from his own conflicting thoughts and emotions, Lahash decided to investigate. Besides, it would do good for Sorin to believe he was gone. It would build an anxiety-filled sense of relief and make Lahash's return that much more devastating for Sorin.

With just a thought, Lahash transported to the courtyard where a large crowd had gathered around the palace steps. He took in the sheer number and estimated that just about the entire population had come together for some event. He didn't have to wait long before the palace doors opened and his daughter stepped out, looking strong and proud. Her golden hair shimmering in the sunlight, she was a magnificent sight. Curious, Lahash drew closer, noticing the trepidation in her turquoise eyes and the slight tremor in her hands. Those were the only signs of her discomfort.

Four members of the Royal Guard stepped out of the palace and formed a wall behind her. Inaya glanced over her shoulder, taking in their presence. Her brother Murdock wore an encouraging smile, and the redhead next to him, Dalek, gave her some kind of hand signal with his thumb in the air. Her mate, Trevin, made no outward gesture, but his intense gaze was locked on her, and she seemed to understand whatever he was silently communicating. Finally, her attention turned to their leader, Caeden. When he gave her an infinitesimal nod, she took a deep breath and turned back to address the crowd. All of this had taken place in just a matter of seconds, but it was clear the bond his daughter had with these males; they brought her support and comfort.

"Thank you all for coming." Inaya's voice rang out strong and confident. "We have all been through so much, and I know many of you are confused and still frightened. I'm hoping I can help eliminate some of your worry and explain what has happened and how we will move forward together and get through this trying time."

As Inaya continued her speech, explaining everything, from the murder of King Vidar to Princess Amira's absence to Sorin's capture, she held the audience in the palm of her hand, each person trusting in her and feeding off her strength. It was clear that his child was a natural leader and well respected.

"In the coming days, we will need to rely on each other more than ever. As you can see"—Inaya lifted her right hand toward the storm building in the distance—"we still have a few challenges left to face. Our sanctuary has never experienced extreme forces of nature such as these, but we will get through this. Preparation is the key. We'll continue to work together and build shelters and gather necessary supplies to weather this storm. I am so very proud of each and every one of you. The captain of the Royal Guard will now guide us on how to best prepare for the difficult road ahead. Thank you."

As Inaya concluded her speech, the crowd erupted

into applause. The energy coming off the Nephilim had shifted from frightened to hopeful and enthusiastic. Lahash's daughter had returned the faith and security that he had stolen from them, and he couldn't have been prouder.

Twenty-Eight

Inaya was more than grateful to step away from the podium and allow Caeden to take over. Somehow, addressing the crowd was both easier and harder than she anticipated. The leadership role came naturally, and she realized that taking charge was second nature to her. In fact, she had been doing it for years on a smaller scale within the palace. Coming to this conclusion, something clicked inside her, like she was seeing herself more clearly. Not just the servants at the palace, but the people of Velius saw her as part of the royal family, just like King Vidar and Princess Amira had always claimed she was. Perhaps she was the only one who didn't accept that as fact... well, and Sorin too. Her gaze drifted in the direction of the cellar where he was currently being held.

It shouldn't matter to her what that villain thought of her. He had proven his true character to the world, and was justly being punished... so why did his hatred of her sting so much? From their very first meeting years ago, his disdain had been apparent, as if he held a preconceived opinion of her, as if he already knew her before she had come to live at the palace after her mother's death. But how could that be? Did he truly know her mother as he had claimed? Inaya didn't remember ever crossing paths with Sorin before coming to the palace, but she couldn't fully trust her memory of that time.

The heaviness in Inaya's chest tightened, making breathing more difficult. It had first begun when she approached the podium to address the crowd, so she had excused it as nerves. But that had gone well and was now over, so why was she feeling this way? Closing her eyes, she took a deep breath and searched her feelings. It was anxiety she was experiencing, as if she were being stalked by a dangerous predator. Yes, that heaviness was eyes upon her. She opened her eyes and scanned the crowd. Almost everyone's attention was locked on Caeden as he spoke... so who was it?

From the corner of her eye, a shimmer caught her attention, but when she turned her head, nothing was there. In fact, there was a break in the crowd, an odd empty space in the group of people. Instinctively, she found herself shifting closer to Trevin. As if sensing her unease, he moved, positioning himself almost in front of her, half blocking her from the crowd and any potential danger therein. Did he feel it too? Was there really a threat, or were they both just on edge because of Eldon's death? Regardless, the idea of him using his body to shield her didn't bring her comfort.

"Don't," he ordered quietly, just as she made the decision to step out from behind him. How did he know her intentions without even looking?

"Do you feel it too?"

He gave a brief nod, but his gaze remained on the crowd, his body tense. Inaya didn't see Trevin give any sort of signal, but Murdock and Dalek each stepped closer to her, poised for action. Inaya waited with bated breath, but nothing happened, and after Caeden concluded his speech and dismissed the crowd, the Royal Guard rushed her into the palace.

"Report," Caeden commanded when they were safely inside.

"Something didn't feel right," Trevin answered matter-of-factly.

Caeden nodded in acceptance and turned to Dalek and Murdock questioningly. Dalek shrugged, and Murdock shook his head, but added, "I trust Trevin's instincts."

"As do I," Caeden agreed, then turned back to Trevin. "What do you suggest?"

"Inaya needs twenty-four-hour protection until we work this out."

"That's—"

"Granted," Caeden said, interrupting Inaya's objection.

"—not necessary."

"The people are depending on you," Caeden stated, once again cutting her off. "As we've talked about before, you are the only member of the royal family here at this time. Your safety is nonnegotiable."

There was that reminder of a higher purpose. Inaya shut her mouth, accepting the responsibility, but one look at the smug expression on Trevin's face had her biting her tongue. If she hadn't felt the threat herself, she might think he was using this as an opportunity to be near her; after all, he did say he'd be pursuing a relationship with her. Could she stand strong against him and fight her feelings if they were together constantly?

No, she wasn't strong enough for that. And Trevin may have decided he was ready for a relationship with her now, but could she really trust that? Could she risk her heart to him again after he had so carelessly trampled on it before? Before she could give it any more thought, she requested, "I want Alyx assigned to my protection."

"No—" Trevin began, but Caeden spoke over him.

"Granted, but Dalek will rotate shifts with him."

"I'd like—" Trevin tried again, but Caeden didn't let him finish.

"Your job is to find the threat and eliminate it. This may very well be connected to Eldon's death."

Trevin nodded, but the look he gave Inaya clearly showed his displeasure.

Dalek sidled up to Inaya and bumped her with his shoulder with a wicked gleam in his eye. "This is gonna be fun."

Inaya may have the reputation of being impulsive, but she had nothing on Dalek. She had to watch him closely; like a puppy, he was making a mess or getting into trouble every few minutes. His favorite pastime seemed to be playing tricks on the other Guard members. At least his mischief kept her busy so she didn't have the time to worry—perhaps that was his intention all along.

"Let's take a field trip." Dalek popped his head up off the couch where he had been sprawling for the last twenty minutes.

"No."

"Aww... I'm bored," he whined.

"You can help me sort out the requests." The citizens had been instructed to submit written requests to petition for their needs, and it was up to Inaya to sort them out by priority and make sure they were then given to the tradesman or volunteer in charge of taking care of the issue in question.

"Don't you need a break? You've been at it for hours. Better yet, why don't you delegate and have some of the volunteers assist for a while?"

The idea held merit. Her head was starting to hurt,

and her eyes blurred the words in front of her. It was only midday, but it had already been a long one, beginning with the meeting with the healer committee and planning the princess's coronation. With a sigh, she laid the form on the desk and turned her full attention to Dalek. "What did you have in mind?"

"Let's go back to the soldiers' keep." He perked up at his own suggestion.

"Absolutely not. I'm already concerned about your safety."

Earlier in the day, Dalek had asked her to walk over there with him to "do something." She was ashamed to say it had taken her at least ten minutes to realize what he was up to, but by that time, he'd already "relocated" every left shoe in the barracks, hiding them under a random soldier's bunk. He'd also loosened the screws on the legs of one of the chairs so it would collapse when someone sat down. Apparently, Dalek was full of juvenile pranks.

Inaya wasn't ashamed to admit that she had joined in hiding Murdock's favorite dagger and creating a treasure hunt for him to go on to recover the item. Dalek had a devious mind, which was demonstrated when he left a ransom note for the release of Trevin's pillow, the price of which was three live chickens, a ham sandwich, a strand of hair from a redheaded virgin, and a blue glass marble, all of which was to be delivered to the second-floor bathroom in the palace by sundown if he wanted the safe return of said pillow.

Inaya didn't see that plan going over well, but it was amusing to witness.

Seeing Dalek's playfulness was somewhat liberating. He seemed to understand that these new responsibilities were weighing on her. He reminded her that just because they were going through a difficult time and they had people depending on them, it didn't mean that they couldn't enjoy the simple pleasures in life—which for him meant annoying his brothers-at-arms. He claimed that, without him, they took life too seriously and his actions were in their best interest.

"Why are you so restless? Aren't you used to guarding the royal family regularly? I've never seen you try to convince Amira to risk the wrath of the soldiers in such a manner."

"I know, just think of all the wasted years!" Dalek's disappointed expression had her smiling. "Had I realized how adventurous the princess could be, I'd have recruited her as an accomplice long ago."

Before the king's death and Sorin's hostile takeover, Amira had hidden behind the façade of the perfect princess. It pleased Inaya that her best friend had finally opened up around the people closest to her and that they could now see her for the person she was.

A pang of guilt slammed into Inaya's chest at the thought of Amira. When Inaya had chased after Trevin to collect the soldiers, she had abandoned her best friend in her time of need. If she had been there, Inaya could have accompanied Amira to the human world and assisted in her mission to find the scout and deter-mine if she was indeed the "natural healer" that Marcelle's journals had prophesized.

"When do you think she'll return?"

"Soon, I'm sure." Dalek jumped to his feet. "Let's get out of here." He seemed oddly serious. Perhaps he was picking up on Inaya's stress.

She decided not to argue and just go with it. "Where are we going?"

"You'll see." Dalek grabbed her hand and led her through the palace and out to the courtyard to where Amira's coronation had been designated to take place.

Inaya was a little surprised that preparations were already underway, considering they had just finalized the plan that morning, or at least everything they could until Amira returned. A smile lit her face at the sound of a sweet melody coming from where the band was set up to practice for the big event.

"May I have this dance?" Dalek bowed in front of her, extending his hand in a gentlemanly gesture.

She couldn't help the giggle that escaped her. Glancing around nervously, she took in all the people working in the courtyard. "Everyone will see."

A wicked smile crossed his lips, and for the first time, Inaya realized Dalek was actually quite handsome with his dark auburn hair that fell in a flattering devil-may-care way, rust-colored eyes, and his easy smile, not to mention his battle-ready, sculpted body. "Indeed they will."

How could she resist? Inaya allowed him to pull her close and lead her around their makeshift dance floor. From the corner of her eye, she noticed the gathering crowd, but kept her focus on her dance partner and found herself relaxing into it. Dalek was an excellent dancer. Who knew he had such hidden talent? When the song came to a close, Dalek pulled away and formally bowed to her once again, really embracing the proper gentleman act.

The smile slipped from her face when she felt the heavy presence behind her, and if that wasn't enough to reveal the person's identity, Dalek's smirk left no doubt. Inaya turned to find Trevin standing behind her, glaring at Dalek, but when his attention fell to her, a small smile graced his lips, making her heart trip over itself.

"May I?" Trevin extended his hand to her as the band began to play their next song.

She may have stepped forward, or he may have just pulled her to him, she wasn't sure, but suddenly she was in his arms. Her body fit his perfectly, and their bodies moved in sync like they had danced together a hundred times. Everything felt more intense—the way the music spoke to her soul, her heavy heartbeat, his gaze locked on hers. The world fell away, and it was just them. She was both at complete peace and tied in knots. It felt as if her soul recognized his. He was the missing piece of her heart that she had been ignoring.

"I should have danced with you before."

His whispered words brought reality crashing back to her, reopening the wound of his past rejection. She hadn't been enough to pull him away from that wall the night of her maturity celebration. He didn't feel the same for her as she did for him. He may have said he wanted her now, but could she trust that? Or would he just pull her back in only to abandon her once again?

"Inaya?" Trevin studied the emotions that crossed her face.

"Yes, you should have." Inaya pulled away as the song concluded. She didn't want to hang on to this pain, but she couldn't help but relive it, couldn't help but once again feel like a fool.

"I'll re-earn your trust," he promised as he let her go.

She forced a smile and nodded. She wanted to believe him but couldn't. "Thanks for the dance." She turned away, and he escorted her to where Dalek was waiting.

"I'll see you soon," Trevin murmured for her ears only. Then he turned to Dalek. His hand shot out lightning fast, plucking a strand of hair from Dalek's head and slapping it into Dalek's hand. "There is the strand of hair from a redheaded virgin. Now return my damn pillow." Without waiting for a response, he stalked off.

Amusement restored, Inaya burst into laughter as Dalek glared at her.

News of Amira's return traveled fast through the people of Velius. Her transport hadn't even landed before tale of her arrival reached the palace. Inaya wanted nothing more than to rush off to meet her, but instead guided the preparations to celebrate her return. Minutes passed like hours, and when there was nothing left to do, Inaya anxiously paced the foyer, her eyes continuously watching the door.

When the princess finally walked inside, Inaya couldn't contain herself. She rushed forward and threw herself at her best friend, almost sending them both tumbling to the ground. Thankfully Trevin was close by to steady them. In that moment, all the fear and anxiety Inaya had been carrying with her over Amira's well-being finally lifted, freeing her of that heavy burden. Amira clutched her just as tightly.

The apology burst from Inaya as she pulled back. "I'm so sorry I abandoned you when you needed me. I've been so worried."

"I've been worried about you, too. We're supposed to go on our adventures together."

Inaya laughed and went to hug Amira again, but was thwarted as Murdock pushed her aside, impatient to greet the princess.

"My turn," he grumbled. "You two can girl talk later." He pulled Amira into a hug and kissed her cheek.

Inaya couldn't help but be amazed at how much had changed as she watched each member of the Royal Guard greet the princess. After Dalek had taken his turn, he shuffled up to Inaya, nudging her shoulder with his. "We're just one big happy family now, huh?"

"That we are," she agreed with a smile, truly feeling like she belonged and grateful that the missing piece of her family had returned. Then it occurred to her, not all of the family was together. "Where is Levi?"

"He stayed behind," Dalek informed her solemnly.

"What do you mean?" A feeling of foreboding settled in her stomach.

"Apparently, not all is as it should be with the scout in the human world. I only had time to get the bare facts from Osmond." Dalek shook his head, a look of disgust crossing his face. "The scout had a rough time of it."

"Is she okay?" Inaya had only met Kearney briefly, but the thought of something happening to her made Inaya sick inside.

"I don't know, but Levi will look after her."

"Why didn't they both return to the island with Amira?"

Dalek moved closer and lowered his voice. "There are Nephilim in the human world."

"What?" Inaya's shock had her near shouting, earning her a few questioning looks from those closest to them.

Dalek nodded to them in acknowledgment and

then grabbed Inaya by the arm and pulled her further from the crowd. "There were Nephilim waiting in the human world to ambush Kearney." Inaya opened her mouth to question him, but he cut her off. "I don't know why or much else, only that she was hurt, badly" —the look of disgust crossed his face again—"and Levi and Kearney stayed behind to investigate who they were, how they got there, and how many more Nephilim have left the island."

Only the scout was allowed to travel to the real world, their mission to observe humanity and gather information. Inaya was stunned at the idea that Nephilim were leaving their sanctuary and choosing to be among the humans who had persecuted them when they first came into existence. How could this happen? And how could they not know?

Trevin and Caeden joined them before she could question Dalek any further. Dalek smirked as Trevin pushed his way between them, and Inaya had to wonder if Trevin felt threatened by him. The preposterous thought made her smile.

"Did you return my pillow?" Trevin glared at Dalek.

"What pillow?"

Inaya was impressed at how well Dalek pulled off the innocent look as he asked that. She struggled to hold back her giggle.

With an exasperated shake of his head, Trevin turned his attention to Caeden. Inaya and Dalek followed suit. "Amira will be taking meetings in the study. We'll start with a full debriefing with the Guard," Caeden informed them. He looked to Dalek. "Get Osmond and Murdock and meet us there." Dalek nodded and rushed off. Caeden turned to Inaya. "She wants to jump right in and address as much as she can immediately. You've been prioritizing the needs of the people and know better than anyone what's been accomplished and what still needs to be done. While the Guard is debriefing, I'd like you to organize the meetings that need to take place and make it happen, but keep in mind she's had a long journey and will need to rest."

"Of course," Inaya agreed, comfortable with falling into a supportive role and being able to help her friend. The last few weeks had been difficult for everyone, but especially for Amira, and they weren't clear of their problems yet. Amira was still bound to Sorin, she was grieving the death of her father, and now she had to transition into the sole leader of the Nephilim, but Inaya and the Royal Guard would be there to help her through it.

Inaya had been surprised when Amira had insisted she attend each meeting after her debriefing with the Royal Guard. It was nearly dark outside by the time they finished up for the day.

"Thank you for all your help," Amira said as they made their way from the study toward the family wing of the palace, Alyx trailing a few feet behind since it was now his turn to stand guard. "And I don't mean just today, Inaya. I guess I never realized how much you actually do around here. You've basically run the palace for years, and I've never even noticed." She grabbed Inaya's arm, pulling her to a stop. "I've taken you for granted, and I'm sorry."

"No, you and your father took me in and gave me a home, a new family. The least I could do was help out."

"All you ever had to do was just be yourself. You were a blessing to us. Thank you for agreeing to help me through this transition." Amira's fear was clearly written on her face.

"Hey, we'll get through this together. Everything will be all right," Inaya assured her.

Nodding, Amira took a deep breath and squared her shoulders. "Get some rest. You look tired."

If only she could. Her nightmares had been relentless, and her complex relationship with Trevin wasn't helping. Sometimes when her mind wandered to him and she found herself contemplating giving him another shot, the voice from her dreams echoed in her head. That deep, masculine voice would remind her, *"It was never meant to be. There is no such thing as love or fate."* And she couldn't help but question if it was right.

Shaking herself from those thoughts, she hugged her friend good night and retired to her room for another restless night.

TWENTY-NINE

Lahash cocked his head and watched the unexpected visitor enter Sorin's holding cell. Well, well, the princess had returned. Confidently, she stepped over the threshold and paused, taking in Sorin's motionless form. For days, Sorin had sat with his back against the wall, blankly staring straight ahead, lost in his mind, attempting to block out Lahash, as if that were even possible.

Lahash was fascinated by the show of emotions that played upon the female's face. She had arrived with expectation, perhaps believing she would find the same Sorin she had always known and detested. But it appeared that neither of them were the people they once were. Sorin was now a broken shell, and Amira exuded an inner strength that she hadn't carried before. When Sorin did not respond as she had expected, fear and worry crossed her features.

But why would she show concern for the enemy? Lahash's eyes narrowed as he studied her as she knelt to Sorin's level.

"Are you all right?" Her voice was soft and pure. "Can you even hear me?"

As if hit by a gust of wind, the princess was pushed to the floor; fear and despair radiated from her as she tried to catch her breath. Lahash's gazed swung to Sorin. What had he done? Was he using the unnatural bond that connected him to the princess to communicate with her?

Movement brought Lahash's attention back to the female as she cautiously approached Sorin, kneeling beside him and hesitantly placing her hand on his shoulder. "I know you're in there. There is nothing to fear here."

Oh, how wrong she was.

"It's safe to talk with me. I can help you. We can help each other."

Why would she do such a thing? Sorin was responsible for the death of her father, he had stolen her kingdom, forged an unholy blood bond with her, and was destroying the Nephilim's sanctuary. She should hate him. She should want retribution! But here she sat trying to give comfort, wanting to help. As much as he tried to understand, her motivation was unclear to him. Lahash had held the rank of a prodigious angel, an arbiter of the Creator's will, the hand of God, and yet, this slip of a female, this abomination, this Nephilim could do as he could not.

Her next words brought something far different than understanding. A blinding pain rocketed through him, nearly sending him to his knees.

"Sorin, you know the demon can't get you here, right?"

Demon....

Was that what he had become? It couldn't be....

For the first time in his existence, Lahash lost control. The building shook as thunder boomed in the distance, and the lights flickered. The keening screech tearing from Sorin's lips made Lahash want to cover his ears and block out the pain, and as the princess crumpled to the floor unconscious, he knew he had to get out of there.

Thirty

Thunder burst through the air, startling Inaya so much that the watering can tumbled from her hand, nearly displacing the plant she had been watering. She wasn't sure how it ended up in the study, but the plant now had the best place to catch some sun in the whole palace. It looked as if it had had a rough time while Sorin had command of the palace, but someone had been nursing it back to health. Inaya had even noticed where it was growing a little pod that would blossom into a beautiful pink and red flower.

After cleaning up the mess, Inaya paced back and forth across the study, having too much pent-up energy to keep still. Her mind was a jumble of chaos, constantly returning to thoughts she didn't want to indulge, particularly regarding Trevin. Was a relationship between them possible? No, of course not, but....

Amira and Caeden seemed to be making it work; in

fact, Inaya was even then awaiting Amira and Francine to arrive for a meeting regarding the changes to Amira's coronation. The princess had decided to make her relationship with the captain of the Royal Guard official and have him crowned king as well. It was clear their love was real and they were meant to be together. Traitorous hope tried to burrow inside her, but she shoved it down.

The door opened, revealing Amira, Alyx, and Murdock.

"Be good, little sis," Alyx said with a wave.

"Where are you off to?" Inaya asked. Perhaps Caeden had decided she no longer needed a guard.

"I'm babysitting you both today," Murdock informed her with a smirk. Inaya had a few things to say about his word choice, but he continued before she could share them. "Now you ladies have fun drinking tea, talking fashion, and doing female stuff." Murdock winked at Amira before shutting the door behind him.

Amira burst into laughter, which was definitely not the reaction Inaya was having. She looked at her friend, judging her state of mind. Amira had been through a lot lately, perhaps the stress was getting to her.

"You think that's funny?" Inaya questioned.

"I didn't the first time I heard it."

Inaya raised an eyebrow and waited on an explanation for that vague comment.

"I just had a visit with Sorin," Amira informed her.

"Sorin said that to you?" Now Inaya was really confused. Last she had heard, Sorin was basically catatonic and not speaking to anyone.

"No, Trevin did." The gleam in Amira's eyes could only be described as wicked.

The thrill at hearing Trevin's name was rapidly replaced with irritation. "Did he?"

A smile spread across Amira's lips. "He did. He wants us to stay out of trouble."

"I guess we'll just have to do that. I'm sure we can come up with some 'female stuff' to do after our meeting."

"That's what I was hoping you'd say," Amira admitted.

Dreading the answer, Inaya still had to ask. "How was your meeting with Sorin?"

Amira's attitude sobered. "He's broken." A look of confusion crossed her face. "Something happened when I touched him.... But I'm not sure—" A knock on the door interrupted their conversation. Amira sighed. "We'll discuss it later."

Murdock leaned inside the doorway, eyebrow raised. "Francine is here to join your meeting."

"Thank you, send her in," Amira requested.

Murdock threw his hands in the air. "Why am I here? Francine could have kept the two of you in line, had Caeden known she would be attending."

"Aww, Murdock, you would have missed all the

fun. Plus, I can't tell him *everything*." Amira's mischievous expression had Inaya smirking.

"There will be no fun!" Murdock declared, giving them both the evil eye before admitting Francine and leaving them to their meeting.

Francine crossed her arms over her excessive bosom and eyed them each, her stern expression enough to make a soldier tremble. "I will have no part in your shenanigans."

"Oh?" Amira asked, fighting a smile. "I was hoping you'd be interested in helping me arrange the new king's coronation. But if you're not interested...."

It took a few seconds for Francine to lose her shocked expression, and she appeared mighty pleased when she announced, "Now, that is something I can get behind. Let's get started, ladies."

It took no time at all for the arrangements to be made. Francine would still need to speak with the healer who would be performing the ceremony, and of course, Amira would need to actually propose to Caeden, but Inaya had no doubt the ceremony would happen flawlessly.

"I'm so happy for you both!" Francine gushed on her way out, her excitement completely out of character for her. "The council and I will have everything ready to take place directly after your coronation."

"Thank you," Amira said, dismissing her.

Inaya walked Francine to the door, and when she turned around, she found Amira somberly staring out the window, apparently in deep thought. "It's your big, *big* day, but you don't seem very excited," she noted, studying her friend.

"I am, but... something happened today. I've been trying to work it out in my head. The conclusion I'm coming up with isn't good... but I'm afraid I'm right," Amira admitted.

"Run it by me, let me see if I can help," Inaya offered.

"When I upset Sorin today, there were physical manifestations of his emotions in the weather. I think... I think he may be responsible for this storm and everything else that's going on."

A chill shivered down Inaya spine. "You're referring to the massive thunder today, right?" She hated to admit it, but it had felt unnatural to her as well. "But couldn't that have just been a coincidence?" Inaya asked, hoping they were wrong.

Amira thought about it for a moment. "It could, but I don't think so." She shook her head. "After my father's death, the shield began to weaken, allowing the cold climate of the northern hemisphere to penetrate. The island's climate shifted so quickly that it set off a series of storms and other natural disasters, but after the bonding ceremony, the shield became stable, and it has remained stable."

That sounded like a good thing to Inaya. If Sorin's forced bond with Amira actually helped secure the shield, then how could Sorin be the cause of the storms now? Instead of voicing her questions, Inaya waited for Amira to explain.

"The only thing that has changed is that Sorin is now responsible for the bond. As his mental status deteriorated, so has our weather."

And there it was. Inaya could see how having an evil lunatic controlling the shield that protected them all could be a problem.

"The moon even became red the night of his capture, the night I...." Amira hesitated, swallowing hard. "The night he withdrew inside of himself."

Inaya briefly wondered what Amira wasn't saying, but she wouldn't push; besides, what she had just shared gave her enough to worry about. Whatever else there was, Amira would disclose it in her own time.

"Wow." Inaya braced herself against the wall, trying to work it all out in her head. She'd love to dismiss Amira's claims as impossible, but how could she when she herself was part of a species that the human world didn't know even existed and their island sanctuary was protected by a blood bond created by angels. Anything was possible. But... "What does this mean? What are we going to do?"

Amira heaved a sigh and once again turned to stare out the window. "I don't know. I'm not sure how much more the island can take... and it looks like this is going to get bad."

"Have you told anyone else?"

"Not yet, there are a couple details I need to work out first."

Inaya clasped her arm around Amira's shoulder, wishing she had the answers. "Whatever you need, I'm here."

"I know."

The door flung open, and Murdock marched in, looking disgruntled, repeating his previous complaint, not bothering with a greeting. "If you had said your meeting included Francine, Caeden wouldn't have assigned you a babysitter."

"But where is the fun in that?" Amira asked, and both females burst into laughter.

"You're both brats," he grumbled, but he couldn't hide his amused grin as he shook his head. "So, is all of your business concluded for the afternoon?"

Amira thought it through. "For now."

"Then what's next?" Murdock asked, and by the look on Amira's face, Inaya knew he wasn't going to like the answer. She decided to sit back and let this play out.

"When is the storm predicted to hit?" Amira asked. That wasn't the direction of conversation either Inaya or Murdock expected.

"It's still out a way over the ocean, so we're estimating early tomorrow evening," Murdock explained.

"The rest of the Guard is out there preparing?" Amira motioned to the window, and the innocent expression on her face had Inaya holding back her laughter. She was starting to see where this was leading.

Apparently, Murdock was beginning to get suspicious as well, because he looked a little apprehensive when he answered. "Yes. Why?"

Amira let out a dramatic sigh. "The tea is gone, and we're out of female stuff to do." She shrugged and turned to Inaya. "Feel like playing with the big boys?"

This was exactly what they needed. Amira required a distraction from the weight of the world she carried on her shoulders, and Inaya could use the distraction as well. Plus, someone needed to demonstrate to Trevin where he could shove his orders and his "female stuff."

"Of course," Inaya agreed, "just let me change."

Before she could make it two steps, Murdock popped in front of her, flinging his arms wide. "Wait, wait, wait! You females want to help weatherproof buildings, stockpile supplies and food, herd and pen animals, and get dirty and sweaty...?"

He was trying to dissuade them, but it wouldn't work. The idea of physical labor and being of service actually appealed to her, and it would be good for Amira too.

Murdock's face lit with hope as he asked, "Don't you need to be getting ready for tonight?"

"It's barely midmorning, we have plenty of time for that," Inaya explained. "Plus, it sounds like fun."

"Fun!" Murdock barked. When he turned his

questioning gaze to Amira, Inaya darted around him and opened the door.

"I need to change as well. Shall we meet you outside?" Amira asked.

Murdock bowed his head, looking defeated. "Meet me in the front hall," he grumbled.

Trevin did a double take. What were Princess Amira and Inaya doing outside the palace walls... and what were they dragging? Was that a crate of food reserves? It had to weigh more than the two of them combined.

With a sigh, he altered his course and marched over to them, but unfortunately, they saw him coming. Inaya abandoned the crate and rushed over to Murdock, who was also carting supplies. She would soon learn that her brother could only be her shield for so long, but he'd let it go for now.

"Princess, I don't believe it's a good idea for you to be outside the palace walls," he offered respectfully.

"No?" she questioned, looking around the makeshift encampment for the refugees. "Dalek is just over there, Osmond is around that corner, and Murdock is staying within fifteen feet. With more than half of my Guard present, I'm perfectly safe."

He knew they couldn't keep her secluded in the palace forever, but it was an unnecessary risk for Amira and Inaya to be working in the encampment. Besides, they were royalty, they shouldn't be doing physical labor anyway.

"I'm sure you are, but there is no need for you to be here."

By her expression, it was clear he had said the wrong thing. And when she opened her mouth, she confirmed it. "Is that right? This is where my people need the most help, this is where I can be of maximum service. Where else should I be?"

"Safe." It was the only argument he had available.

"I think we've already covered that."

"Eldon's killer still has yet to be apprehended," he reminded her.

"Have there been any more leads?"

"No." He had spent the last two days trying to figure it out but had come up empty so far.

"Have there been any more crimes committed?"

"No." He saw where this was heading.

"Has anything happened that would lead you to believe there is a specific threat to me at this time?" she asked.

"No, Princess, but—"

She didn't let him continue. "Okay, please inform me if anything changes." And just like that, he was dismissed.

He hated to do it, but she left him with no choice…. He was going to get the captain. If anyone could talk some sense into her, it would be Caeden. If nothing else, he would sympathize and share Trevin's frustration. When his eyes met Inaya's across the way, he tried to communicate his displeasure. He almost swallowed his tongue when she winked at him and went back to what she was doing.

It didn't take much to get Caeden involved. By the time they had stalked back to the encampment, the females were no longer carting around crates of food. No, they were now on a freaking roof! These ladies had absolutely no sense. Neither had any kind of training, and yet they felt it was a good idea to attempt to weatherproof a roof? The fools were going to break their necks.

The moment Inaya spotted him, a look of trepidation crossed her face and she darted to the back of the building and disappeared, abandoning Amira. Trevin could only assume there was a ladder on that side. She was running from him again, but this time he wasn't accepting it. No, it was time they settled things once and for all. They belonged together, and they were both miserable with the current state of their relationship. That would end now. He had wanted to give her space and time to make her own decision and come to him, but he realized that was a mistake. Deep down, she knew they belonged together, she had always known, but he had messed things up, and now she was using it as an excuse to lie to herself.

Inaya marched through the encampment toward the palace walls, her paced clipped. Although she refused to look behind her, it was clear she knew Trevin was following. Her shoulders thrown back, chin tilted up, indignant pride radiating from her. But more than that, there was an extra sway to her hips. Trevin didn't bother hiding his grin. Yes, she knew he was following—and gaining ground—and it excited her. They both wanted this.

Trevin planned his approach perfectly. He could have snatched her up at any time, but he waited. Their paths intersected just as she was about to pass the entrance to the soldiers' keep. With a firm grip on her arm, he steered her inside, ignoring her gasp of surprise, and led her straight to his room on the second floor. She never said a word, keeping pace the entire way. As the bedroom door shut behind them, she ripped herself away from him and turned to face him, hands on her hips, attitude on full display. This time he thought it prudent not to show his amusement.

"Just what do you think you're doing?" she demanded.

Back to the door to prevent any ideas of escape, Trevin took his time answering. Instead, he allowed his eyes a leisurely trek down her body, taking in the rapid rise and fall of her breasts that gave away her excitement and enjoying the way her formfitting pants hugged her curves. When his eyes finally made their way back up her beautiful body and reached her face, the sexual tension was clear. Her bottom lip was pinned between her teeth, and her eyes shone with excitement.

"I was going to ask you the same thing, but I know exactly what you were doing on that roof. You wanted my attention. You have it."

Inaya's mouth fell open, appearing shocked that he could so easily see through her. He stalked forward, making his intention clear, not hiding anything, and when he wrapped his arm around her and pulled her body flush against his, she didn't protest.

"I wasn't avoiding you. I had thought you needed time. I was wrong. That's not what you need at all." He brought his mouth closer to her ear. His voice emerged deep and husky as he informed her, "You needed me." A shiver ran through her, confirming his words. He pulled her closer, nuzzling her throat. "You need me to prove how much I want you, that I need you...."

His erection pressed into her side, emphasizing his words, and the most beautiful sound he'd ever heard escaped her lips. She moaned, soft and needy, but he wasn't finished. With one arm wrapped around her hips, the other slid up her body and into her hair. Securing a handful at the back of her head, he used it to tug her head back so that they were face-to-face, so close their lips were almost touching. The passion in her eyes was almost his undoing; she liked his dominance, craved it, but he had a point to make and he was not going to be distracted.

"All of you." He allowed his lips to brush against hers. "Every day. Always. You're mine and I'm yours, and I'm not going to put up with this distance you've put between us anymore. I messed up in the past and hurt you. I won't do it again." He hated to bring it up, but he had to clear the air between them once and for all. This would be his last apology.

When a hint of sadness filled her eyes, he claimed her lips fully. It took her a second to open to him, but when she did, her tongue danced with his with equal and untamed passion, heightening his need to a level he had never experienced before. Breaking the kiss, he pressed his forehead to hers, giving them a moment to catch their breaths, only then noticing that he had maneuvered them so that her back was pressed to the wall, his body blanketing hers from the front.

"Now, admit you're mine and let me replace that pain with pleasure. Let me prove to you what we can be together." Not able to keep his lips off her, he brought his mouth to her neck, sucking gently at first before allowing his teeth to sink into her flesh. A moan tore from her throat and she arched further into him, seeking more of him. Granting her silent demand, he pushed himself against her, more firmly pinning her to the wall. He knew just what she needed, and he was going to give it to her. "I'm going to make you feel so good." It wasn't a boast; it was a vow. "Now tell me."

He pulled back so he could look into her eyes. They were still glazed with desire, but there was also a bit of trepidation. This wasn't easy for her, but they both needed this, and he wasn't about to allow her to deny them. His hand tangled in her hair again, tugging lightly. Her mouth parted in a needy sigh.

"It's okay. You can tell me. Trust me," he urged, somewhere between a command and a plea.

Biting her bottom lip, she looked away. Just as he was about to demand her attention, her eyes shot back to his, fire and determination blazing through, and for a moment, he worried she'd tell him to go to hell.

"I'm yours, and you're mine." The last part came out as a growl.

Elation roared through him. "You're damn right." He gently kissed her forehead. "Now are you going to let me make you feel good?"

Trapping her bottom lip between her teeth again, she nodded once. That was all the permission he needed. His mouth swooped down to hers, desire controlling the pace of their kiss, only breaking to pull the shirt over her head. His quickly followed before their lips met again. His hand caressed her skin, memorizing the shape and feel of her. Her kiss became ravenous the firmer his hands on her breast became. When he tightly pinched her nipple, giving it a small tug, her back arched off the wall and she broke the kiss with a deep moan. As he suspected, she liked a little pain with her pleasure. She suited him perfectly.

He buried his face in her neck, repeating the pinch on her other nipple. "That feel good, sweetheart?" He already knew the answer, but he needed her to admit it.

"Yes." Her voice was a breathless groan.

His mouth trailed from her neck down to her breast, biting, licking, sucking as he went. When he reached the erect tip, he circled it gently at first with his tongue before sucking it in his mouth, giving it a firm tug. Without warning, he bit down. Her cry of pain and pleasure mixed had his control threatening to snap. Her hands flew to his hair, tangling, a firm grasp holding him to her, as if she feared he'd abandon his task. That wasn't going to happen. He'd fantasized about her beautiful breasts more times than he could count, and now that he had access to them and realized the pleasure he could bring to her, he was going to take his time, making sure to give each equal attention and the proper homage they deserved.

Inaya's desire had taken her over, and she became restless and needy, clawing at his back, grinding her hips against him. She was ready for more. His mouth returned to her lips, the passion of their kiss momentarily distracting him before he remembered his goal. His hands slipped down her body to the front of her pants, making quick work of the fastening and sliding them past her hips to the floor, supporting her as she kicked them off. There was no denying himself, he had to see her. Stepping back, he took in her perfection.

Her curvy body had been crafted by the angels them-selves. She was magnificent.

When his eyes made it back to her face, her uncertainty was clear. He couldn't allow that. "You're gorgeous, every bit of you." Her eyes lit at his compliment, and her face bloomed with heat.

"Thank you," she returned softly. Determination flashed in her eyes, instantly putting Trevin on alert. Breath held, he let her do as she willed. Her hand landed on his chest and began its slow trek down his abs before reaching the fastening of his pants. Her eyes darted back to his, seeking permission. His brief nod gave her the confidence she needed. She fumbled through unbuttoning his pants, but finally succeeded; Trevin patiently appreciated her efforts. As she pushed his clothes down his hips, his manhood sprang free, thick, proud, and long.

A smirk came to his lips at Inaya's indrawn breath but fell away at the sight of her fear.

"Look at me." His tone left no room for hesitation. His palms cupped her cheeks, and he kissed her forehead. "This is just you and me, physically expressing our feelings for one another. There is nothing to be afraid of." Eyes locked with hers, he asked, "You trust me, right?"

She hesitated for half a second and then nodded.

"Then kiss me," he demanded, and she immediately complied.

It didn't take long before she was lost to their

passion once more. He kept his hands firm and soothing as they traveled her body, exploring every inch of her silky skin, and when he reached her center, he found her hot and wet for him. Her hips arched forward, and a needy whimper left her lips as his fingers slipped through her heat, caressing the bundle of nerves before sliding further back to slip inside her. Preparing her with first one and then two fingers, he thrust into her as she instinctively rode his hand.

Breaking their kiss and panting heavily, she begged, "More. I need something more."

Hand never ceasing, he trailed his lips down her neck, licking, sucking. When he reached the sensitive area where her neck met her shoulder, he growled, "I'll give you exactly what you need." And then he struck, biting down as his fingers inside her became more forceful, his palm rubbing her clit with just the right amount of pressure. Her body tensed, and she let out a scream of pleasure and pain that soon transformed into a moan of ecstasy as she clenched around his fingers, finding release. "Good girl," he praised. "That was beautiful." His voice was husky and rough with need.

As she sagged against him, he supported her weight and maneuvered her to the bed. The sight of her sprawled across his bed did something weird to his heart; it felt both heavy and light at the same time. This was where she was meant to be. With him. He lay beside her, gently kissing her anywhere he could reach, using his hands to work her back up. When her body once again began responding to his touch with need, he crawled down her body, kissing, sucking, nipping the whole way. When his destination became clear to her, her body tensed and her thighs clenched.

"Trevin?" she asked, sounding unsure.

"I'm going to taste you," he stated firmly. When she didn't open for him immediately, he bit down on her thigh, reminding her who was in charge. She yelped, but her legs opened, granting him access to what he craved most in this world at the moment. He kissed away the pain on her thigh as a reward before moving on. Letting her get used to this new form of intimacy, he started slow, taking his time with gentle licks from the bottom to the top of her core. When she fully relaxed into his ministrations, moaning and clutching at his shoulders and hair, he delved deeper, seeking her cream and savoring every drop.

He needed to make her come as much as he needed his next breath. Once again, he slipped two fingers inside her, curving upward and thrusting, massaging that bundle of nerves deep inside her. Her hips arched off the bed and a cry of ecstasy burst from her at first contact, but he was nowhere near done with her. Lowering his head, he brought his mouth to her clit, sucking and licking. He nearly came undone as she began to ride his face, losing all inhibition as she grasped his hair and held his face to her. Her second climax hit, and it was even more beautiful than the last.

He wanted to bring her down gently and then build her back up before continuing, but he just didn't have it in him. She had destroyed his willpower, and all he could think about was his need to be inside her. He crawled back up her body, positioning himself on top of her.

"Legs around my hips, sweetheart, and arms around my shoulders," he commanded. Looking dazed and blissful, she complied. Trevin knew this was her first time, and he had prepared her the best he could, but this next part would still be uncomfortable for her. "Deep breath." He entered with one firm push on her inhale, covering her mouth with his when she cried out in discomfort, trying to distract Inaya as her body adjusted to his. She bit down on his bottom lip, sending a shot of adrenaline through his body. He needed to claim her, to dominate her body, but he held back, moving slowly, being gentle, fanning the flames of her desire as the pain receded. Her body moved in sync with his, building the tempo.

"Honey, I'm going to come again," she cried out breathlessly, clenching around him, and that's when he lost all control. He gathered her close, wrapping his arms around her as his hips slammed into hers, fucking her relentlessly. Inaya was just as wild, moaning and screaming out her pleasure as her hands grasped at his body, trying to pull him closer, making two bodies become one.

Trevin had never experienced anything as amazing

as coming inside of Inaya. It went far beyond physical pleasure. His heart and soul felt whole and complete and just as sated as his body. Rolling to the side, he gathered her close, holding her and caressing her soft skin as their bodies cooled and their breathing returned to normal.

Thirty-One

"Inaya, are you all right?"

She jumped at the sound of her name, turning back to face Amira. It took her mind a moment to catch up and figure out what she had asked. "Oh, yes, of course."

"Really?" Amira watched her skeptically. "Because you seem like something is bothering you."

"I'm sorry. I guess I'm just a little distracted."

"Want to talk about it?"

"No, no, this is your day. I'm supposed to be helping you get ready for your coronation... and hopefully your wedding, if you ever get around to asking the groom."

A blush stained Amira's cheeks. "I'll ask him." She sounded nervous.

"Are you scared? You know he'll say yes, right?"

"Caeden loves me, I know this, but he has a strange

sense of duty.... I've tried to get up the nerve all day, but it just hasn't seemed like the right time."

"You're almost out of time. The ceremony is in less than an hour."

"I know. I'll do it as soon as I see him, but for now, let's talk about you. What happened today? Your mind has been somewhere else since you arrived. Did you and Trevin have a fight? Was he angry about the roof thing?"

It was Inaya's turn to blush. "He was...." She didn't know quite how to answer. She didn't want to share the intimate details of what she shared with Trevin, not because she was ashamed or anything, but because it was special and felt sacred, but she could use some advice. "He.... We made love," she finally blurted.

Amira's eyes widened in shock, and then a smug grin spread across her face. Squealing, she ran at Inaya, nearly tackling her to the ground as she wrapped her in a hug. "I'm so happy for you!"

Inaya chuckled at her friend's enthusiasm, and oddly, a weight lifted from her shoulders at having her friend's approval. As amazing as the experience had been, in the back of her mind, she had worried she had made a mistake. "He wants us to be together," Inaya admitted.

Amira pulled away, studying Inaya's face. "I should hope so... but is that what you want?" she asked, looking unsure.

"Yes... no... I don't know," Inaya admitted.

Amira took her by the hand, leading her to the couch in the dressing room. After they were settled, she asked, "What's wrong?"

Tears clogged Inaya's throat, but she swallowed them down. "He... he's broken my heart before. Who's to say he won't do it again?" Those words were so hard to say.

"Oh, honey, trust is scary—for all of us—but there are no guarantees in life, no completely safe choices. No one knows what the future holds, but if we allow fear to prevent us from taking chances, we'll miss out on so much. Enjoy life while you can. Grab this moment of happiness and savor it while it lasts, and let the future work itself out." Amira paused for a moment, then grinned. "Plus, I think he realized what a fool he was for rejecting you before. I don't think he'll mess up again and risk losing you. You're amazing, and there is no way he hasn't figured that out by now."

Inaya was humbled by her friend's words. Amira was right; there were no guarantees in life. For all she knew, the world could end tomorrow, and she didn't want to have any regrets. "Thank you, Amira."

"Anytime. So... what's happening between the two of you?"

Inaya's mind flashed back to the last image she had of Trevin—bare-chested, lying in bed as he watched her dress. He looked so sexy and tempting, Inaya wasn't sure how she had found the willpower to leave his bedroom. If fear hadn't propelled her out the door, she probably would have thrown herself at him and demanded a repeat performance of all the amazing things he could do to her body.

"I kinda freaked out and ran away, telling him you needed my help," Inaya admitted.

"You used me as an excuse to escape?" Amira asked, chuckling.

"Well... I didn't know what else to do. I mean, making love to him was amazing... and the connection between us, it's not just physical, and then he wanted to talk about the future.... It all just became too much."

"Inaya, you need to decide what you want, what's best for you, and then go after it. Be the amazing, impulsive, brave woman that we all know and love. Jump right in and live life to its fullest. And if you ever stumble, those of us who love you—and that includes Trevin—will be here to steady you."

In that moment, Inaya realized how incredibly blessed she was, but there were no words she could come up with that could fully express her appreciation, so she just nodded and smiled at her best friend.

"Okay, so stop hiding behind me and go get your man, and I'm gonna go do the same. I have a future husband to propose to!"

Inaya didn't like the look of uncertainty on Trevin's face as he watched her rush down the stairs toward him. But before she could reach him, his expression morphed into one of pure determination, and somehow, that just reaffirmed her decision. She was jumping in with both feet... literally. She launched herself into his arms and kissed him as if it would be the last chance she'd have to show him how she felt. Holding her tight, he kissed her back just as fiercely.

When they were forced to part for air, he pressed his forehead to hers and breathed, "Marry me."

She pulled back in shock, staring into his intense, dark brown eyes. "What?"

"You're going to marry me." It wasn't a question this time.

"I am?" She meant to sound indignant at his high-handedness, but it came out breathy and excited instead.

Trevin nodded once. "I've already spoken to Murdock and received his blessing—"

"You asked for my brother's permission?" Inaya was shocked.

"Of course."

"And he gave it?" That was even more shocking. Murdock tended to be overprotective where she was concerned.

"He did, but it wouldn't have mattered."

"Why not?" If her brother's opinion didn't matter, then why did he ask him?

"Because you're already mine." Trevin kissed her forehead. "The marriage and bonding ceremonies are just a formality."

Excitement and peace warred within her. This felt right. This was what she wanted. It was the path she was meant to travel. Meeting his eyes, she beamed up at him. "I'll marry you."

"Damn right you will."

Their lips fused together in a soul-searing kiss.

"Ahem!"

The loud interruption would have had Inaya jumping guiltily away had it not been for Trevin's arms holding her to him, refusing to let her put distance between them.

"If you're done mauling my little sister," Murdock began, glaring at Trevin, "the coronation is about to begin."

Trevin glared right back at Murdock before pressing a kiss to Inaya's forehead. "We'll finish this after the ceremony."

Inaya's heart beat faster as images of their time in Trevin's bed flashed through her mind. Continuing later sounded like a fantastic idea. Her nipples beaded as she pictured him lavishing attention on them, sucking and biting, before trailing down her body, using his tongue to—

"Inaya?" The questioning tone in Trevin's voice told her she must have gotten lost in her daydreams.

Who knew how long she'd been standing there with a stupid grin on her face.

"Are you all right?" Murdock added.

Heat flooded her cheeks. She'd been having naughty thoughts in front of her brother! "I... I'm fine, just a little excited—" Well, that could be misconstrued—although technically correct—so she rushed to add, "—about tonight's celebration. It's a big day for Amira."

"I see...." Unfortunately, it sounded like Murdock did see—a little too well.

Thankfully, Trevin stepped in and saved her. With a knowing grin, he said, "Go join the fun. Murdock will escort you." He turned to her brother expectantly.

"Of course." Murdock took her by the elbow to lead her out to the courtyard where the ceremony would be held. She glanced over her shoulder to see Trevin's eyes locked on her. She wasn't even out of the room and she was already beginning to miss him. It occurred to her that this turn of events didn't bode well for her future. She forced herself to face forward and put one foot in front of the other.

With candlelight illuminating the courtyard and stars shimmering as a backdrop, the courtyard had been transformed into the perfect romantic setting for a wedding. Soft music played in the background as the guests gathered in their designated spots.

The Royal Guard was technically on duty, along with many of the soldiers. Osmond and Dalek were already surveying the crowd, and Trevin would escort Caeden and Amira. Apparently, Murdock had been assigned her supervision. He escorted her to the front of the stage, where Maryse and baby Elijah waited.

She didn't have to wait long before Caeden and Amira emerged, Trevin following discreetly behind them. And it was clear by Amira's jubilation that all had gone well with her proposal. Tonight, Cashile would be getting a new queen and a king, and Inaya's best friend would be marrying the man of her dreams.

With that thought, Inaya's eye sought out Trevin. It hadn't yet sunk in that someday soon she would be getting married as well. The thought both terrified and thrilled her, but as the ceremony began, Inaya let that all go and watched as her best friend's dreams came true; she even teared up during the wedding, having never seen Amira so happy.

Afterward, a large feast was served and the dancing began. Inaya would have envied how much in love Caeden and Amira looked if she hadn't caught Trevin staring at her more than once with a look that was more than raw hunger; it was pure possession. A shiver trailed down her spine just thinking about it.

With everything they had all been through lately, and with the dangerous storm looming, the Nephilim needed this night of celebration and happiness. Inaya allowed herself to release all of the stress and worry she normally carried with her as she danced and enjoyed the festivities. The only thing that could have made it better would have been Trevin at her side, but she understood he was performing his duty.

As her eyes locked on the newly married couple on the dance floor, Inaya felt a familiar presence at her back, her body so attuned to his, she didn't need to turn to know Trevin was there. An arm slid around her chest, pulling her back against him, and she instinctively relaxed, her body melding to his.

"Are you ready?" his husky voice rumbled in her ear, reminding her he'd promised to finish what they had started. Her breath caught at the idea, and she nodded her acceptance. His hand slid down her arm until he linked their fingers together so he could lead her away from the celebration. Desire had begun to cloud her mind the moment he had touched her, so it took a minute for their destination to register in her brain. They were not headed to the soldiers' keep like she had expected; instead, they were headed to the orchard near the stables.

A lone figure stood in the clearing, candlelight shining on the trees, providing a romantic, beautiful backdrop. As they approached, Inaya recognized the figure to be a woman with her back turned toward them as she arranged something on a table that had been set up. She looked up at Trevin in question, but he just continued to guide her forward, walking directly toward the female. She turned before they reached her, and Inaya recognized her as the healer who had performed Caeden and Amira's wedding ceremony. Inaya didn't know Lyra well and had only been acquainted with her since she had begun helping to establish the healers council that had formed to make up for the loss of the Supreme Healer.

It took Trevin a moment to realize Inaya had stopped abruptly, and he nearly dragged her a few steps before following suit.

"What's the matter?" he asked.

"Wh-what's happening?"

"What do you mean?" Trevin answered, sending a tingle of frustration through her.

"I thought we were going to finish what we started?" Inaya kept her voice low, but sent a brief smile to Lyra, who was waiting patiently just out of earshot.

Trevin's eyebrows furrowed. "We are."

"In the orchard? With an audience?"

Trevin glanced around. "It's a beautiful spot. I thought you'd appreciate it, but if you prefer we do it somewhere else, that isn't a problem, as long as it happens now."

"Well... I thought we'd go back to your room... and be alone."

"You want to do it alone?" Trevin sounded confused, which was starting to piss her off.

"Of course I want to do it alone. It's a private matter between the two of us, not something we would share with others, and if you expect me to, you're out of your damn mind." Inaya's voice had risen, but she didn't care. Anger and hurt warred within her.

Trevin's hands landed on her shoulders and held her firmly, as if afraid she was about to run away, which wasn't far from the truth; the thought had crossed her mind. She couldn't believe what was happening.

"Sweetheart, calm down. If you want it to be just the two of us, I can arrange that."

"Of course that's what I want," she snapped.

"Okay," he said slowly, drawing the word out. "And you want to do it in my room?"

"Why is that a problem? I know I have limited experience, but don't most people do it in a bed?"

"You want to do it in the bed?"

Something about the way Trevin tilted his head and looked at her oddly sent warning bells off in the back of her mind, but she was too worked up to pay it any attention. "Well, yeah."

His eyes closed, and he shook his head. "Okay, we'll get married while in bed."

"Thank y—wait, what?" Now Inaya was the one confused. "Why would we get married in bed?"

"That's what I've been trying to figure out." His hand flung out in a frustrated gesture.

Inaya took in her surroundings once again, seeing it from a different perspective. "So... you brought me out here to marry me?"

"What else did you think was happening? We're

finishing what we started earlier. I'm not giving you a chance to overthink this and run away."

"Oh...."

A wicked smiled curved his lips. "What were you thinking?" he asked, but it was obvious he had already figured it out.

Heat flooded her cheeks. "I... uh...."

He stepped up closer, their bodies brushing against one another. Bending close, he whispered in her ear, "That eager to bed me again, huh, sweetheart?"

How was she supposed to answer that? "I... uh, no," she lied.

His deep chuckle rumbled through his chest. "No worries, that's gonna happen too, but first we formally make you mine. Then I'll take care of your other needs." His whispered words came out like a promise, sending a shiver of anticipation down her spine.

"Okay" was the only word her brain could form. He chuckled again and stepped back, then proceeded to lead her to Lyra.

THIRTY-TWO

By the way Lyra struggled to keep the smile off her face, it was clear she had heard at least a part of their argument. "Lady Inaya," she greeted, bowing her head. "I'm honored to be allowed to preside over your vows."

That's when the reality of the situation finally hit. They were really doing this... now. Panic rose inside her, and Inaya's eyes darted to Trevin's. Not saying a word, he held her gaze, his steady presence more reassuring than any words he could give. After only a moment, the tightness in her chest eased and she was able to take a deep, cleansing breath. As if able to sense her resolve, he nodded once and turned to Lyra.

Inaya followed suit, finally remembering her manners. "We appreciate you taking the time to do this for us."

Lyra smiled brightly. "Shall we begin?"

"Please," Inaya answered.

Turning to the supplies set up on the table, Lyra picked up two long, white candles, handing one each to Trevin and Inaya. "Marriage is more than a partnership, more than just deciding to live with someone else for the rest of your life, and for us Nephilim, that can be a really long time, so this is not a decision we make lightly. We bond our lives, merge our souls, in a sacred bond passed down to us by the very angels themselves. Two become one, in this life and whatever comes next. As a symbol of this commitment, of this unification, I invite you to create the flame of unity." She gestured to an unlit red candle in the center of the table.

Trevin and Inaya's eyes met briefly before they moved as one, each pressing their flame to the wick of the red candle.

"Red," Lyra continued, her voice soft and melodic, "the color of passion in all its many forms, and may you experience them all together, as one, supporting the other with love and unwavering dedication.

"The past"—Lyra motioned to the white candles each still held, as the red candle burned brightly between them—"is a lesson that prepares us for what is to come. Please blow out your individual candles, as you now embrace the future, a future you will experience together, through both the joyful and the challenging times."

They blew out their candles, laying them on the table. Lyra picked up the ceremonial dagger, its wickedly sharp blade gleaming in the candlelight, and passed it to Trevin, who took it without hesitation.

"The blood flowing through our veins gives life to the flesh, and this night it will give life to the union between you. Trevin, if it is your will, please draw forth your life force from your left hand."

In a swift slash, he made a shallow cut on the palm of his left hand. Lyra retrieved the dagger, passing it along to Inaya. "Lady Inaya, if it is your will, please draw forth your life force from your left hand."

Inaya's heart beat a mile a minute, but she didn't hesitate. The blade burned through her palm as it easily cut through her flesh, blood immediately beading from the wound. She barely noticed Lyra taking the dagger from her and placing it on the table.

"Please clasp hands," Lyra instructed. As they did, she intricately wrapped a green, gold, and pink braided cord, the same one she had used in Caeden and Amira's ceremony, around their arms from elbow to wrist. "Let the strength of your will bind you together and the life that courses through your blood make you inseparable in this life and beyond, where you shall meet, remember, and love again."

Trevin became blurry as tears filled Inaya's eyes at those sacred words, but she refused to break eye contact. From this moment on, her life would never be the same, nor did she want it to be. And then she felt it; the blood bond between them became a tangible entity, lighting up her insides, giving her strength, making her feel whole for the first time in her life. And from the look on Trevin's face, he was feeling it too.

"This is no longer needed," Lyra whispered, understanding the gravity of the moment. With ease, she slipped the cord from their bound arms. "You are one." She turned and blew out the red candle before placing her hand on top of their clasped hands. "Love each other above all else and be happy." And then she was gone.

Thirty-Three

As much as he had wanted to, Lahash couldn't stay away. He found himself back in Sorin's cell. Anger and another emotion, which he refused to name, warred within him, making him relentless and remorseless in his mental assault on the pathetic waste of space in front of him. Sorin hadn't outwardly acknowledged his presence in any manner, but Lahash was in the one place where Sorin couldn't hide—his mind.

"You have failed us both," Lahash growled as he paced the small confines of the cellar, his eyes never leaving Sorin. "No matter, it will be over soon." His words were punctuated by thunder rumbling in the distance.

Sorin knew exactly what he meant by that. Lahash had revealed his plan and shown him the part he had played in the downfall of the Nephilim, showing him how the tainted bond Sorin had created that tied him to the island sanctuary was corroded and would soon destroy the island and everyone on it. And yet... watching the thoughts filter through Sorin's mind, it appeared he believed Lahash to be the wicked one.

An angry laugh tore through him, sounding cruel to his own ears. "If you wish to play pretend, you may do so, but we both know the true nature of your character." Lahash crouched in front of him, making sure his wings were tucked close to him and not touching the soiled ground beneath his feet. Tilting his head, he examined the pathetic being before him. "I never could comprehend why the Nephilim were granted sanctuary. Such flawed creatures. Creatures who never should have been, and yet here you are. Protected... cherished even. An accepted deviation, whereas we, the progenitors, we were punished, banished, and exposed." Lahash flared his wings, displaying the pearly white abominations. "So fitting that one of the beloved be the determinant of restitution," he said, more as a reminder to himself.

"I'll wake up soon. This is all a dream. All of this will cease to exist," Sorin promised himself in his mental pep talk.

Lahash couldn't help but smirk at his chosen verbiage. How right he was—soon this would all cease to exist. A nagging voice in his own mind asked, *What then?* He forced that lingering doubt from his mind.

"Soon your desire will be granted," Lahash

answered Sorin's mental dialogue. "I am a gracious master after all. This sin will be amended, and the by-product will perish. This island will cease to exist, along with all of its inhabitants." With that final word, a mental image of a golden-haired beauty with flashing turquoise eyes and courageous spirit came to his mind. Inaya... his daughter, she would cease to exist as well. Pain flared within his chest; the anguish so great, his eyes closed of their own accord. It only took him a second to get himself under control, but when he did, he discovered they were no longer alone.

"Interesting...," he murmured.

Apparently, in his fear, Sorin had used his bond to Amira and brought her essence forth. She wasn't physically in the room with them, but a manifestation of her consciousness was. At his voice, she turned toward Lahash, expression one of total awe. "Magnificent" fell from her lips, and Lahash nearly laughed. This female had no idea what he once was, how truly magnificent he had been before his fall, when he had taken for granted this life, his purpose, and thrown it all away by making the wrong decision, by giving in to the needs of the flesh... by making a mistake.

Outwardly, he let none of his thoughts show. Sorin's fear beat at him. Apparently, he had not meant to call the female forth and he actually worried for her safety. Interesting.

With a peaceful expression, Lahash spread his wings to show their full glory and stretched his arms out, reaching for her, beckoning her to come to him. "Come here, child."

As if in a daze, Amira stumbled forward, but before she could reach him, Sorin finally pulled himself out of his trancelike state and lunged for her, wrapping his arms around her waist and propelling them across the room as far away from Lahash as possible.

"That's the demon."

Sorin's words echoed in Lahash's head. There was that word again. Anger flared white-hot through him, and he dropped his façade. He knew his eyes burned crimson as a hateful laugh burst from him.

"How touching," he taunted between laughs. "In your own perverse way, you actually care for her. How delightful, for it will be you who destroys everything and everyone she cares for, simply by being you. Apropos, if I must say so myself."

"Who are you?" the female demanded, shifting her stance and placing herself between Sorin and Lahash, using her body to protect him.

"Why, child, don't you recognize your own father?" He couldn't help but toy with her.

"You are not my father." By her tone, he knew he had hit his mark.

"Oh, but in a way, I am. I am one of the fathers to you all." Her body jerked as realization hit her, bringing a smile to his face. All the while, Sorin hid behind her, trembling in fear as she bravely faced him. "If you won't call me 'papa,' you may call me Lahash." He couldn't remember the last time he had introduced himself, the last time he had actually cared about being seen.

"What do you want?" she demanded, her courage impressing him.

"What anyone would want. Retribution," he answered honestly... or what used to be honestly. Now he wasn't so sure.

"By destroying Cashile?" Sorin asked, finally joining the conversation and attempting to step around Amira, but she refused to allow him to put himself in danger.

"By undoing what was never meant to be," Lahash growled, his frustration getting the best of him. Why couldn't they understand? Taking a deep breath, he reminded them, "Besides, I'm not destroying Cashile... you are."

Sorin's face lost all color, the truth slapping him in the face. Still keeping an eye on Lahash, Amira turned so she could see Sorin as well. Lahash could see her mind working; she was putting together the pieces. "He's referring to the storm, isn't he?" The guilty look in Sorin's face was answer enough, but he nodded anyway. "Can you stop it?" The hope in her voice had even Lahash wincing.

"It's not something I'm doing purposely," Sorin confessed.

"Of course it's not," Lahash agreed, "it's just who

you are... what you are." *What I made you*, he added silently.

Amira ignored Lahash's comment and remained focused on what was important. "How do we reverse the bond?"

That was a good question.... Was it possible? The bond was designed by the angels, and Lahash was an angel... or he used to be. Was it too late to change their fate?

He didn't let these questions or his doubts show as he answered the female. "Darling child, being of 'royal blood,' you of all people should understand the sanctity of a blood bond. What is done cannot be undone. Sorin controls this bond because you are weak, but his very nature will destroy it. It can do nothing less."

"There has got to be a way!" Amira pleaded, looking to Sorin to save them.

No one has ever looked to me to be the savior... the hero instead of the villain. Sorin's thoughts were unexpected. Lahash had never know Sorin to care about doing the right thing. He only cared about himself and what felt good at the moment.

"That's because that isn't your role." Lahash gave him the hard truth. "You will never be the hero."

"But you could be."

The new voice had Lahash whirling around, nearly stumbling over himself.

"Briathos...."

The angel stood not ten feet away, his obsidian

wings tucked behind him, his amber eyes sharp and alert, his head tilted to the side as he studied Lahash. The way he held himself told Lahash he was ready for any outcome of this interaction.

"Why are you here?" Lahash demanded. What he meant was, *Why now after all this time? Where were you when I needed you most?* But he refused to ask. Gusion had foretold the arrival of a light bearer, but Lahash hadn't let himself believe it was possible. After his fall from grace, he had called out to his former brothers, seeking help, but none had heeded.

"You wanted our attention. You have it."

"It was never about—" Before he finished his denial, he realized Briathos was baiting him. Changing tactics, trying to regain control of the situation, he asked, "What shall you do?"

Lahash's gaze shot to the two Nephilim as Briathos turned his attention to them. They seemed to be communicating telepathically through their bond, completely oblivious to everything around them.

"What would you have me do?" Briathos countered almost absently before turning his back to Lahash.

"There is nothing to be done." The words sounded belligerent to his own ears.

Briathos cocked his head to the side, once again studying him. "Is that what you truly believe? Better yet, is that truly what you desire? Shall I walk away and allow you to destroy them, your children?"

Inaya's image sprang to mind—the stubborn expression she wore when standing up for what she believed to be right, the beautiful smile she reserved for those she truly cared about, the way she looked as she tenderly held her brother's newborn baby in her arms. His daughter would never bear a child of her own.... She would cease to exist.

"It's not too late." Briathos's voice was low, almost pleading.

Lahash almost believed the light bearer cared. And in that moment, he made a decision. "Save them."

And then he was gone, but if he had stayed just a moment longer, he would have heard the rest of Briathos's revelation.

"For you, Lahash. It's not too late for you."

Thirty-Four

Waking up with his naked wife tucked up close against him was one of the best experiences of his life. His body stirred as he nuzzled her neck, and she instinctively rubbed against him, her body seeking his even in sleep. They had made love deep into the night, taking the time to learn each other's body, but that wasn't enough. He knew he would never get enough of her. Inaya's turquoise eyes opened slowly, and the sleepy smile she bestowed upon him filled his heart with love to the point he feared it might burst. His lips brushed hers—

Desperate pounding rattled the door, followed by, "Trevin, we gotta go. It's the queen."

Both Trevin and Inaya jumped from the bed. Inaya scrambled to put clothes on, but Trevin headed straight for the door, uncaring about his state of undress. He checked over his shoulder to verify she was decently covered before he opened the door, and he couldn't help but admire how sexy she looked wearing only his button-up shirt from the night before.

He jerked the door open just as Dalek was preparing to pound on it once more. "About damn time," Dalek grumbled.

"What's happened?"

"The queen killed Sorin," Dalek announced. Inaya's sharp intake of breath had Dalek's head swinging in her direction. A look of shock crossed his face before it transformed into a smirk and he turned back to Trevin. "Looks like you'll be the next to die when Murdock finds out his sister was in your room."

"Murdock is well aware of *my wife's* location." That wiped the cocky grin off Dalek's face. "I'm assuming our new queen survived Sorin's death?"

Dalek was once again all business. "Yeah, she had a hell of a night, but she's safe. Get dressed, and bring your *wife*. We're meeting for a debriefing at the palace." And then he was off.

They were dressed and at the palace in no time. Dalek had been right, Amira was a little shaken up, but she seemed to be handling the situation, and the news of Inaya and Trevin's wedding brought a little joy to the atmosphere. After everyone arrived, Caeden and Amira shared their incredible tale about how Sorin had been manipulated by a fallen angel set on destroying the Nephilim and how the entire island was in danger of being destroyed as long as Sorin retained control of the shield that protected their sanctuary. The most astonishing part was hearing about Amira's interaction with not just one but two angels.

"So the storm is gone, and so is the fallen angel?" Murdock asked, looking as shocked and overwhelmed as Trevin felt.

"Yes," Amira answered. "When I killed Sorin, and the angel completed the bond between me and Caeden, the shield once again became stable. As for the fallen...."

"We don't know where he is," Caeden finished when Amira's words faltered. "The angel warned us that there is much dissension and corruption within our people. Amira and I can feel it within our bond that ties us to all of the Nephilim, but we're unable to know the full extent of what is going on."

"We're going to need some help," Amira added, looking to Inaya, causing a heavy feeling to sink to Trevin's stomach.

"What can I do?" Inaya asked, her hand tightening on Trevin's under the table.

"Since the storm has subsided, the people who have come to Velius to seek shelter will be returning to their homes in the other territories. Those territories no longer have leaders, with Sorin's death and Lady Ferrara's and Lord Donovan's disappearances. Caeden and I will need to remain here for the time being, but there needs to be a royal presence in the other territories. Specifically in Ammon." Amira's eyes darted to

Trevin, and his whole body tensed. "With Ammon's past, it's clear that the fallen angel's presence has had the most profound effect in that area. Inaya, we'd like you to take control of that territory."

Trevin was well aware of Ammon's history, having played a vital part in it. He was not excited about the idea of going back, but he knew his wife would not shirk her responsibility and loyalty to Amira, so he would be confronting his past.

"Of course," Inaya agreed, sealing their fate.

"Trevin, we know what we're asking of you," Caeden added, not one to beat around the bush. "We'll be sending a unit of soldiers with you. Discover what threat, if any, is still in place there. Under the rule of Sorin and his father before him, the people of Ammon have suffered. We need to provide safety and security to our people."

Trevin nodded his acceptance. "When do we leave?"

"Take today to get your affairs in order. You can leave in the morning. Plan for an extended trip, possibly a permanent one."

Inaya's hand once again tightened on his. His wife was frightened, but the look on her face gave nothing away.

"What about the other territories? You know, I could pass for royalty," Dalek informed them, bouncing his eyebrow in an excited manner.

"You could also pass for a simpleton," Osmond grumbled.

Trevin couldn't help but smile at the sound of his wife's giggle, and in that moment, he almost regretted every time he'd wanted to strangle Dalek.

When Amira stopped laughing, she informed them, "Kimi and Zefania received the most damage from the storms and earthquakes. We will be sending soldiers and craftsmen to those territories to help rebuild and get people back into their homes. It'll be a long process. We'll take it one step at a time for now."

"Will returning to Ammon be a problem for you?" Inaya asked Trevin once they were alone in her room.

"No. It is just a place."

"But it is a place that holds painful memories for you," she countered as she began packing up her belongings.

"Memories aren't stationary. They live inside of us. I have those memories here, just as I will in Ammon."

Inaya thought about that for a moment and realized he was right, but still.... "You don't have to go with me."

"The hell I don't." Trevin grabbed her arm, pulling her around to face him. "You are my wife. You're needed in Ammon; therefore, that's where I'm needed as well. With you." He studied her face for a moment. "What is this really about?"

Inaya hesitated before hedging, "You're part of the Royal Guard...."

"I am. What of it?"

"You heard Amira, this position in Ammon might be permanent for me. How are you supposed to do your duty as a member of the Royal Guard if you are in Ammon with me?" Her fears and insecurities swirled inside of her. She knew how important being part of the Royal Guard was to him. It gave him purpose; it was his life. Guilt ate at her at the thought of him giving that up for her.

"What do you suggest? I give up my wife for my job?" he asked, looking incredulous.

"I just... I just know how much it means to you."

"I don't think you realize how much you mean to me, Inaya," he said, his words coming out in a frustrated growl. "When I married you, it wasn't just for a night, or just when things were easy and convenient. It was forever. No matter what path life leads us on, we do it together."

Her heart melted at his words, and looking into his eyes, she knew he meant it. He wouldn't abandon her when things became difficult, and he wouldn't put duty or anything else before her.

Surging forward, she crashed her lips into his for a passionate kiss. She needed to show him she understood, that she valued this gift he was giving her, because to her, it was a gift. Desire flared between them as Trevin took control, hand tangling in her hair as he angled her head in a way that allowed him to deepen the kiss before exposing her neck and trailing biting kisses down her throat. When he reached the juncture of her neck and shoulder, he bit down, the sharp pain sending a wave of unadulterated lust through her, soaking her core, preparing her to be taken, dominated, owned by the man she loved.

Without warning, he stepped back, releasing her. "Clothes off," he commanded. The hungry look in his eyes had her scurrying to obey. Once she was naked, she reached for him, hands going to the buttons on his shirt. But before she could undress him, he shook his head. "On the bed, ass in the air." His voice was soft, but no less commanding. A shiver ran through her as she positioned herself as directed. They had made love many times in the last two days, and each time was a new experience for her, teaching her all the different ways a man could love a woman's body.

Trevin's warm hand trailed down her spine, slowly caressing her until he reached her ass. The first firm swat to her behind shocked her. It didn't hurt exactly, but it stung. She turned her head to look over her shoulder, her body held in place by Trevin's hand on the middle of her back. He met and held her gaze. There was no anger in his eyes, just determination and intensity, and, underneath that, love. He watched her closely as he used his hand to rub the sting away. No words were said as his fingers inched closer to her wet core, reviving her need for him, only to slide away before giving her what she wanted. Just as her eyes drifted closed and she lost herself to the moment, his hand lifted and came back down on her ass again.

This time, the sharp sting of pain didn't shock her... it excited her, adding to the pleasure of the moment, but more than that, it centered her, keeping her tied to the moment. He didn't give her time to recover; instead, he spanked her over and over again, his hand never landing in the same spot twice, each hit just a little harder than the last, until her entire bottom burned with delicious heat and she was begging for more. The chaos, the doubts and insecurities, all faded away. They had no room in this moment. Every slap grounded her more firmly to the moment, until all that was left was her and Trevin and the love and intimacy they shared.

She knew it excited her when Trevin was forceful and dominant, but she'd never dreamed she would enjoy being spanked, yet she did.

Without warning, his fingers were inside her, thrusting. "So damn wet for me," he growled, and then his control snapped. Inaya was vaguely aware of him pulling his fingers from her and ripping his pants open. And then he was inside her, filling her completely. Seated firmly, he stopped, as if just the act of being inside her was enough for him to regain his control. One arm slid around her chest as he bent over her, pulling her up slightly. The other hand tugged at her hair, angling her head so he could devour her mouth. The kiss was hard, deep, full of ownership. "Don't ever question my devotion to you again," he commanded after breaking the kiss.

He waited, watching her closely, expecting an answer. So she nodded, but that wasn't enough for him.

"Words, Inaya."

"I... I won't," she promised.

"Good." And then he began to move in long, deep thrusts, their tempo gaining as lust took control, both seeking fulfillment... but it was more than that. It was a connection they shared as their bodies found completion and satisfaction within the other.

There was one more loose end Trevin needed to tie up on the way... Isaac. He hadn't forgotten how he had hurt Inaya, and he was going to make damn sure he never had the opportunity to do so again. And since Isaac's only living relative, his sister, lived in a small village on the outskirts of Ammon, now was the perfect time to take care of the problem. Trevin didn't like the idea of Inaya tagging along on this task, but her traveling ahead was an even more unappealing option.

His caution turned to dread as they approached and he noticed the mourning shroud in the windows of not just one house, but practically all of them. That custom was rarely used anymore, making the scene that much more eerie. Inaya nudged her horse a little closer to his. Trevin had ordered the majority of the soldiers traveling with them to remain on the edge of the village, not wanting to announce their arrival to their quarry, but the few who were escorting them shifted closer as well, perhaps feeling the unusual heaviness in the air.

They didn't bother with stabling their horses at the public barn; instead, they rode directly up to Lyrissa's, Isaac's sister, house. The curtains moved, and a face peeked out at them before vanishing. "Stay here," Trevin requested and waited until he had Inaya's nod of acceptance. She was impulsive and sometimes acted without thinking things through, but he was learning to trust her after everything they had been through. If she agreed to stay behind, she would.

He gave her a grateful smile before dismounting, but he only made it one step before she added, "Unless I think you need me, and then I'm coming in."

Trevin groaned inwardly. Of course she would. But that was one thing that both endeared her to him and drove him crazy. She wouldn't hesitate to put herself in danger to protect a loved one. He met her gaze and recognized the love and worry mixed within it, and all he could do was agree, and make sure he didn't find himself in a position where she felt like he needed her assistance. "Okay."

Accompanied by two armed soldiers, leaving the remaining two with Inaya, Trevin cautiously approached the house, but before he made it up the stairs, the front door opened, revealing a tall blonde with wary eyes.

"Can... can I help you?"

"Are you Lyrissa?"

"I am." Her eyes scanned him closely as she answered, obviously trying to place him.

"I'm Trevin. I come on behalf of Queen Amira and the Royal Guard—"

"Oh!" She rushed forward, grabbing his hand. Trevin wasn't sure what to make of her behavior, but she didn't appear to be a threat. "You received my request."

"Ma'am—"

It seemed as life had returned to her after hearing who he was, and in her excitement, she wasn't allowing him to get a word in. "You're going to find out who... who slaughtered my brother, aren't you? You'll make them pay." A tear rolled down her cheek, but she angrily brushed it away as she stared hopefully up at Trevin.

"Isaac?" he questioned. A sob escaped her at the mention of her brother's name as she nodded. "Isaac is dead?" He needed to be sure.

"Y-yes."

Trevin turned to look over his shoulder, his eyes locking with Inaya's. Clearly having heard, she slid from her mount and rushed to Trevin's side. "Lyrissa, I'm Inaya. I'm so sorry for your loss." And to Trevin's ears, she actually sounded like she meant that. "Do you mind if we come inside? We have some questions before we can help find out what happened to your brother."

Inaya's presence seemed to calm the female. Lyrissa took a deep breath and invited them into her home, offering them refreshments as they made themselves comfortable on the sofa.

"No, thank you," Trevin answered for both of them. "Can you tell us what you know?" He thought it best not to explain that they had come to her home to take her brother into custody and try him for treason.

Lyrissa shook her head, as if the images in her mind were almost too much to take. Then she opened her eyes and met Trevin's gaze. "No one knows what happened. No one even heard him scream, and by—" She gulped. "—and by the looks of him, he screamed a lot." Her voice wavered at the end of that statement, and she took a deep breath before continuing, but was unable to maintain eye contact. "He was ripped apart, his body scattered throughout the market square, left for the birds to pick apart. The entire village was traumatized. The elders of the community believe it was an omen, a sign of a deep evil in our midst. And who can argue? What other than something evil could do that to my br-brother?

Who besides something truly evil and superhuman is physically capable?" Sobs rocked her shoulders, and she was unable to continue.

Inaya rushed to her side, wrapping the mourning woman in her arms and murmuring words of comfort. When Lyrissa finally regained control of herself, Inaya remained beside her, holding her hand. "How was your brother the days leading up to his death? Was he behaving differently?"

Lyrissa thought about it for a moment. "Actually, his visit was a bit random. He just showed up one day, and he didn't want to talk about any of the recent events happening in Velius. We've all heard rumors after the king's death. Some said the princess had married Lord Sorin, others said she had been killed as well, but Isaac refused to say anything. He was a soldier of the king's personal army, so I thought maybe the king's passing was too painful for him. I had believed his grief was responsible for his bad attitude, but now I'm not so sure. Looking back, he seemed more angry and perhaps a bit worried." Lyrissa shrugged.

"So he never spoke of anything that was happening in Velius or what he or the other soldiers were doing?" Trevin asked, wanting to be certain Lyrissa wasn't an accomplice in her brother's treason.

"No." She shook her head. "He rarely spoke, and he didn't want to leave my house."

Trevin believed her. He knew his next question probably wouldn't be helpful, but he had to ask. "Do you know of anyone who would want to hurt your brother?"

Her answer was immediate. "Oh no. As part of the Royal Guard, you must have known my brother. He was a dedicated soldier, loyal and brave. Everyone loved him."

Apparently, she didn't know her brother well, but Trevin wasn't about to correct her. So instead of outright lying, he just nodded.

"You said he seemed worried," Inaya interjected. "Any idea why?"

Perhaps because he helped Sorin overthrow the kingdom and physically assaulted a member of the royal family when he tried to kill Inaya? Again, Trevin kept his thoughts to himself.

"No, I'm sorry. I don't...." She trailed off and tilted her head to the side, as if a thought had just occurred to her. "Do you think his murderer was the same person who killed the king?"

It wasn't common knowledge that Marcelle had murdered the king, and it wasn't Trevin's place to disclose that information, so he vaguely stated, "We'll look into all possibilities. In the meantime, is there anything else you can tell us that might help us identify your brother's killer?"

The look of concentration on her face was short-lived before she shook her head once again. "Not that I can think of."

Trevin rubbed his pocket as a thought occurred to

him. Isaac and Eldon had been close friends, but more than that, they were partners in crime. Both of them were murdered, and there was only one clue left at Eldon's crime scene—an unnatural pearly white feather, a feather he now knew belonged to the fallen angel. On a hunch, he pulled the feather out of his pocket, where he'd been carrying it ever since its discovery, and held it up for Lyrissa's inspection. "Have you ever seen anything like this before?"

Lyrissa reached out, sliding her finger down the silky-smooth feather. "No. What kind of bird did that come from? I've never seen *anything* that color before."

Although it had been a long shot, Trevin couldn't help but feel disappointed. After hearing about Amira's interaction with the fallen angel and her description, he was positive Lahash was responsible for Eldon's death, even if he didn't understand the fallen's motivation. Isaac's brutal death would have been another piece to the puzzle. But even though there was no physical evidence tying Lahash to Isaac's death, who else was physically capable of such a horrendous act?

"It's not a creature native to Cashile," Trevin answered vaguely. "Who discovered the body?"

"The baker, Constance, but half the village witnessed what was left of his body."

"I'd like to speak with her. Can you show us the way?"

"I'm sorry, but I just can't... I can't bring myself to return to the place he was killed." Lyrissa was visibly shaking once again.

"No, it's okay," Inaya soothed. "We understand how difficult this is for you. If you could just point us in the right direction, that would be great."

After getting directions and assuring her they would do what they could to bring her brother's murderer to justice, they said their goodbyes. Trevin's gut told him it wouldn't be so easy to find the criminal and serve punishment.

Unfortunately, the only additional information Constance could provide was a more in-depth description of the body. Not only was Isaac torn limb from limb, but the murderer had also disemboweled him by ripping his ribcage apart and allowing his organs to spill out of the body. No Nephilim was capable of such a feat... but a fallen angel was. But why would Lahash kill Eldon and Isaac when he had gone out of his way to ensure the Nephilim perished by their own hands in his main goal to destroy them all? He could have just killed everyone himself, but he hadn't. What made it acceptable for Lahash to get his hands dirty when it came to Eldon and Isaac? It wasn't because they were traitors to Velius, because that played into his ultimate goal. And why were the deaths carried out so vastly differently? Eldon's death appeared to be quick and painless, but Isaac was made to suffer, and then his body was displayed to the village. Was it somehow a warning to others? What message was the fallen trying to convey? The more Trevin thought about it, the more questions arose.

"No wonder most of the town has mourning shrouds hanging in their windows, and did you notice the talisman hanging in the doorway of the baker's?" Inaya asked as they prepared to leave and continue on their journey.

"Unfortunately, that talisman will serve no purpose against the evil that has visited this village."

"What do you mean?" Inaya froze just as she was about to mount her horse. "Do you know what happened here?"

"I have an idea." Trevin moved closer to her, careful not to be overheard. Amira had briefed Inaya and the Royal Guard about the fallen angel and his plan to destroy the Nephilim, but that information was not being released to the public. "Lahash."

His one-word answer had her drawing in a sharp breath. "But why would he do that?"

"I don't know, but I think he is responsible for Eldon's death too."

"The feather...," Inaya murmured, putting it all together.

"Yes, I found the feather in Eldon's cell after his death."

"So there really isn't anything we can do for this town to bring them closure?" Inaya's voice rang with disappointment.

Trevin pulled her into his arms and kissed the top of her head, not having an answer that would comfort her. "It's time to move on."

They met back up with the rest of their soldiers and began the last leg of their journey to Ammon. Tension was thick in the air as each person was lost in thought, considering the nature of the brutal murder.

"Do you think he's still around? Now that his plan has failed, maybe he left." Inaya didn't have to explain to Trevin who she was referring to, and even in her whispered tone, he could hear the hope in her voice.

"We should hope for the best and prepare for the worst. The nature of such beings is out of the scope of our knowledge, so it's difficult to predict what actions he will take next, but my guess is he's still around." Trevin couldn't explain it, but that's what his gut was telling him.

Inaya fell quiet once again and remained so until they reached Ammon. It had been many years since Trevin had been back to this territory, but the way to the sovereign manor was a path he'd never forget. The manor was a huge monstrosity, mimicking a palace, but lacking the elegance needed to be beautiful. Instead, it was ostentatious.

"This was Sorin's home?" Inaya's distaste was clear in her tone as she eyed the building as if afraid to take her eyes off it.

"Yes, and his father's before him," Trevin answered. "Have you not been here before?"

"No." She shook her head. "There was never a need." As they made their way to the stables along the right side of the manor, she finally tore her eyes free and turned to study Trevin. "You lived here?"

"In the soldiers' barracks." He pointed to the run-down building just beyond the practice field. She didn't ask him any more questions about his life in Ammon, for which Trevin was grateful. She knew of "the games" Sorin's father, Malcolm, had conducted with his soldiers. She may not fully comprehend the brutality and the horrendous nature of them, but she knew enough to understand it had been a dark time in his life and not something he wanted to relive.

Dread formed a hard knot in the pit of Inaya's stomach as they approached the manor. The laborers and pedestrians paused to warily watch their approach. She felt the need to cower under their gaze, but instead held her head high and continued forward, nodding in greeting to anyone who met her eye.

Wanting to be cautious, but not have her arrival appear to be an act of aggression, only three soldiers accompanied them to the manor. The rest had split up within the town to evaluate the morale and get a feel of everyday life in Ammon. They would meet up with Inaya and Trevin later in the evening to discuss their findings and begin planning how they could improve the quality of life for the citizens of Ammon.

It felt awkward knowing she was basically coming to take over someone else's home, even if the dwelling technically belonged to the territory leader, whomever that may be at the time, instead of the current resident. Although she had no desire to live there, she could only hope that the transition went smoothly. More than just its unwelcoming outward appearance bothered her. Just knowing this was where Sorin had called home made it that much more unappealing. Between Malcolm and Sorin, who knew what depraved acts were committed behind those doors. She refused to let her mind wander in that direction; if she did, she doubted she'd have the fortitude to cross the threshold.

Part of her duty was to inform Sorin's family, as well as the people of Ammon, of his passing. How the people would respond, she had no idea. From what she knew, Sorin was not a kind and helpful territory leader, and his father before him was even worse.

At that thought, something occurred to her. She had failed to get the full scope of what she was walking into. At her abrupt stop, Trevin halted and turned a questioning look toward her. They were less than ten feet from the door, and she was just thinking to ask, "Where is Malcolm?" She had heard the stories of his misdeeds and his removal from authority, but nothing more.

When Trevin's gaze flickered to the manor and then back to her, her unease shifted to nausea, and she knew she wasn't going to like his answer. "Inside, I imagine."

Yeah, she didn't like that response. "How is he still in the place of authority?"

"He's not. He was removed from power over a century ago."

"Then why is he here?"

Trevin studied her a moment, as if trying to unravel her thought process. "Where would you have him be?" There was no judgment in his tone, just genuine curiosity.

There was no hesitation in her answer. "In exile."

Trevin's lips turned up at the corners. "That might have been a fitting punishment, but where would we exile him to?" Trevin had a point. They couldn't just release him on the human world. Before Inaya could come up with a better solution, Trevin continued. "If it were up to me, I would have preferred something a little more permanent, having seen firsthand what he is capable of."

"What was his punishment?"

"Removal from power and imprisonment for half a century. Upon his release, he was placed under the care of his wife."

"Why would King Vidar settle for such a lenient punishment?" Inaya had known him to be a kind and fair ruler, but this didn't seem like justice.

"At the time, his mental stability was in question. Malcolm claimed to be under the direct command of an angel."

"Lahash." She whispered the name on an exhale.

Trevin nodded but said nothing more. Inaya turned her attention to the front door, her mind racing with what might greet them on the other side. "Do you think he'll cause trouble?"

Trevin reached for her hand, entwining their fingers. "Let's go find out."

Hand in hand, they reached the massive, uninviting hardwood door. As if they had all the time in the world, Trevin waited patiently as she took a deep breath to steady her nerves before knocking. The wait felt like forever, but surely was only minutes, before a timid-looking male opened the door and peeked around, his eyes growing big as he took in Trevin's intimidating stature and muscular build. Then his gaze traveled to the three soldiers standing just a few feet behind them, his throat bobbing as he swallowed deeply.

"Lord Sorin is away," the man said quickly, before attempting to shut the door. Thankfully, Trevin was quicker, his large hand firmly holding the door open.

"Yes, we know that," Inaya informed him. "I come on behalf of the queen." That gave the man pause, making him cease his fruitless effort to overpower Trevin's one-handed hold on the door.

"The queen?"

"Queen Amira," Inaya clarified. Apparently, the news of her coronation had not yet reached these parts.

"So has she married our lord then?"

"Umm... no." Inaya hoped her repulsion at the

idea didn't show on her face. "Please allow us entrance, and we would be glad to explain. Are his parents available? We would like to speak with them first."

"Yes, both Lady Elise and Lord Malcolm are in residence." He stepped back, allowing them inside. "Who may I tell them is calling?"

"Lady Inaya and Lord Trevin." She ignored the pointed look and raised eyebrow Trevin shot her.

"Very good, my lady. Please wait here a moment." Then the timid man scurried off.

"Lord Trevin?" Trevin asked her, looking slightly amused, and a deep chuckle came from one of the soldiers behind them.

Inaya chose to ignore them and addressed her husband. "Of course, isn't that why you married me, for my title?" she teased.

Trevin bent his head close to her, his voice deep and gravelly, his words coming out as a purr that caressed her nerve endings. "I married you for a lot of reasons." His breath brushing against her neck did wicked things to her imagination. "And I'll be more than willing to give you a demonstration of a few of those things later tonight, but your title was never a factor in my decision." Her body was on fire with her desire, and he had yet to even touch her.

Before she could find the words to respond, the man returned. "The lord and lady will see you now."

They followed him into the receiving hall, which was set up much like a throne room in a palace. On a raised dais sat a stocky male with dark brown hair and eyes. His scowl and hostile aura had Inaya nearly tripping over her feet. She shifted her gaze to the elegant female beside him. She appeared fragile and timid, avoiding eye contact as she forced a smile in place.

"Lord Trevin and Lady Inaya," the servant announced before bowing and backing away.

"Why have you come?" Malcolm barked, forgoing pleasantries.

Something in his voice triggered a memory for her, but it remained just out of grasp. Determined not to be intimidated, Inaya met his gaze and answered in a strong voice, "We come on behalf of Queen Amira and bring news of your son."

Inaya nodded to the Velius soldier standing on her right, instructing him to deliver the handwritten message from the queen. Malcolm looked reluctant to take the paper out of the soldier's outstretched hand, but after a moment, he conceded with a loud sigh. Breaking open the royal seal, he quickly scanned its contents. A nerve ticked in his jaw, the only outward reaction he displayed to discovering his son was dead and Inaya would be taking over as territory ruler for the time being.

Malcolm didn't attempt to pass the letter to his wife, nor did he communicate its contents. Instead, he sat for a moment staring at the ground. The heavy air, filled with tension and expectation, weighed on Inaya's nerves, but she remained quiet for as long as she could.

When the wait became unbearable, she expressed her condolences. "I'm sorry for your loss. If—"

He didn't allow her to finish. Instead, he jumped to his feet, bellowing, "You think to take my territory from me?"

Before he could make a move toward her, she was surrounded by her soldiers, with Trevin standing before her, bringing Malcolm's full attention to him for the first time.

"You!" Malcolm shouted. "I know you. You ungrateful whelp, this was all your fault. You stole my territory to begin with, and now you think to come and finish the job? Did you kill my boy too?" He didn't wait for Trevin to answer his outrageous question, he continued to rant, but was smart enough to stay where he was, not making any move to approach them. Regardless, neither Trevin nor her soldiers relaxed their stances; they remained at the ready, weapons in hand. Inaya had just enough room to peek around Trevin's shoulder to see the red-faced Malcolm glaring at them. "You're pathetic. How could you ever believe that you could take what is mine?"

"There is no such thing as love or fate. You're pathetic. How could you ever believe that I would want you?" The words from her nightmare echoed in her head, coming in Malcolm's voice. Her whole body froze, and the breath ceased in her lungs. How could he be the villain from her nightmare? Then the rest of the memory clicked into place.

From a child's point of view, she hid behind her momma's skirt as a red-faced Malcolm towered over them, screaming. "You are nothing but a whore, an object to be used and discarded at my discretion."

Her momma's sobs shook her entire body. "You don't mean that. You love me. We are fated mates."

An evil sneer twisted his face. "There is no such thing as love or fate. You're pathetic. How could you ever believe that I would want you?"

"B-but—"

He didn't let her finish. "Dispose of the child." He grasped her by the throat and pushed her backward, causing her to trip over Inaya's small body. They both tumbled to the hard, unforgiving floor. "If you don't, I'll return and dispose of you both." Without another word or a backward glance, he stormed out of their small home, slamming the front door behind him.

For hours, her momma didn't move from the floor. Instead, she remained where he had tossed her and cried herself to sleep. When it became dark outside, Inaya covered her momma with a soft blanket, hoping to bring her some amount of comfort, and then crawled into her own bed for the night, feeling alone and empty.

Sometime later, a strange thump awoke her from a deep sleep. Terrified the man had returned to carry out his threat, Inaya huddled under her blankie, curling herself into a tight ball. Minutes or hours passed, she didn't know which, but the man's voice never echoed through their home, nor did he burst in to drag her from her bed. Gathering her courage, she wrapped the blankie around herself and forced one foot in front of the other to check on her momma.

The first thing she noticed was the chair that lay crashed over on the floor; that must have been what had woken her. Just above that, at Inaya's eye level, were a pair of bare feet suspended in the air. Breathing suddenly became difficult, and as much as she didn't want them to, her eyes traveled up from the feet, to the legs, up past the torso, to land on her momma's once-beautiful face, now tinted blue with bloodshot eyes that seemed to stare right through her.

Inaya's bottom hit the floor, and she scurried backward until she hit a wall.

Malcolm's bellow brought her back to the present. "My family was gifted this territory by the angels themselves, and I will die before I allow you to take control."

"Very well." Trevin's voice was calm and controlled, but clearly conveyed his deadly acceptance.

That gave Malcolm pause. His yelling must have alerted the Ammon soldiers stationed within the manor, because half a dozen came rushing into the room, hands on their weapons, seeking the danger. A wicked smile crossed Malcolm's lips. "Seize them," he commanded.

Thirty-Six

Lahash watched as a silent observer from the corner of the room, ready to step in as needed. He had followed the newlyweds on their journey to Ammon, his mind a jumbled mess as he tried to reconcile his recent actions and his forsaken dream. The conflicting emotions within him only eased while in his offspring's presence. Since the beginning, he had realized that their destinies were intertwined, but at the moment, it felt like his sanity was tied to her as well.

Seeing the despair and pain on her face as they investigated Isaac's death was almost his undoing. She didn't understand that he had done it for her. Lahash had sought vengeance in her name, but all she saw was a brutal murder committed by "evil." He yearned to make her understand, but revealing himself to her would accomplish nothing, so he remained in the shadows, a silent observer.

And once again, he found his offspring pitted against one another. The knowledge of Sorin's death didn't seem to be a factor, but Malcolm's pride wouldn't allow his family to be removed from power. If only he'd open his eyes, he'd realize his bloodline would still reign, the fool.

As the scene unfolded before him, Lahash's frustration smoldered. His plans, his future, everything he'd worked for was in ruins. He floundered in a sea of uncertainty, adrift without a purpose, and more than anything, he desired a moment of peace, time to come to terms with the wreckage that was his life. But here he was, watching Malcolm's tantrum as he made the dire misstep of threatening Lahash's only anchor. It would be a simple matter to remove Malcolm from the equation and rid them all of the hassle, but the mental image of Inaya's distraught face as she discovered Lahash's punishment of Isaac was seared into his brain, shaming him, making him question his moral compass, effectively staying his hand.

Lahash cocked his head and studied Inaya closely as her face twisted in anguish as she listened to Malcolm rant. She was obviously in distress, and with her mate standing protectively in front of her, he was unaware.

And then Malcolm sealed his death warrant with two words. "Seize them."

Lahash had had enough of lurking in the shadows. He had sacrificed too much to allow Inaya to be harmed in any way, the consequences of his actions be damned.

A firm hand landed on his shoulder just as he took his first step forward, the shock enough to halt him in his tracks. He spun around to discover Briathos, once again appearing without warning.

"Wait" was all the angel said, as he nodded for Lahash to return his attention to the spectacle playing out before them. As uncomfortable as it was having the angel at his back, concern had him dividing his attention.

Time slowed as the Ammon soldiers stepped forward, following Malcolm's order and advancing on Inaya, Trevin, and the Velius soldiers. A growl rumbled in his throat as he attempted to break Briathos's hold on him. "Release me."

"This is not your fight." The angel's voice was low, controlled, and if Lahash didn't know any better, he'd describe it as uninvested, but that wasn't the case. There was a reason Briathos was involving himself. Angels always had a reason.

But that didn't mean Lahash could trust his motives. "The hell it isn't. I—"

"Stop," rang out the confident command, freezing the soldiers in midaction, all eyes darting to Inaya. She didn't need to yell, the authority was clear in her voice. She stepped forward, away from the protective circle her guards had formed around her. "Malcolm has no authority here. Lord Sorin is dead. I am Lady Inaya, envoy to the queen, and the new ruler of Ammon, and I'm ordering you to stand down."

The soldiers exchanged quick glances before lowering their weapons and bowing their heads in submission.

"See." Briathos released his hold on Lahash and stepped beside him. "Your child is strong and capable. We each must walk our own path. Allow her that dignity."

Lahash nodded his understanding, but before he could ask the questions burning in his mind, movement from the corner of his eye grabbed his attention as Malcolm made the stupidest mistake of his life. He ripped the sword away from the closest soldier to him, grumbling, "I'll do it myself." Raising the sword, he rushed forward, headed straight for Inaya. It was almost comical how effortlessly Trevin took him to his knees before he got anywhere close to his target.

"And it looks as though she already has a capable protector," Briathos added.

Even on his knees, a sword held to his throat, Malcolm refused to yield. "Do it, boy," he taunted. "I lost my rulership because of you, but even then you weren't man enough to take it yourself. You ran to the king like a scared child seeking someone stronger to fight your battles. Tell me, are you still that weakling?"

Trevin's moral character never wavered. The disgust was apparent in his expression, but it was clear Malcolm's insults missed their mark. Trevin simply did his duty. "Restrain him and take him into custody." His voice held no emotion as he gave the order. Once Malcolm was dragged away, he turned to his wife, giving her a nod, a silent acknowledgment that she was safe and once more in command. Her smile was brilliant, and then she turned her attention to the silent woman still sitting meekly in the chair at the front of the room, having been informed her son was dead and then watching as her husband committed treason and was taken away.

With the danger averted, Lahash granted the angel his full attention. "Why are you here?"

"Why are *you* here?" Briathos countered.

"Do not play games with me." Impotent anger flared inside him.

Briathos took in a deep breath as his eyes surveyed their surroundings, and just when Lahash began to give up hope, the angel met his stare. "You made the right choice, letting go of your plan for vengeance. It would not have brought you what you seek."

That cold truth was a knife to his heart. His eyes closed briefly against the pain as he centered himself. "Your presence forced my hand."

"No, I simply facilitated the exit strategy you were searching for. It was your choice."

Lahash decided not to argue with his assessment, but he wasn't yet willing to admit the truth.

Briathos sighed at Lahash's stubbornness. "You made a mistake... many mistakes—"

"You think?" Lahash sneered.

Ignoring him, Briathos continued. "It's not too late to choose a different path. When things don't turn out as we originally planned, it's not because we failed. It's because that was not the outcome that was meant for us. There is a bigger plan at work, something far more important than you or me, and we all must play our part."

"Are you trying to say this was all destined?" The skepticism was clear in his voice.

"I'm saying there is a reason we are here, now, at this point in time, exactly where we are. And you have a choice to make."

Lahash snorted. "Now you sound like Gusion."

"Do I?" Briathos's head cocked to the side as he studied Lahash. "The seer is correct about many things, but falls short where it counts most." Briathos looked away as something close to pain flashed across his features. When he met Lahash's gaze once more, there was only steely resolve in his eye. "The others are truly lost to us, choosing a path for which there is no return, but you, brother"—a bittersweet ache lanced through Lahash with that one word, threatening to send him to his knees—"you still have a choice."

"What is it you would have me do?"

"Stop them." Briathos stated this near-impossible task as if it were simple and easy.

"Why should I? I care nothing for humans."

"You once cared very much for a human," Briathos countered.

"Leave her out of this."

"Very well. Then do it because it is right. Or if moral integrity is not motivation enough, do it for your children." Lahash tried to interrupt, but Briathos powered on. "They are all your children, and they are in danger. You are not the only fallen to have taken an interest in the Nephilim. Even now, your brethren are using them as pawns in the downfall of mankind. And if they succeed, your children will perish as well."

A strange possessiveness expanded in his chest. *How dare the fallen toy with the Nephilim.* And with that thought, Lahash conceded that Briathos was right. The creatures he once saw as abominations now had value to him. They were not the mistakes he once believed them to be. That wasn't to say that he liked them all; in fact, there might be some that he actually despised, but he found the idea of harm coming to even those was unacceptable. They were his children, and they needed him, for who else could stand up against the fallen angels?

It didn't matter that the few Nephilim who knew of him thought him to be a demon; they were his family, which meant he was no longer alone in this world. Lahash would do what was necessary to protect his children, and hopefully, make up for the mistakes he had made along the way.

"What would you have me do?"

For the first time, a real smile flitted across Briathos's lips. "Satan is waiting."

I naya had considered confronting her father, but what would be the purpose? It wouldn't change the past, and there was so much hate in his heart, she couldn't trust a word that came from his mouth. In the end, she decided that he didn't deserve the privilege of knowing her. Malcolm would never be the father she had dreamed of having as a child. But that was okay. She'd had King Vidar's love and guidance when she'd needed it most. She would cherish his memory and be grateful for the honor of having him step into the void Malcolm had left in her life.

As for her mother, now that Inaya's memory of the past was clear, she could see her mother for the broken soul that she was. And although she had abused and neglected Inaya for years, in the end, perhaps she protected Inaya in the only way she knew how. Facing a situation that she perceived as hopeless, she'd taken her own life instead of that of her child. Was it the right decision, no, but Inaya could see why she did it. So instead of holding on to her anger and hurt, Inaya decided to have compassion for her mentally ill mother. Once she made peace with the past, her nightmares ceased.

Inaya stared out the window of her new home, watching the progress being made as workers remodeled the sovereign manor into the new soldiers' barracks. She had been unable to feel at ease in that pretentious mansion and was grateful when Trevin had proposed the idea of putting it to better use. Although she and Trevin were now the permanent leaders of the territory of Ammon, their four-bedroom cottage suited her and their growing family perfectly.

As if reading her mind, Trevin stepped up behind her, wrapping his arms around her stomach, which was just beginning to show signs of the life nestled securely inside her. "It's coming along nicely," he murmured before pressing a kiss to her head.

"Which one?" Inaya laughed. "The baby or the building?"

"Both." He chuckled, giving her a squeeze.

She turned in his arms, sliding hers around his waist. "The whole territory is." Shortly after arriving in Ammon, it became clear that many of the people lived in poverty and fear. Malcolm and Sorin had neglected the needs of the populace and abused their roles to feed their own greed. It had taken a while for the citizens to trust in Trevin and Inaya, but their economy and the overall morale of the people were improving. The role of territory leaders suited both Inaya and Trevin, giving them purpose, and they worked well together, trusting and supporting one another.

Gazing up at her husband, it occurred to her that everything they had experienced in life—the tragedies and the heartbreak, combined with the joy and blessings—had led them to this place in time, where they were meant to be, on a journey they would travel hand in hand.

Acknowledgments

Divine Grace took way longer to write than it should have. I'd almost given up on being a writer, and this book never would have seen the light of day. But there are a few amazing people in my life who believed in me and pushed me to continue.

Becky Johnson, thank you for not giving up on me. And thank you for giving me a deadline, especially since I cussed you the entire time and missed the first one (oops!).

Nicole Bowen, your endless love and support keep me sane—okay, sane-ish. I don't know where I'd be without you, and I never want to find out.

Michael "Shane" Grove, thank you for believing in me, especially when I don't believe in myself. You've kept me grounded and connected to my characters. This story is better because of you.

Jacqueline Flanders, everyone needs a cheerleader and a partner in crime, you must have drawn the short straw, because you're mine.

And finally, to my children, Jacobi and Marek, making you proud is the best feeling in the world.

Thank you for supporting me while I follow my dreams. I love you more than anything... even tacos!

About the Author

Virginia's greatest passion has always been fiction, particularly romance. The innocent in her loves the idea of a happily ever after, but she has a massive soft spot for the bad boys. If you ask her, she'll tell you she's living her dream—getting paid to read and helping indie authors to create beauty by working as an editor for Hot Tree Editing. She's inspired by the many amazing indie authors she has met and has (finally) found the courage to follow her other dream by becoming a published author.

About the Publisher

Hot Tree Publishing loves love. Publishing adult romantic fiction, HTPubs are all about diverse reads featuring heroes and heroines to swoon over. Since opening in 2015, HTPubs have published more than 300 titles across the wide and diverse range of romantic genres. If you're chasing a happily ever after in your favourite subgenre, HTPubs have you covered.

Interested in discovering more amazing reads brought to you by Hot Tree Publishing? Head over to the website for information:

WWW.HOTTREEPUBLISHING.COM

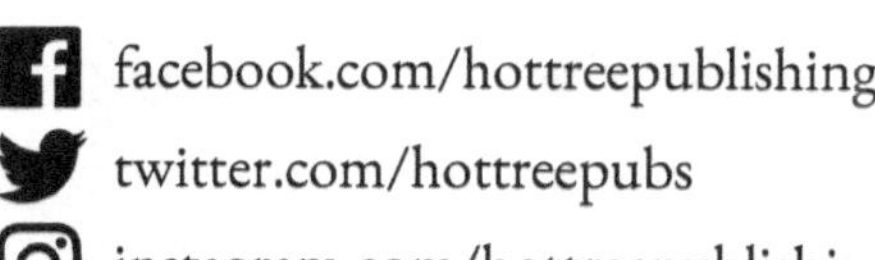

facebook.com/hottreepublishing

twitter.com/hottreepubs

instagram.com/hottreepublishing

www.ingramcontent.com/pod-product-compliance
Lightning Source LLC
Chambersburg PA
CBHW032203180726
48284CB00001B/172